Praise for Hotwire

"Every spare minute I had was spent reading, including during my lunch breaks at work. Solid and very well written."

~MaKaela Howell, reviewer

"Christy is a character that will make you want to be stronger, try harder at whatever you do, and learn how to disarm an enemy."

~Tamara Borden, reviewer

"This book has it all. Romance. Danger. Christy. Action. Adventure. Subterfuge. Christy. I can't say enough about how much I love Christy, her character just gets better and better with each new story."

~Cathy Jeppson, reviewer

"Hotwire kept me quickly turning the pages as I couldn't wait to finish. Keeps you biting your nails while on the edge of your seat. Hogan cleverly created characters with detail, who are both relatable and grounded, making it easy to transport to the world of the high school students."

~The Bookstalker Review

"It's a thriller that reminded me of a mix between *Gone in 60 Seconds* and the *Gallagher Girls* books."

~Canda Mortensen, reviewer

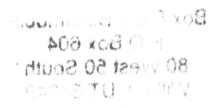

"A captivating novel that I couldn't put down. Seriously, you'll have to put aside house work and consider getting a baby sitter so that you don't have to put the book down until you read the last word."
~Brooke Stephenson at familyisfriendship. blogspot.com

"A spellbinding, action-packed series of twisted events that lead our favorite agent into the clutches of the world's most feared group of formidable, crass, and malignant men. Make your popcorn, unearth your horde of favorite snacks and drinks because you will not want to walk away from this intense series of events."
~T. Russell, Summerfield, Florida, reviewer

"Christy is like the female version of James Bond, only better! A clean spy novel that will have your heart racing, hands sweating, and feelings out of control!"
~Konstanz Silverbow, reviewer

"A wild ride you won't want to get off until the very end."
~Cindy Roland Anderson, author of the bestselling novels *Fair Catch*

a Christy novel

Cindy M. Hogan

Also by Cindy M. Hogan
Audio, Print, and eBook

Watched Trilogy:
Watched
Protected
Created

Adrenaline Rush
Gravediggers

Sweet and Sour Kisses:
First Kiss
Stolen Kiss
Rebound Kiss
Rejected Kiss
Dream Kiss

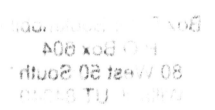

a Christy novel

Cindy M. Hogan

O'neal Publishing

In honor of the beautiful and eclectic city of New York

Chapter 1

I stretched out a kink in my neck, readjusting my heavy surveillance headphones *again*, exasperated that none fit me right. "Ugh!"

Agent Halluis Moreau whacked me on the shoulder bracingly. "Don't worry, it'll only be about ten years until big people things actually fit you," he said, his lightly accented voice dripping with mockery.

I turned and scowled at him, but it didn't take long looking at his goofy face before I was fighting a smile. I blamed the mustache—who could take a guy seriously when he was sporting a pencil-thin mustache? It didn't help that he insisted on always wearing all black, from his tight turtleneck to his shiny shoes. He looked more like a little boy playing spy than an actual spook. I turned back to my monitor before he could catch my lips twitching.

"Really funny, Halluis." I let the sarcasm drip from my voice to cover the smile. "Just pay attention to your feed. You don't want to miss anything."

He scoffed and tossed his own headphones down on the table. "*Mon oeil.* As if these kids ever say anything important. Our time would be better spent practicing your French."

"My French? What's wrong with my French?"

"Your accent is terrible."

The van door slid open and slammed shut quickly, letting in a burst of frigid air. "You're a Parisian, so you're obligated to say that." It was Agent Amédée Renaud, always known as Ace, returning from a quick bathroom break.

The three of us were positioned inside a cramped surveillance van, parked on a crowded New York City street, listening to various audio feeds coming out of A.G. Bell Academy, an engineering prep school. The team had been monitoring activity at the school ever since they'd pinpointed it as a hub for car theft activity.

"I find it hard to believe that any kids in this school could be stealing expensive, high profile cars all around the city. They're kids." Halluis looked at me, a sheepish look on his face, before tilting his head to the side. "What? They're in high school. Sure, it's an elite engineering high school, but still a high school."

"If it is them," Ace said. "I can't wait to see how they're doing it. Whoever they are, they're good at hiding their tracks."

"I don't get why Division 57 is even involved in this. Shouldn't the police be dealing with this?" I said, voicing a concern I'd had since they'd brought me on board a week before.

"Yeah, but we're not after all the cars. Just one. The police don't seem to have a great handle on this—they've been after this group for months, with no leads. Our client, whoever he is, wants his car back, and he doesn't want to wait around for the police to get it together."

"Well, I'm up for a quick in-and-out mission after the last one." I leaned back and pushed a big breath of air through my nose. "Still, I don't see why anyone would make such a big deal over one car."

"Do you have any idea what kind of car it is? A 1959 Mercedes Benz 300 SL Gullwing Coupe!" Ace whistled. "If someone stole it from me, I'd be hot to get it back no matter the cost."

"But Division doesn't send us on operations to benefit one person."

"Ours is not to reason why," Halluis cut in. "We don't question our mission orders. But rest assured, we wouldn't take on a client just for money. The car must be very important, or Division wouldn't have invested all the resources, man-power, and money into tracking it down that they have, don't you think?"

I nodded. Everything I'd seen Division 57 do had huge impact.

"I'm sure you're right," Ace said. "I might even get out from behind the computer to touch that beauty when we find it, but only for a second."

I considered the two men in the van with me. Before I'd joined them, Halluis and Ace had been a two-man team—Halluis as jack-of-all-trades, doing most of the actual intelligence gathering, and Ace as tech genius extraordinaire. He liked to call himself "glorified tech support," but it was Ace who had found the only solid lead thus far. He'd written a computer algorithm that had analyzed the locations of the car thefts and had identified the academy as the center of the theft activity. The two of them had been trying to gather intel from the school and learn anything that would help track down the illusive car. But so far, no luck.

That's when they'd brought me on board.

At nineteen, I was one of the youngest spies on Division 57's payroll, making me a perfect candidate to go undercover in the school and learn things that surveillance feeds and computer algorithms could not. It was Friday, so we had one more day of monitoring the feeds, learning as much as possible. On Monday, I was going in, joining the ranks of future engineers as Amber Smith, transfer student.

Only a few knew it, but my unique photographic memory had taken me through spy school and my other trainings in under a year. I had a natural knack for it. I only wished it hadn't taken witnessing a murder when I was sixteen to put me on this path. I never wanted another terrorist or madman to hurt so many people. I loved being one of the good guys.

Ace shook his shaggy blond hair, which despite being streaked with gray had a boyish quality to it—maybe because it always seemed to be in his face. "I could really go for a hot dog right now. What's the point of being in New York if we can't take part in all the beauty of the city?"

Halluis just rolled his eyes. "You Americans. I can't believe you call that food."

"Hey, I'm Canadian. *French* Canadian," Ace protested. The two of them started to argue about what exactly it meant to be French, and I tuned them out, turning my attention back to the audio feed.

What Halluis had said was true—we'd placed audio feeds as carefully as possible, using Ace's algorithm to locate likely students to monitor, but so far all we'd caught was the typical teenage conversations about school, bands, TV shows, and of course the opposite sex.

The one I was listening in on now, in fact, was a fine specimen of banal adolescent conversation.

"...come on, man, it's gonna be tight. We're putting it on the big screen, four players, blowing up zombies all night long." That was Nick Harris, one of the kids we'd tagged as a possible suspect. I sighed. Sounded like he'd be playing video games all night—no car theft activity there.

I was about to change the feed and focus on one of our other targets when I heard the response.

"Sorry—it sounds like a lot of fun, but I'm busy tonight. Got a hot date with a German model."

My scalp twitched, and my hand tingled; I waited another second before switching the feed.

"Aw, what? Jericho—there's no way you're going out with a model. I call BS."

"Believe what you want. Doesn't bother me. I'm just telling you I'm busy."

"Right, right. Still, man, you're seriously gonna ditch us for some chick? I can't believe you'd do that to your boys."

"Ha! I'd leave you in the dust for this one any day. She's more than worth it. Older, high class, you know. Usually spends her nights with a rich doctor, but she's seen my charm now. She's as good as mine. And the payoff is gonna be so good."

Nick made the expected response of combined disbelief and awe, but I was too distracted by the storm

5

inside me to pay much attention to his words. In my head, it was if alarm bells were going off. My senses were on high alert, and everything inside me screamed that something was going on here. It may have seemed like a totally normal conversation, typical teenage boy bravado and brag, but I knew—I just *knew*—there was more to it than that.

"Quiet, quiet," I hissed at Ace and Halluis, who were still arguing. "Pull up everything you've got on a kid named Jericho."

"Jericho Roman?" Halluis asked, turning back to his keyboard. "No, it's a dead end. We looked into that kid. Total straight arrow. Class president, good student, *très populaire*, all that."

I shook my head. "I think something's up with him." I pulled my heavy headphones down and stared at the info sheet Halluis pulled up on his monitor. This Jericho kid certainly seemed clean—from a well-off family, good grades, everything Halluis had said. Yet, I still felt this intense pull, telling me to pay attention. Something occurred to me. "You did look into him, though. That means Ace's algorithm tagged him."

Ace shrugged. "It's not perfect, you know. The algorithm tags potential suspects, it doesn't handcuff the culprits. There's still some work actual agents have to do. We ruled him out."

I nodded slowly, but something still felt off. I sighed, massaging my neck. The giant headphones had really put a strain on my muscles.

Ace chuckled. "Don't worry, Christy, I'm working on some things that should make your life easier," he said.

I smiled distractedly. There was something Jericho

had said...

"Hey, Ace—didn't you also make a list of possible targeted cars?"

"Yeah, it was just a variation on the same algorithm I designed to—"

I cut him off before he could get too wound up in techy-talk. "Will you pull that up for me?"

A look passed between my two team members, then Ace shrugged as if to say, "Humor her."

Halluis pulled it up, and I scanned it quickly. "There!" I shouted, pointing at one of the cars on the list.

"The Mercedes S63?"

"Yes. Jericho said he had a hot date tonight with a German model, one who usually dates a doctor. And look, you tagged this Mercedes—a German car—owned by Dr. Robert Madison."

Ace shook his shaggy head, "I don't know, Christy. That seems a bit of a stretch. It's probably just a coincidence."

"The kid's just trying to look good for his friends— dating a model. Please," Halluis snorted.

I held my ground. "No, listen—it was something he said. 'The *payoff* is gonna be good.' Something about that phrase... it just isn't sitting right with me."

Halluis raised one eyebrow, his mustache making his face look exasperatingly smug.

I threw my hands in the air. "Fine—you guys think it's nothing? How about a wager, then?"

Halluis leaned back in his chair and crossed his arms, eyeing me appraisingly. Ace just grinned, his boyish face alight with glee.

"Name your terms," Halluis said.

"All right, here's how it's going to go down. Tonight, I'll tail Jericho while you monitor the Mercedes. Ace, you'll monitor the operation from the van. If I'm wrong—if Jericho really does just have a date tonight and the car is nothing but a snooze-fest—then I'll eat those fried crickets and snails we saw the other day in Chinatown."

Ace's grin widened.

"But if I'm right," I quickly added, "Then you guys have to eat them—dressed up like sexy women."

Halluis's eyes flashed. "You're on if you do it dressed up like a bum."

"Fine."

Ace looked from Halluis's face to mine. "So, who's going to tell our fearless leader?"

Chapter 2

A few hours later, we were all sitting around our kitchen table in the brownstone townhouse Division had procured as our mission headquarters. There was an official conference room in the brownstone, but more often than not we found ourselves hashing out important mission details around the table over a meal. Jeremy McGinnis, my handler—the fearless leader Ace had mentioned—had brought a pizza, and we were now arguing over the evening's particulars between bites.

It was insane to think that witnessing a political murder while on a school trip in D.C. three years ago had brought us together and propelled me into my life as a spy. I tried not to stare at the ropey muscles of his arms as he ate his pizza. A picture of him lying in a hospital bed after saving me from the murderer flashed through my mind.

Maybe it was the fact that he'd saved my life more than once that made me feel such a strong connection to him. His calm voice always calmed me, and something in his earnest eyes assured me. I stared at them until he noticed me looking. I glanced away from him, pretending to look out the window, as his sexy, dark brown eyes fell on me. And when his hand brushed through his ever-so-perfectly rumpled light brown hair, I took a sharp breath in and forced myself not to think about my own hand doing that very thing.

"If you're right and he's involved with the car thefts, we can't risk him seeing you tail him. It would completely blow your cover at the school," Jeremy said. Halluis and Ace had agreed to keep the bet just between us and to act supportive of the plan, and to my great relief Jeremy was immediately on board. That fact only slightly tempered my irritation at his objections to my tail.

"He won't see me! Come on, Jeremy, I'm a trained operative, same as the rest of you. I know what I'm doing."

I watched his jaw tighten, the only outward sign he gave that he was getting impatient. "It's just not a risk I'm willing to take—he could catch a glimpse of you, just enough to make him wary of you later when he meets you at school. It could undermine your cover, and I just don't think it's worth it."

"Don't worry, Christy, we have the car—you're so certain it's the target, all we need is a classic stake out. We don't even need to tail the boy," Halluis said, his eyes wide in mock sincerity. I glared at him.

"I never said that," Jeremy interjected, missing the sarcasm in Halluis's tone. "I'll tail Jericho. Halluis—you put a tracker on the car, which Ace can monitor from the van. Christy, you'll be in position across the street, ready to step in if anything goes wrong." He saw my smile and held up a warning hand. "But mostly, your job is just to watch."

"Got it, boss," I grinned.

***

11:30 that night found me crouched in the snow under some dense bushes, staring at Dr. Robert Madison's coal black Mercedes S63 through ill-fitting night vision goggles. The street was dark—the street lights were inexplicably out—and I was glad for the improved vision the goggles gave me, even if they were nearly as painful to wear as the surveillance headphones had been. The car was parked outside the good doctor's mistress's apartment—the fact that he was a cheater made me feel slightly better about simply watching as his car was stolen. Hopefully stolen, anyway.

"I'm not sure what I'm wishing for right now," Halluis's voice came over the com in my ear. Through the goggles, I could see his black shape silhouetted in green, darting under the car to place the tracker. "On the one hand, it would be lovely to see you eat crow on this one—or should I say, eat crickets? But we need a break in this case." He grunted as he rolled out from under the car and slunk away. In a second he was gone, ghost-like, to take up position in a nearby alley. "Am I crazy to hope that you're right?"

I was surprised to hear a little anxiety in his normally flippant tone. He was actually hoping for this to succeed, despite his skepticism. I smiled to myself. I was really growing fond of these guys. This was my first time working with a real team, and it felt good.

"Less chatter on the line," Jeremy's voice cut in.

"Everyone needs to be on alert."

I could see Halluis's eyes roll in my mind's eye, and I smiled again.

"Any movement, yet?" I asked quietly.

"Still watching his door. Nothing."

I sighed inwardly. Could I have been wrong about Jericho? The feeling I'd gotten was so strong—I just couldn't shake it. Even now, with no movement on the car or on Jericho, I had this sense that something was about to happen. I couldn't explain it, but I knew it.

"Hold it—he's exiting the home. I'm on his tail. Ace, take me out of the com grid. Going radio silent. Contact me only if there's an emergency." With that, his line went dead.

I waited for a snarky comment from Halluis, but there was nothing. I breathed out slowly. The moment of truth. If Jericho was really just on his way to a date, the night would be wasted, and I'd have no more information going in to the school on Monday than I did right now. And that would not be good. I really needed something to go on.

It felt like an eternity of waiting, but it was only twenty minutes later that a hint of movement caught my attention. I whipped my head toward it, focusing my green pool of vision on the shape—it was a man, a kid really, walking silently down the street toward the Mercedes.

I pushed up higher on my elbows, the snow crunching under my coat.

"You see something, Christy?" Ace asked.

I shifted the goggles and whispered, "There's someone approaching the Mercedes. Is it Jericho?"

12

I heard some tapping over the line, probably Ace performing some kind of analysis on the feed from my goggles. "That's a negative. But it is one of our tagged suspects. Mikado Kawaguchi, another student at the school. This could be good."

I held my breath and watched the kid—Mikado—nonchalantly pass right by the car. I sighed, disappointed, until I noticed he was slowing down. He stopped at a street lamp about ten feet away from the car and just stood there, standing almost inhumanly still. His straight, chin-length hair hung loose around his face, and he was wearing dark clothing. The darkened street lights, and now this suspicious behavior—it was looking good for the car being a target at least.

Five minutes after midnight, Mikado shifted slightly, straightening his shoulders in anticipation.

"Incoming," Ace said. "On your ten."

I turned my head farther to the left, up the street from where Mikado stood, and saw another kid approach the darkened street lamp.

"Positive ID," Ace's voice chirped in my ear. "It's Jericho."

Yes. I celebrated inwardly. Finally, the break we needed!

He walked up to Mikado, and I could tell they were talking, though I couldn't hear what they were saying. Jericho slapped Mikado on the back, and Mikado nodded, then they approached the Mercedes. I watched, nearly in awe, as they expertly broke past its defenses. All it took was a roll of sticky film slapped on the driver's side window, a computer, a blank key, and a GPS jammer, and in three minutes flat they were inside. Even I couldn't do that.

"I can't believe it. The kid was right." Halluis's flippant tone was back.

"Hey, that's Wonder Kid to you. Show some respect."

"I'm activating the tracker now. See you at the van."

"I'll expect some humble words of apology when you get there."

Halluis snorted. "Not likely."

I let the night vision goggles fall around my neck and watched the lights of the Mercedes as it sped away down 69th Street and skidded onto 5th Ave. The headlights shone right at my position for a few quick seconds before darkness descended on me once again.

"Tracker activated," Halluis said. "Those kids are fast."

"We've got them on the screen," Ace said. "Their days of stealing cars are numbered. Great job, Christy. We finally got a break in this case, and it's all thanks to you."

"Now, that's what I like to hear," I said as I climbed out from under the bushes and stretched before brushing off the snow from the front of my jeans and jacket. After lifting off the goggles and depositing them into my go bag, I pulled out a Ritter Sport mint chocolate bar and took a big bite before depositing it back into the pack. The chocolate melted slowly in my mouth, and I savored the rich flavor in celebration. I looked back down 69th street and then out at the sprawling black pit that was Central Park at night before jogging to Park Avenue to join Ace and Halluis in the van.

I beat Halluis there.

"Shotgun!" I cried as I pulled the door shut, the slow beep of a tracker sounding in the background. Once I sat down, I flipped the heater on full blast to clear the frosted windshield. I rubbed my hands together and held them in the warm blast. "In fact, I think I get shotgun for life—what with me being totally right, and you two being totally wrong."

Ace didn't respond. I glanced back at him and saw that his brow was furrowed and he was staring intently at the screen. It was only then that I noticed that the beeping had stopped.

"I don't get it," he said, brushing his hand through his shaggy blond hair. "The tracker stopped working."

"What?" I said, climbing into the back to look at the monitor, too. Sure enough, the tracker was dead, and we were no longer tracking the Mercedes. Sirens wailed in the background.

Halluis crashed into the front passenger seat yelling out, "Shotgun!" as he did.

"I already claimed it, you dork. What took you so long?" I made a face at him.

"I'm not as young and sprightly as you, my little chicken. The real question is why is this van still so cold? Have we decided to start selling ice cream?"

We didn't answer, but Ace asked, "Any way that tracker wasn't secure, Hal?"

"No. It was totally secure, as all my bugs are. Why?"

"We lost the signal. I thought maybe it fell off the car." Ace bit the corner of his lip as he looked at the screen. I leaned back against the van wall and exhaled

15

loudly.

"I can't believe we lost it. It would have done so much for us if we could find out where they're taking the cars." I pulled my knees up to my chest and hugged them.

"It was secure. They must have found it and disabled it," Halluis said, looking at the monitor.

"They must be actively looking for bugs, then. I'm going to have to step up my game." Ace rubbed his hands over his face, obviously angry with himself for losing the tracker.

I shrugged my shoulders. "It's all right. I mean, it's not great I know, but we've now identified two of the thieves. I can get in with them, learn how the operation works, and get to the cars that way. We'll find our target in no time, you'll see. Where's Jeremy, shouldn't he be back by now?" I glanced out the window, hoping to see him. "Ace, can you put him back on the com?"

"Oh, yeah. Right. Got it." Ace typed quickly then looked up at me with a nod. "You should be able to get him now."

"Jeremy? Did you see? We got them!"

There was a pause over the line, then Jeremy's voice came in, rough and clipped.

"We need to talk."

Chapter 3

"We still have to send her in," Halluis argued, his face screwed up in anger, eyes shooting daggers at Jeremy. It was an hour later, and we were once again gathered around the kitchen table. No food this time, just angry, tense voices and a whole heap of trouble.

"I'm telling you, the kid is a psycho. There's no way I'm sending her in to that mess." Jeremy sat up straighter in his seat.

"It's not only your decision—we are a team, and we all have a mission to accomplish. You can't just override everyone else's opinions." Halluis slammed his fist on the table, his face bright red. I needed to do something to diffuse this situation, quick. The relationship between Jeremy and Halluis had already been tense, but this was the first time Halluis had actively challenged Jeremy's authority. Jeremy had joined the mission when I had, and the director had made him team leader. I got the impression that before then, Halluis had been calling the shots.

I cut in, trying to keep my voice reasonable.

"Jeremy," I said, placing my hand on his arm. He was so tense, his muscles felt like rocks. "I'm a trained operative. I've been in dangerous situations before, as you very well know. I can handle a couple of teenage boys."

Jeremy shook his head. "You didn't see what I saw. I don't want you messing with these guys, Christy. There's something seriously wrong with that Jericho kid. And Ace, you guys gathered some pretty nasty stuff on Mikado, too. Back me up."

Ace glanced down, avoiding Jeremy's eye. "I'm just the tech guy. I don't make mission decisions."

Jeremy glowered at him. "Fine, just pull up the audio feed from tonight."

"You had audio?" I demanded. "Why didn't you tell us that right away?"

"I thought you'd trust my judgment."

I winced. "Just...show us the feed."

Ace opened his laptop, typed in a few commands, and soon we were listening to the sounds of the city—distant horns blaring, the scuffling of feet, and various unidentifiable sounds.

"What are we hearing?" I looked at Jeremy questioningly.

"Just wait for it. It didn't take long. This happened a few streets away from where they lifted the car."

A moment later, a muffled voice came onto the feed, rough-sounding and a little garbled, like maybe the guy was missing more than a few teeth.

"Hey, man. Can you spare a dollar? Just trying to catch the train home, know what I'm sayin'?"

"Of course, friend, of course." That was Jericho's

voice; I recognized it from the feed earlier. "Just step over here with me for a second, okay?"

"Oh thank you, man, that's real nice of you. You got a good heart, I can tell—hey, what the—? Hey!"

After that, all we could hear was the sound of fists connecting with flesh and cries of pain and alarm.

Jeremy nodded, and Ace stopped the feed. "He took that guy into an alley and just whaled on him." Jeremy's face looked grim. "When he'd stopped moving, Jericho opened his wallet, pulled out a dollar and dropped it on the guy's chest. Then he just walked away like nothing had happened."

I shuddered. "That was... awful. I..." I didn't know what to say. What could I say? I still had to go in, and Jeremy knew it.

"He wasn't even anywhere near the crime scene. It's not as if he could have been a witness or caused Jericho any harm. Do you see what I'm saying? The kid just did it for the fun of it. A guy like that—you just never know what he's capable of."

"Was there any more?" Halluis interjected.

Jeremy looked confused. "I got the guy help, if that's what you mean. I called an ambulance. I think he's going to be all right, but I can't be sure. He was beaten pretty badly."

Halluis was shaking his head. "I mean on the feed. Did you hear anything else?"

We all stared at him.

"Look, I'm not trying to be callous, but somebody here has to be the practical one. We have a mission to accomplish. We need every bit of information we can get. Was there anything else on the feed to go off?"

Jeremy scowled, but then he shrugged. "Roll it forward, Ace. He didn't talk again until he met up with the other kid."

Ace complied, and the audio skipped ahead. A new voice joined the feed, a quiet, impassive voice that must have belonged to Mikado. "You're late."

"Don't take it hard, Mikey, you know you're my best girl." Jericho's tone was mocking. "I just gotta spread the wealth, you know? The J-Love's gotta make the rounds."

Mikado didn't respond. I remembered the stillness of his stance, his curt nod. This kid wasn't one to respond to mockery. He knew when to keep his silence.

Jericho snorted. "Come on, where's this lady we're lifting tonight?" A moment passed, then there was a faint, low whistle. "Day-am! Ol' S-Dub doesn't mess around, does he? Jeez, that car is sweet."

Jeremy nodded at Ace, and he cut the feed. "That's it. After that, they just take the car." He sighed and rubbed his eyes.

"We still have to send her in," Halluis repeated. "These are the only guys we've found with a solid connection to the thefts. It's the only choice."

That started Jeremy off arguing again, and I sighed. It was so frustrating to have them squabbling over me like they were my parents or something. I was a trained Division operative. Shouldn't I have a say in this? But neither of them was even asking my opinion. I checked out of the conversation and let my mind wander back to what I'd heard on the feed.

Yes, Jericho sounded scary. And Mikado was so poker-faced it was hard to know what to expect from him. I'd have to look into the intel they'd gathered on him, find out what I'd be dealing with. He hadn't responded at all to Jericho's goading or to his exclamations over the car.

"Hang on," I interjected, forcing my way into the argument. "There was something in that feed we need to pay attention to. Jericho named their leader."

"What? No, he didn't," Halluis started, but fell silent when I held up my hand.

"He did. He said, 'Ol' S-Dub doesn't mess around'— S-Dub. That's gotta be their leader, or at least the one who assigned them their target. The next guy up on the totem pole."

Jeremy pursed his lips. "Sure, I can see that, but S-Dub? That's not much to go on—it could be anyone, anywhere. Sounds like a nickname, maybe like dubstep? Like a deejay or something?"

"Or initials," Ace cut in. "SW, perhaps?"

"More likely than a deejay." Jeremy shrugged. "But how are we supposed to find someone with just initials?"

Ace had already started typing away at his computer, and we all turned to him expectantly.

"There are 32 students at A.G. Bell Academy with the initials SW. Three teachers."

"Subjects?" Jeremy asked. Of course, I had the list of faculty and students memorized, and I pulled it out of its little folder in my brain, studying its contents for clues.

Ace typed again. "American History, Spanish, and— oh, this one's a counselor."

"Hmmm...I mean, it's possible," Jeremy said, but he

still looked skeptical. Halluis shook his head again, and I could tell he was gearing up for another go at the argument.

One of the names stood out to me—I could see it as clearly as if I were reading it off a paper in front of me. I didn't want anyone else to know about this uncanny ability of mine—some things were better kept secret— so I had to bring it up a little carefully.

"What about the auto engineering teacher? He would likely know a little something about cars. If it was going to be anyone at the school..." I trailed off as Ace pulled up the information.

He frowned. "Not likely, first name Robert, last name Shareweather. Not S-Dub."

"Shareweather!" I exclaimed. "There's your S-Dub. *Share, weather.* Not initials, just a nickname."

I let the idea sink in for a minute. Halluis still seemed unconvinced, but Jeremy and Ace started nodding.

"It's worth investigating anyway," I said. "I'll start there on Monday. If Shareweather doesn't pan out, I'll investigate the other SWs. But then..." I didn't have to say the rest. If those leads didn't pan out, I'd have to go back to Jericho and Mikado. "Look, I'm not excited about it either, but we have a job to do."

Jeremy shook his head. I couldn't be sure, but I had the uncanny feeling that there was something he wasn't telling us. "I don't want you to get in with those boys if you don't have to." Jeremy stood. "If you can find some of the other lifters at the school—we know there are more—then I think that's the wiser route."

Halluis sniffed but held his tongue, for which I was

grateful. I didn't want to listen to another round of their bickering.

"So, it's a plan then," I said, forcing a smile. I stood up from the table, hoping that would be enough to quell any further conversation. "It's getting pretty late. I think we all need some sleep."

"It *is* a little late for a child to be up," Halluis said, slipping back into his usual teasing tone. "Let's get you in bed before your parents find out." He smirked at me, and I shot him a truly grateful smile. It was good of him to let it go, let things get back to normal. Whatever that meant for a bunch of spies.

Chapter 4

I spent the weekend studying everything the team had collected on Jericho and Mikado, plus just general information about the school and the teachers whose classes I'd be in. For good measure, I studied up on engineering as well. Amber, my alias, would have had to pass tests and qualify to attend the school, so I couldn't come in looking completely clueless. Not for the first time, I had reason to be grateful for my photographic memory. Even with that skill, after an entire Saturday of cramming my head full of facts, I was exhausted and ready for a break.

I'd considered going sight-seeing on Sunday, since it was probably the only chance I'd get, but the boys were busy with mission preparations—conveniently ducking my invitation to visit Chinatown—and Jeremy was nowhere to be found. When I thought about it, I realized I didn't want to go sight-seeing on my own. What I really wanted was to go to church. I recognized that it was pretty weird for a spy to want to attend church, but I found so much peace there, peace that wasn't found in my job. I probably wouldn't get a chance to go once the mission began, so it felt all the more important to take this opportunity now.

After the service, I was feeling much more at peace with the task in front of me. If only I could impart a little of that peace to Jeremy. When I returned to the brownstone, he was back, poring over information in the conference room. I watched him from the door. Tension was evident in the way he hunched his strong shoulders and the way he bit down on his knuckles whenever he wasn't typing. I wished I could pull him into a hug, but I wasn't sure such a gesture would be entirely welcome. Sure, we'd been through so much together, but he was my mission leader—and I'd never seen him hug Halluis or Ace.

"Jeremy," I said gently, trying not to startle him. He turned and looked at me, and the circles beneath his reassuring eyes made it clear that he had hardly slept. His strong jaw sported the perfect five o'clock shadow. I sighed. "It's going to be okay," I said. "You can trust me. I really can do this. Don't you know that by now?"

Jeremy opened his mouth, then shook his head. "It's not that—I do trust you."

I raised an eyebrow at him. "Then, why so worried?"

He just shook his head again. "Forget about it. You're gonna be great. You always are."

I smiled, but inside I was still perplexed. There was something he wasn't saying. I wished I knew how to break past that stoic barrier. "Thanks, Jeremy. I won't let you down. I promise."

***

Bright and early Monday morning, I took the

crowded subway to the school and made my way to the auto engineering outbuilding.

It was a single-story building directly behind the school, sandwiched inside a block of brownstones. Two adjacent brownstones had been remodeled into the A. G. Bell Engineering Academy. A narrow driveway led from the street to a small parking garage below the outbuilding and to a small, paved, open space where students could hang out on breaks and at lunch. I still had a hard time accepting that it was a school. I was used to the sprawling campuses in the west and south and had never attended a school in a huge metropolitan city.

New Yorkers were magicians with space. Every inch everywhere was used to maximum capacity. The block surrounding the school was full of residential brownstones and small businesses. There was no football field, no soccer field, and certainly no baseball field. These private schools didn't offer extracurricular sports, so none was needed. Of course, Central Park was only a block away, so no one could complain about green space.

If you wanted your kids to become something, it was pretty much a necessity to send them to a private school of some sort. Parents actually put their kids on waiting lists from the time they were born to get into the school they thought best. A.G. Bell Academy prepared kids with either the aptitude or the fortitude to become some type of engineer.

I tugged at the uncomfortable uniform I had to wear: a starched white button-up shirt, tucked crisply into a red and blue plaid wool skirt. Knee-high socks and ridiculously shiny Mary Janes polished off the ensemble. My long, straight hair had been dyed red, and I wore it up in a high ponytail.

I'd gone to the school early, my go bag disguised as a high schooler's backpack, hoping to get a chance to snoop around in Mr. Shareweather's office, adjacent to the auto engineering outbuilding. However, as I approached the squat building, I realized my hope for some alone time was in vain. I could hear muffled voices coming from the building as I walked past some windows. I groaned inwardly. Was detention or an early study hall held in the building each morning? At least I could listen in and maybe learn a little more about Shareweather. Ace's algorithm hadn't tagged him, so there wasn't any surveillance data on him. All I'd been able to learn about him was what was in his official school file, and that hadn't been too helpful.

I stepped lightly toward the outside door of his office. A careful tug on the door handle proved it was locked. I tried the back door. Locked. I searched for an open window. I didn't find one, but I could see into the shop area because some blinds had been damaged, the thin metal slats sticking out in an odd way.

I put my nose up to the closed window, careful not to let my uniform brush up against the dirty outer wall, and watched as Mr. Shareweather spoke to a small class of students. His thick, bushy, salt-and-pepper hair clashed slightly with his more youthful brownish-red mustache and beard, although his well-trimmed beard did fade to gray and white near the ends. He seemed to have a permanent worried look on his face, making his eyes seem smaller than they already were. The creases in his deeply tanned forehead seemed more like the mountains one might find on an eighty-year-old man and not one who was fifty, tops.

I watched as he stepped toward a nearby car door and demonstrated what no ethical teacher should: how to break into a car that didn't have a smart key. I smiled inwardly: I'd found S-Dub. I didn't even need to hear what he was saying, I knew the movements. It hadn't been that long ago that I had learned to do that very thing as part of my training for this mission.

I wished desperately I was still connected to the team over com. I would have loved in that moment to gloat to Halluis over this little triumph. Score another one for Christy. Of course, it was completely impractical to have a com device in my ear at school—even a subtle one could be spotted and cause me no end of trouble. I wore a wire, though, so the team was listening in back at headquarters. I resisted the urge to whisper "Ha!"—it would have been unprofessional. I didn't want to undermine my team's confidence in me.

I turned my focus back to the classroom. There was a small group of kids gathered around S-Dub's hulking mass—seven in all. After his demonstration, five students practiced on several different cars while two other students seemed to be helping them, mentoring them. One of them had this strut. He was one confident guy.

It wasn't like the building could house a bunch of cars, but it had sections of cars throughout the room. Five students were male and two female. I scanned five faces quickly, committing them to memory. The two student mentors never turned toward me, so I wasn't able to memorize their faces. I had to memorize their clothing and build instead. Neither Jericho nor Mikado was present. Maybe they were in the advanced class, I thought ruefully.

They all shouted out once they figured it out and were successful. I watched, wondering if S-Dub would teach them something I didn't know. As S-Dub's formidable shape moved toward one student, a waif-like girl, she visibly trembled. Apparently, she'd been unable to start even one of the simplest of cars. I'd be a bit scared if he were stomping toward me, too.

A light went on in the building behind the school. As it did, Mr. Shareweather walked in front of the section of windows I was looking through, and though he was a good twenty feet from me, my shadow fell across his face. I took a sharp breath. He paused, turning his head in my direction.

Crap! I ducked and then cruised out of there without a sound. For about half a second, I thought I should stick around and pretend I had only been curious about what was going on, but I was sure S-Dub wouldn't stand for that. If he was the car gang's leader, he'd be too smart to believe that. Instead I ran, heading for the corner of the building.

My heart thundered as I ran, adrenaline and training making me fast. Once I'd made it into the narrow alleyway next to the outbuilding, I heard the back door to the shop click open and the pounding of feet headed my way. My whole body was on alert, all muscles tight and ready to fight. I sprinted along the side of the building and ran without a sound around the other corner to get to the front of the building and get the heck out of there. Had others beside Mr. Shareweather caught a glimpse of me? I wasn't going to stick around to find out. I was about to round the corner to the front of the building when I heard feet inside the building pounding my way. I looked at the door at the front of the building. I was cornered.

S-Dub was smart. I couldn't double back to the back of the building, and I couldn't escape anywhere from the side I was on—I was surrounded by buildings that I couldn't enter. And from the sounds of pounding feet, I wouldn't have time to run to the front of the building and slip into the small parking garage either. I licked my lips and tasted the salt of sweat beading on my upper lip.

In a rush, I looked all around; my only option was to climb the rain gutter spout. I wiggled it. It was old. Would it support my weight? I had to chance it. I jumped up as far as I could and shimmied up the pipe, sure my white button-up shirt was getting all kinds of dirty. I cut my hand on one of the brackets that braced the pipe to the building, but I couldn't stop and check it out. I bit down on the pain and pulled myself further up the pipe, feeling my skirt get caught on the same bracket I'd cut my hand on. I was almost to the roof. The sound of feet from the back of the building pounded nearer, and the door just to the side of where I was opened wide. They'd be upon me any second. I pulled hard, hearing the skirt rip. I gripped the edge of the roof just as my pursuers rounded the corner. I could feel their presence below me, hear their heavy breathing.

I didn't dare move. One sound and they'd look up.

My arm strained, and my grip loosened as sweat slicked my hand. I closed my eyes and said a prayer that no one would look up. The two groups of kids were directly below me.

"No one's here," one male voice said.

"S-Dub's imagining things." Someone kicked a rock and sent it rolling down the sidewalk.

"He usually doesn't do that." There was scorn in this boy's voice. "He's got a sharp eye."

I could feel them looking all around.

Please don't look up! I glanced at my white-knuckled hand and its precarious hold on the edge of the roof, my other gripping the pipe. I watched helplessly as a drop of blood pooled on the edge of my hand and then dropped to the ground right behind one of the kids, barely missing his head.

"Let's get back in," the first voice chimed in. "We've only got half an hour to perfect this. Tonight's the night, and we won't have another chance. We can't let S-Dub down."

I heard murmurs of assent and footsteps moving toward the front of the building just as my hand slipped. I pressed my legs hard into the pole and pushed my shoes even harder into the brick exterior of the building, latching my now-loose hand on the pole in hopes of gaining some stability. I held my breath until I was sure they'd had enough time to get back inside. With renewed effort, I made my way down the pole and, once on the ground, with utmost stealth, I made my way into the parking garage to wait it out.

Chapter 5

Blood dripped from the deep cut on my hand. I ripped my dirty shirt and wrapped the strip of cloth around the gash, hoping to stem the tide. It stung. Leaning against the cement wall, out of the path of the masses walking on the sidewalk, I thought about what I'd seen and heard. *Tonight's the night.* What were they doing tonight? Stealing cars? Putting their learning to good use? I waited ten anxious minutes before venturing back out of the garage and melting into the foot traffic on the sidewalk.

I walked casually, bumping along the crowded sidewalk to the next block. The noise of the city pressed in on me: people chatted on phones, vendors shouted, and obviously frustrated drivers honked their horns, urging the cars in front of them to drive faster even though it was impossible. I ducked into a little alcove, trying to muffle some of the noise and pulled out my phone. I cringed a little as I dialed Jeremy. The day had barely even started and I was already calling for help. It definitely dulled a little of the triumph I'd felt at being right about S-Dub. There was nothing for it, though—I needed a new uniform, not to mention some mild medical attention. I bit my lip and hit *call*.

A few minutes later, Jeremy met me near a subway hole, a bag of supplies in his hand.

It might have been my imagination, but it seemed he was barely containing the urge to shout, "I told you so." This was not how this day was supposed to go at all. I was supposed to be calming Jeremy's fears, showing him I had this mission easily under control. Instead, my disheveled uniform and gashed hand must have screamed, "She's completely inept!" I didn't think it would help if I explained that it was quick thinking and pretty amazing physical prowess that had helped me avoid getting caught. The fact was I'd nearly blown my cover in the first half hour of the mission. Not good.

"Don't beat yourself up, Christy," Jeremy's voice cut into my thoughts, taking me by surprise. Had he read my mind? "Things go wrong sometimes. You handled yourself well, though. That took some quick thinking not to get made."

"Thanks," I said, hesitantly. Had I misread his facial expression? I thought he'd be ready to lay on the lecture, but he hadn't.

"Come on. Let's take care of that hand." We walked to the park and sat on a secluded bench. He numbed my hand and stitched it up. He worked quickly with strong, expert hands.

"It wasn't as deep as I'd thought when you first showed it to me."

"Yeah, the blood made it seem worse than it really was. It barely even hurts."

"Next task," Jeremy said, holding up a bag with fresh clothes and nodding to a nearby café. "You can get changed in there."

He ordered a coffee and a croissant, and I ducked into the restroom with the bag he'd brought. I changed into the new uniform and changed my hairstyle. I'd had my hair in a tight ponytail, and now it hung loose about my face. Instead of the white button-up shirt, plaid wool skirt, and knee socks, I now wore solid khaki pants and a navy blue polo shirt. If anything, this getup was even worse than the last. I felt like an idiot, but we didn't want to chance the auto engineering teacher or any of the kids identifying me from the quick glance they may have gotten at the shop. Sometimes it took seeing someone again to figure out you'd seen them before.

"Now that we know Shareweather is our man," Jeremy said, "all you need to do is find an in."

"I saw two girls in the classroom this morning. S-Dub was training them to break into cheaper cars. I think they might be my way in. I'll befriend them and play up the poor-me-I-need-money angle and see if they won't get me an audience with S-Dub. I'll also make myself sympathetic to him when I have his class, making sure he knows I could use some extra cash. If he's looking for new recruits, maybe he'll approach me."

"I like the sound of that a lot better than you getting mixed up with those boys."

"Me, too." I shook my head and tried to ignore the throbbing that had begun in my hand.

"I've asked Halluis to start shadowing you."

"What? Jeremy, I do not need—" I could feel heat rising in my chest.

He spoke over my objections. "Look, if you're getting involved with this group that involves Mikado and Jericho, then I'd like a little more assurance of your safety than a wire and an electronic feed."

I grimaced, but kept my voice low to avoid being overheard. "Jeremy, my safety is not the number one concern. I am a spy. Not a witness, not an asset—a spy. I don't need any extra protection. I can complete this mission without being babysat."

"No one is babysitting you. To be honest, Halluis needs something to do. I'm sure you've noticed he's been a little—tense, lately. I think he needs to feel more involved in the day-to-day aspect of the mission, or he's going to go insane. He's making me insane, at the very least."

I narrowed my eyes. It felt like an excuse, but there wasn't any more time to argue about it now. "Fine." My voice was flat, and I hoped he heard the irritation in it.

"I knew you'd see it my way. You should be fine at school—provided you avoid climbing up any more walls—but anywhere else, Halluis will be shadowing you."

I sighed.

He smiled. "Go get 'em."

***

Checking in with the office and picking up my class schedule made me late to second period, which turned out to be a very bad thing. And if I thought being the new kid at the school was going to help me, I couldn't have been more wrong. I was now the center of

Cindy M. Hogan

attention.

The meanest, most old-fashioned teacher in the world peered down at my excuse note over her boondoggled glasses. I smiled my best smile, but she didn't reach out for the note. Instead, in her clipped, proper voice, she said, "Miss Smith, seeing as this is your first day of school here at the academy I would have expected you to show up on time. I do not like to be interrupted. I would appreciate you waiting outside the door until I am finished directing the class."

I blinked, not quite sure what she meant. I decided my best course of action was to wait in the hall until she invited me back in, possibly after giving the class instructions? I let the arm holding the note fall to my side and backed up, out of the classroom. She watched me intently until I slipped around the corner where she couldn't see me. I sighed and resigned myself to waiting until she was finished directing the class.

I soon learned, however, that by *directing* she must have meant *lecturing*, and she wasn't going to *finish* at all.

Listening to her gravelly voice made me sleepy, so I slid down the wall and closed my eyes. Next thing I knew, students rushed by me with quick steps, never quite running, because that would be bad here at A.G. Bell Academy.

Before I'd quite gotten my bearings, a hand was thrust into my face. "Need some help?"

I looked up to find a boy with piercing blue eyes that contrasted nicely with his caramel-colored skin, dark, obviously professionally sculpted eyebrows, and very short hair. I blinked twice. I started to reach up with my injured hand, but thought better of it and gave him my left instead. He was strong, and I popped quickly to my feet.

"I'm Viktor." He looked me hard in the eyes.

"Amber."

"Ms. Milner is awful, isn't she?"

"You could say that." I shifted from one foot to the other, wondering when he planned on letting my hand go. His glassy blue eyes traveled over my body appraisingly.

"Uh, I better get going. I'm sure Mr. Ramos won't excuse a tardy, either."

"Where's your cell?" He held out his other hand and winked at me.

I stiffened and started tugging on the hand he still held. His thumb caressed the inside of my palm, sending a sickening feeling to my gut.

"I'll punch my number in. You can call me later, and we could, ya know, discuss what I learned today in the old hag's class." He licked his bottom lip.

I pulled my hand back hard. "Uh. I can't be late. You saw what that got me with Milner." I didn't let my stare waver. "I'm sure I'll see you around." I walked away. I could feel his eyes watching me. I didn't like it one bit and sped up.

It felt good to be in the safety of Mr. Ramos' classroom. Viktor had given me a seriously ugly feeling. I took my seat just as the bell rang and looked up to see a female teacher writing her name on the board. A substitute, then. It irritated me—I'd studied all my teachers' files, and now here was a perfect stranger standing in front of me. It didn't really matter, but it was annoying anyway.

Both Jericho and Mikado were in this class. From the way they acted, you'd never know they stole cars together at night. Jericho sat across the room from Mikado, and they didn't acknowledge each other even once.

We watched a film on the dissection of a mouse to ready us for our dissection the next day. I kept my eyes on my notebook. I definitely didn't need to see that. I could hear all the crass comments from the boys about doing even worse things to those poor mice. I focused on the worst of them, spoken by none other than Jericho, and he wasn't talking about mice, but fictional people he'd like to gut. It was easy to pay attention to Jericho when he spoke. There was something pleasant about the strong set of his jaw and his smoky, deep brown eyes. They were all laughing, making loud dying noises and acting out deaths. The substitute kept shushing the kids, but they ignored her, and she finally gave up and focused on reading a book.

Normally, I wouldn't take stock in what a teenage boy said about slicing up action heroes from the movies, but there was something serious in Jericho's voice—violent and real. As the video ended, the sub left her desk to hand out the worksheets that went with the video. Jericho made his way to her desk and asked if he could borrow a pen. She told him he could. I watched him intently. There was something in his eye, a mischievous light that held my attention. The rest of the class talked or passed the papers to the person behind them. Jericho grabbed a pen and dropped it. He leaned down behind the desk to retrieve the pen and when he stood back up, a brief look of triumph crossed his face. He made his way back to his seat sans a pen.

The sub finished passing out the papers and sat back down. As she did, the office chair fell back onto the floor, sending her feet flying up into the air and her head crashing into the wall. While the rest of the class laughed, Jericho rushed to her, helping her get up and fixing the chair for her. She thanked him profusely and rubbed at her head. Heat seared my gut. He had engineered that whole scenario. Why? Why would he put her in danger and then come to her aid, acting the hero? I stared at the satisfied look on his face, and I watched as the girls in the class stared at him, admiring his very being.

Jeremy was right about this guy. There was something disturbing going on. First the homeless man, and then this strange display. And yet, he was class president—*trés populaire*, as Halluis had put it. It was like he had a split personality. He was scary. That was all there was to it.

As for Mikado, there had been some interesting things in his file. He never got in anyone's way and tended to keep a low profile, except at his martial arts lessons every day after school. I figured that was the "nasty stuff" Jeremy had mentioned. He was one powerful fighter. The file said he could take down three opponents without much effort, and that it looked like he could have taken down a couple more before having to breathe hard. As I watched him in class, I noticed that same inhuman stillness that had caught my attention the night they'd stolen the S63. He reminded me of a panther, crouched and waiting to strike. It made me shudder inwardly.

***

My first opportunity to make contact with my targets was at lunch. I scanned the cafeteria, quickly finding the five kids I had identified from S-Dub's car theft training. None of them sat with each other except for two, the most unlikely girls I thought I would find in auto engineering class. In my mind, I pictured manly girls, or at least ones who wore ties and stern faces, and stiff, straight-laced boys who lacked imagination as the preferred type for auto engineering. So much for stereotypes. The one girl had all pointy features: a pointy chin, a pointy nose, pointy ears, and even her head seemed a bit pointy. If anyone could have been an elf masquerading as a human, it was this girl. Even the odd shade of her green eyes against her dark skin made her seem otherworldly. They were a bit too clear and bright. Her friend was also small in build, but much rounder. I guess you'd call the shape of her face a heart shape. Her large, sullen, gray eyes betrayed no emotion, and her cheeks were puffy and rosy.

I headed for their table, my sack lunch in hand. Both sat eating without speaking. When I plopped down next to them, they didn't even look up. With their heads angled down, they ate their school lunch voraciously, like they never got to eat.

I checked out their clothes and saw the telltale signs of poverty. Their uniforms were dingy, slightly fraying, and a bit thin. These girls were scholarship girls for sure. And I was Amber Smith, a scholarship girl, too. That meant these girls were smart, or they wouldn't be here. I wondered what S-Dub had promised them to get them into early-morning auto class for car thieves. It had to be money related. I wondered if he'd invite me. Maybe he targeted scholarship kids. Then I thought of Jericho, who was extremely well-off. Why had Shareweather targeted him?

"Hi!" I said, not wanting to waste any time.

Neither said a word.

"I'm Amber. I just moved here and—"

Hands pushed firmly on my shoulders. "I've been looking all over for you," a familiar voice said, sending chills of revulsion down my spine. "I didn't expect you to be sitting with the riff-raff, though."

"Hey," I said, standing up and facing him—Viktor. "You should apologize to..." I realized I didn't know their names and stuttered, "tttheese fine young women. I don't see any riff-raff."

With eyes the size of apricots, he said, "Are you blind?"

The boldness and utter meanness of his question made me ball up my fists.

"Look, Viktor." I took a step away from the table and poked him in the chest with my index finger over and over again while I spoke. "I want you to leave, and I wouldn't mind never seeing your ugly mug again." He was anything but ugly, but I was referring to his insides.

He threw his arms in the air like he was being held up at gunpoint and said, "No problem, sweet thing. Just trying to help the new girl out." He had this slight accent to some of his words, and I wondered where he was from. His head made sweeping motions from side to side, checking to see who was watching, I'm sure. He didn't turn away from me until he was at least ten yards away. A scowl seemed to present itself the farther away from me he got. Something played at the back of my mind as I watched him continue to walk away once his back was to me, but I couldn't put my finger on it. I turned and sat, only to find I was alone at the table. Those two girls had abandoned me. My face burned. Rejected by the rejects. What next?

I looked around, thinking about moving to another table so I wouldn't feel like such a loser, the feelings of sitting alone during my real high school experience threatening me once again. Then I remembered that I was no longer that bullied girl, but a killer spy. I stayed put, laughing inside.

To my surprise, a blond boy followed by three others came and sat down at my table. "I'm Hank," the boy said, patting his completely unmuscular chest. He and his friends all looked young, freshmen probably. And all looked like they skipped sports in favor of books.

"Have you come to save me from my complete loserness?"

All four smiled at me, but the blond was obviously the spokesman. "Actually, we were hoping you could save us from that fate." He and two others wore braces.

"I'll do my best."

From that point on, their chatter was unstoppable, and I knew I'd never sit alone here at lunch again. I admired these kids for taking a stand against bullying and reaching out to the new kid.

I used the time to get more insider information on the school and how the social structure worked. One thing was for certain. The majority of the student body loved Jericho.

Chapter 6

Fourth period was auto engineering, with Mr. Shareweather, of course. Ace, listening to the feed from my wire, had pulled some quick computer magic and changed my schedule to get me into the same class as the two girls I was hoping to befriend. I'd gotten a note from the office during my third period with an apology for the confusion and my corrected schedule. Once again, I was grateful for my team. It was pretty awesome having someone to rely on behind the scenes. I wished he'd been able to give me more information on the girls, but I'd take what I could get.

After getting class materials from Shareweather, I went straight for the two girls.

"What the heck?" I asked, stepping right in front of them. "I was sticking up for you two, and you do a Houdini on me? I felt pretty dumb sitting there after that."

They both stared at me. The round girl seemed to stand guard, a few inches in front of the elf-like girl.

I stood, hands on my hips, narrowing my eyes at

them to show them I meant business. Neither spoke before S-Dub's booming voice filled the room. "We will be discussing lock mechanisms and how they typically function as well as discussing possible ways to improve them."

I stared at the two girls. What was their deal? Why wouldn't they talk to me?

They tried to avoid me all class period as we inspected different mechanisms in the various sections of cars in the room, but I stuck to them like tar to a shoe the whole period. I hoped my persistence would pay off.

We got into groups to discuss changes that could be made, and class flew by. My hands got grimier and grimier the more car parts I touched. At the end of class, we used a good amount of Goop to clean our hands in the locker room. Even after three scrubbings, they seemed to still have a slight gray tinge to them, not to mention the terrible smell left behind. I pulled out some fresh-smelling hand cream and rubbed it in. When I looked up, it shocked me to see both girls staring at me. Their focus seemed to be the lotion bottle.

"You want some? That Goop made my hands reek." I held the bottle out to them.

I saw the slightest upturn in their mouths as they made their way over to me. They greedily rubbed the lotion into their hands and up their arms. The bell rang, and I turned to go.

"Hey, wait." It was the round girl who spoke.

"Yeah?" I said, continuing to walk but looking back over my shoulder at them.

"I'm Gina, and this is Karina." She motioned toward the pointy girl.

I stopped and smiled. "Like I said before," I gave them a meaningful look. "I'm Amber." I smiled again, and my insides celebrated the much-needed win.

"Wait!" Gina grabbed my arm. "You forgot your lotion."

"You want it?" I asked. "I accidentally brought two to school today. It's totally weighing me down. You're welcome to it." I turned to go before they could protest.

A deep, warm feeling spread through my chest. I bounded down the hall.

I had physics next, and Viktor sat at the other end of the room. I could have sworn I saw him scowl at me more than once. I guess I'd made an enemy. I didn't care. He gave me the creeps.

Three kids from the incident at the shop were in that class with me. I made sure to pay attention to them and try to overhear their conversations.

There was an anxiousness in their words, but it was hard to make anything out. Something was going down and soon. I had to find out what.

Just when I thought I was going to have to follow one of these students for the rest of the day, I caught part of a rushed conversation between Gina and Karina as they were leaving school.

"Just make sure you bring the tools tonight," Karina was saying. "We can't afford for anything to go wrong. I can't stand how S-Dub looks at me when I screw up."

"Nothing's going to go wrong," Gina said confidently. "We've been practicing. We can do this."

"Okay—meet at my place at 6:30? We'll have to ride

the train."

The girls kept talking as they left the building. I considered following them home, but I realized there wasn't much more I could learn. The mention of tools and S-Dub together was a pretty strong indication that something involving the car theft gang was going to happen tonight. I'd just have to follow the girls as they met up at 6:30, and go from there.

***

I was preoccupied as I walked into the brownstone, considering how best to strengthen my tentative connection with Gina and Karina, so at first I didn't notice the angry voices coming from the kitchen. I only clued in when I heard my name.

"...brought in Christy. She shouldn't be involved in this," Jeremy was saying. He wasn't shouting, but I could hear the heat in his voice. I pushed the front door shut as quietly as possible and crept nearer to the kitchen, making no sound.

Halluis answered, and there was venom in his clipped tone. "Agent Hadden has the requisite skills and training needed for this mission. That is why I requested her. Your concern over her involvement is unprofessional."

"Unprofessional? This whole mission is unprofessional—nothing is being done according to protocol. There's no cross-talk between us and other agencies—why haven't we been able to get any of the intel from local law enforcement, or from the FBI? Why haven't we been given any of the extra resources we've asked for—every time I ask for help from Division, my request is denied. Why is there no official Division record of this mission even existing? Something isn't right, and you know it."

"Do you even hear yourself? Cross-talk with other agencies? Official records? We are a black ops organization—we live by secrets. Obviously, there's something we are not privileged to know, and that is the nature of our business. We do as we are told. That's it."

"And that's enough for you?"

"You are young, Agent McGinnis. In my opinion, too young to be running an op like this one. But no one asked my opinion, and I am not going to stand around whining about it. I do what I am told. I suggest you do the same."

There was a momentary silence, and I belatedly realized that the argument was over. Halluis stormed out of the kitchen, took one glance at me, and stomped up the stairs. The argument echoed through my thoughts—Jeremy thought I shouldn't have been brought in? He was concerned I wasn't good enough for the mission? I thought he knew me well enough to trust me by now. Even though we had never before worked as closely as we were now, he had seen me in action. That thought sent a wave of icy cold anxiety through me. Was that the problem? Jeremy *had* seen what I could do—and it wasn't enough.

I didn't want to face him—how could I look him in the eye, knowing he didn't want me on this mission? I quickly backtracked, retreating to the entryway to take off my bag and coat before Jeremy emerged from the kitchen, hoping to make it seem like I had only just come in.

It didn't matter anyway, because Jeremy never came out. I approached the kitchen gingerly, wondering if I should bring up what I'd heard or pretend to be entirely ignorant of the argument. But when I entered the kitchen, Jeremy was gone.

"I think he left," said a voice from behind me.

I whirled around to find Ace standing awkwardly in the doorway. His hands were shoved deep into his pockets, his short-sleeve T-shirt emphasizing the tattoos up and down his arms. He smiled uncomfortably.

"You heard that, too, then?" I swallowed, hard. I didn't want Ace to know just how much Jeremy's words had affected me. I decided to focus on the second half of the argument. "Jeremy thinks there's something strange about the mission. What should we do?"

He shrugged. "I don't get involved. All this stuff goes over my head, really. I'm just the analyst, glorified tech support, remember? They put me out in the field because it's easier than having me answer questions over the phone, but I'm not one of you guys. I just hand out the gadgets and keep my mouth shut."

"But don't you think we should talk about this?"

He shook his head. "Come on, I've got some new toys for you." He turned around and headed up the stairs.

I stood in the kitchen for a moment, trying to process what had just happened. I scowled, then followed Ace up the stairs, shoving the disturbing argument from my mind. I'd have to figure this out later. I had to focus on the one thing I had any control over right now—my own mission.

***

"Just stick this little dot somewhere on one of the girls' upper body." Ace handed me a piece of stiff paper that had a little clear dot on it. "The closer to the mouth you get it, the clearer it will be." He lifted up another stiff piece of paper, but this one was blue instead of white. "You can stick this anywhere on whichever girl you want. It's the tracker. I didn't have time to get more than one of each made."

"I'll be shadowing you tonight," Halluis said. He acted completely nonchalant, as if he had not caught me eavesdropping on his argument with Jeremy moments before. He held up a little metal device and said, "If the kids are going after a car, I'll put this little baby on there, and it'll lead us to their storage facility or chop shop. Done and done. And Jeremy will be in the shadows, waiting for the girls or someone to make a move on cars. I'll stick to you and the girls, and he'll watch out for S-Dub, the boss, or even the boys."

"Sounds like a plan. Do you have an earpiece for me?"

Ace handed me a tiny com to stick into my ear. "There's only one problem."

I raised my eyebrows.

"You won't be able to talk to me or Halluis once the listening device is active on the girls. I couldn't figure out how to stop the terrible feedback from having both active at the same time. Only know that Halluis will be somewhere in the shadows following you. You can't have better backup than Halluis."

I smiled, but the fact that Jeremy thought I needed a shadow at all pricked at me. When he'd first suggested

Halluis shadow me, I'd thought he was being overprotective. I'd even found it a little charming, if irritating. But now, realizing that he'd assigned Halluis to follow me because he was concerned I couldn't do my job—I had to fight back the blush of shame that threatened to creep over my face.

Well, whatever Jeremy thought, I'd have to prove him wrong. And I couldn't let his doubt affect me, or the rest of my team.

"Thank you," I said. "I'll do my best not to need any backup."

Chapter 7

At 6:15, I sat on a bench about a block away from the entrance to the girls' building, disguised as a bum—an outfit inspired by one of my trainers, Cort. Ace had accessed the school's directory and found the addresses for both girls. It turned out they both lived in Prospect Park, in a massive apartment complex built on what had once been the Brooklyn Dodgers' Ebbets Field— one of the infamous New York City projects.

We'd agreed that it would be less conspicuous to watch for the girls out here—they'd have to pass right by me to get to the nearest subway hole—rather than try to catch them at Karina's apartment. Even though I would have done it, I was glad I didn't have to go inside. The run-down apartments had an ominous feeling.

In my disguise, I'd be able to place the trackers and then follow them the whole night, hopefully to watch them steal a car and follow them to the car's end destination. Sure enough, at 6:40, the girls walked by, heading for the subway, Gina in a puffy black parka, a royal blue dress underneath it, and Karina in a pea coat with a hint of red poking out. I furrowed my brow. They were supposed to be stealing cars tonight, unless I'd completely misinterpreted their conversation. Why were they dressed for a dance?

Before entering the subway, Karina spun around, throwing her arms into the air.

Gina laughed and said, "The guys won't be able to take their eyes off of you tonight!"

"You either, Gina!"

They stood under a streetlamp, and the delight on their faces and the way they walked, as if walking on air, made me smile. They looked happy. A tall, husky man with a black leather jacket over a black hoodie, followed close behind them, a ski cap pulled down tight against his head. He'd been behind them since they'd left the projects. Did they know each other? My heart sped up. If he tried anything, I'd have to stop him.

"Do you really think this dress makes me look skinny?" Gina asked.

"Girl, it doesn't make you look skinny. You *are* skinny. If I were a guy, I'd be all over your sexy self." After a few minutes, Karina added, "I barely ate anything for dinner I was so nervous."

"Don't be nervous. You got this. Those boys won't know what hit them." Gina looked from side to side like she didn't believe her own words. They were definitely going to the dance I'd heard kids talking about all day. This complicated things.

I didn't have time to worry about the implications of this change in plans. The husky man was getting closer, and it was obvious he was headed in the same direction as the girls. He moved quickly in front of them just as they were about to take the steps down into the subway. I darted forward, ready to strike, but then had to redirect myself down the steps at the last second, brushing against him slightly. I mumbled an apology.

"You can't go into the subway without first giving Uncle Laron a goodbye hug. I know you won't be so willing outside the school or on the train. I'll be close enough to help you if you need it. Don't worry, your friends won't know I'm there." He hugged Gina. They knew him. He'd been their escort. I felt pretty foolish listening to them follow me down the steps, Laron still talking.

"Have a good time. I'll meet you at the school at 10:20. Be safe."

If they were planning on doing something illegal tonight, no one would have expected it. They took a seat facing the middle of the train. I held onto a pole only feet from them. Uncle Laron sat at the other end of the car.

"I can't wait to dance with Mateo," Karina said. "Sure, I'll only come up to his waist, but he's so hot."

"You can say that again," Gina said. "And he smells so yummy."

They nodded and giggled. Was I following the wrong girls? I wished I could consult Jeremy, but he'd never come back after the argument with Halluis. I had to go with the intel I had, and that was that the girls were involved with something tonight, something more than a dance. I'd just have to trust my gut and follow through with the plan. I'd figure out what to do about the dance when the time came. For now, I needed to plant the trackers.

I pretended to lose my balance on the train when it took a curve, and I plopped the flat locator bug onto Gina's sleeve, then pressed a listening device on Karina's collar. They both screamed and squealed, standing up and brushing themselves off as I stumbled away. Laron made his way over to them, so I hurried into the next car.

I sat in the train car next to theirs, body hunched over, earpiece in, listening to the two girls talk about how disgusting it was to get groped by some bum and lamenting the fact that they had to ride the subway at night to the school. That *would* suck. Most kids would find a ride in a taxi or with someone who owned a car, especially at an expensive school like Bell. I opened the GPS function on my watch and made sure that the locator I'd put on Gina was transmitting. A purple dot flashed hot on the screen. They were mine.

Now I had to figure out how to blend in at the dance, when I'd planned to be disguised as a bum the entire night.

Gina, Karina, and their escort exited the station at the stop nearest the school, and I slunk out behind them, making sure they didn't notice me. I watched them exit the subway and head toward the school.

I made my way to the back stall of the closest restroom in a deli, cleaned off the makeup on my face with a wet wipe, and pulled out the clothes in my go bag.

First, I selected a plain white blouse—the type commonly used by waiters and valets, a convenient disguise in a city like New York. I quickly shed the coat, scarf, T-shirt, and torn-up sweater that was my bum disguise and yanked on the white shirt. It looked a little austere, so I rolled up the sleeves, then unbuttoned the bottom five buttons and tied the ends into a chic little knot. I went through my options for the bottom half of my body, but they all seemed wrong—the muddy, baggy jeans I was currently wearing were definitely out. The black dress slacks that normally accompanied the white shirt were definitely too formal, and the only other pants I had were a pair of wool uniform pants. I grimaced.

Just as I was about to despair—I couldn't show up at a school dance in my uniform!—my eyes lit on the scarf I'd discarded. An idea struck. I quickly slipped out of the jeans and started wrapping and tucking the scarf around my waist. In one minute flat, I had a stylish draped skirt—perhaps a little shorter than I would have preferred, but still school-dance appropriate. A few well-placed safety pins ensured the skirt would stay in place the whole night. I smiled in satisfaction.

Luckily, I had a pair of slim, strappy black heels in my go bag—they didn't take up much space, and they took the waiter disguise upscale if necessary. I quickly traded them for my raggedy sneakers, then I used my mirror and wipes to completely clear myself of the disguise makeup and put my normal teenage makeup back on. After carefully arranging my go bag so that if anyone looked inside they'd think it merely a high-schooler's bag, I brushed my teeth. After a quick once-over with the mirror, I deemed myself completely transformed and hurried out of the deli.

I listened in on the girls the whole time, figuring out

a new plan for the evening. If they were going to the dance, perhaps all the other thieves would be at the dance, too. Maybe I'd be able to ID the two I'd seen in Shareweather's class, but didn't recognize. If I could figure out who they were, that would give us nine kids to track, including Jericho and Mikado. More bodies to track would be a definite bonus. I could also keep track of all the thieves and give the team a heads up when they left the building in case of equipment failure. Maybe I'd overhear something that would give us a jump on the gang.

The only interesting thing I heard from the girls was a comment about how they hoped no one would be by a particular door. I figured that was my only clue. They would most likely be sneaking out a door at the dance to go do whatever it was they were going to do. I hoped it had to do with stealing cars. Best case scenario, Halluis would place his tracker on whatever car they stole, and then the tracker would lead us to the storage facility where they kept all the stolen cars. We could then go in, retrieve the Mercedes 300 we'd been assigned to retrieve, and send the authorities to get the rest.

I let my team know about the change in plans as I continued on my way to the school. Since we weren't able to use the com except to listen in on the girls, I pulled out my phone and sent a coded text.

The girls are going to the school dance. If they leave, Halluis will have to follow. I'll be at the dance, trying to learn everything I can about S-Dub's gang. There may be more kids involved than just the ones I saw this morning.

A moment later, my phone buzzed, and I read the coded response. *Got it. Halluis is in position to tail the girls.*

I heard the girls arrive at the school and enter the main lobby, where the dance was held. I had to promptly turn the volume down on my earpiece. I wouldn't be able to understand most of what they were saying unless they left the room. That was when I wanted to hear them anyway.

Once I arrived, I listened to the same spiel given to Karina and Gina from the people at the door.

"Once you enter the dance, you are obligated to stay until nine. No ins and outs." I wouldn't be leaving. My job was to keep track of anyone else who left the dance.

I signed in and went through the doors to the sound of pounding bass. Tables and chairs lined the walls, but only a smattering of kids sat in them. I stood back and perused the crowd. I found the five kids I had ID'd from Mr. Shareweather's auto theft class. Only Gina and Karina were together, but they were all dancing their hearts out. I set my bag under a chair by the bathroom and turned back to the dancing mass, intending on working my way over to the girls.

Before I could do that, though, a curious thing happened as I looked over the crowd. A teacher made her way out to the dance floor and tapped a guy on the shoulder. He stepped out of the dancing mass and leaned down to listen to the woman, then they both looked my way. He immediately started toward me. I turned my head to see if someone was behind me, but no one was. He kept on the path to intersect with me. I felt my face flame for some reason as I started to walk out onto the dance floor.

The guy heading my way was in no way knock-your-heart-out gorgeous, but the idea he was heading for me made my insides buzz. As he got closer, I squeezed my hands together and realized this guy was slightly cuter than average—someone I could easily talk to and not worry that I was about to come face-to-face with someone way out of my league. He could make a good cover as I tried to inconspicuously keep track of the thieves at the dance. By the time he reached me, I had calmed my thudding heart and was able to give him a genuine smile.

He spoke first. "Hi. I'm Carson. Would you like to dance?" He cocked his head to the side, the minimal light dancing off the light blond highlights in his dark blond hair.

"Sure." I smiled at him. Dancing would give me plenty of casual-seeming eye contact on all the different elements of S-Dub's little group. This would be a piece of cake surveillance job.

He bit his bottom lip with his front teeth, and I took quick stock of my dancing partner. I couldn't tell if the close-cropped beard and mustache were permanent or if he'd simply chosen not to shave today. Permanent was good in this case. It would be nice to have a good-looking guy on my arm while I kept an eye on the crowd.

"Great." He held out his hand to me, and I took it. He led me out to the herd of dancing students, and I took a mental snapshot of the crowd. As I twirled around with him, I noticed everything. The longer we danced, though, I felt a momentary silliness come over me. I knew I knew how to dance, but I hadn't been to a high school dance in forever and didn't want to look like a fool. I reminded myself that I was Amber, a high school student, not Christy, an agent for D57. The deejay played a familiar pop-rock song that eased my tension in a hurry. Carson totally got all into the music, singing along while he danced. His self-assuredness made him slightly better-looking. When the song ended, he led me away from the dance floor.

"So," I said, leaning toward him so he could hear me over the music. He leaned down toward me. "That teacher made you ask me to dance?" There was no way a guy like this wouldn't have multiple girls after him. He had to have been forced to seek me out.

He chuckled. "Yeah. Sorry. I should have noticed you before she did."

I looked at him in question.

"I'm one of ten ambassadors at the school. It's part of an Honor Society project. We're supposed to help new students feel at home."

I lifted an eyebrow. "Gotcha." A ping of sadness hit me that he hadn't asked me of his own accord. I quickly pushed that silly idea out of my mind. This was not about me. It was about the car thieves. We hadn't had long to dance before the next song had started and the changing of dance partners was in full swing. My eyes took everything in, and I counted all the people there. Jericho was missing, but the six others I could recognize were all there—Gina and Karina, three of the auto shop boys, and the mysterious Mikado.

"Want to dance again?"

I looked out into the crowd--I hadn't seen the faces

of the other two auto shop boys, but I hoped to uncover their identities tonight. Maybe I could catch one of the three boys' attention and dance with them. Maybe I'd get some more insight into the car thieves before they all disappeared. "Sure."

After that, I danced with Greg and then Tanner, neither of them were my marks, but both guys were fun and interesting and kept me near two of my marks. By the end of the second dance, Mikado had gone missing. Before the music stopped, the deejay called out, "See ya back in ten for some good ole country line dancing."

The group dispersed, and I caught a glimpse of Gina heading for the bathroom. I scanned the crowd and found Karina heading for the drink table and one of the guys from S-Dub's *class* heading for the men's room. The other two boys had scattered about the room. While Karina talked to a few people, I walked in her direction. She turned toward the bathroom, but then carefully detoured to a doorway that led out of the room. She stood in front of it, holding a cup and drinking with one hand, while the other was behind her back. Was she picking the lock?

I looked away for no more than a few seconds, and when I turned back, she was gone. Three of the seven were now gone. I glanced at my watch monitor and could see Gina had made it out of the building and was walking along the side of the school. Karina's ragged breathing told me she was running down the hallway she'd just entered and would probably be joining Gina any minute.

I made my way to the door Karina had gone out. With my back leaning on it, I tried to push it open. It was locked. I slipped a bobby pin out of my hair and made quick work of unlocking the door. I pushed on it, ready to disappear for a few minutes into the hall and give the team an update, when I saw Carson heading my way. I took the pressure off the door and smiled at him, assuming a relaxed posture. I even took a half-step toward him, letting my hands fall to my sides. I hated not being able to just follow the girls. It made me feel pretty helpless to stay inside at the dance, and I was curious how they would do. But Halluis and Jeremy were out there with their eyes on the girls and guys. They would be able to tell me everything.

"You know, if you wanted to dance with me again tonight, you could have just told me instead of acting the wallflower again." He gave me a flirtatious look.

"When something works for me, I milk it." Having him around was so convenient. It was easy not to look out of place. I counted the remaining marks with a quick glance around the room.

He chuckled. "I had a feeling you're someone who always gets what she wants."

"You had a *feeling*, huh?" I gave him a wry smile and checked for the three guys. They were still there. The one that had headed for the bathroom had returned. "Actually, I was hoping to get some fresh air." I pretended to push on the door. "But they've successfully locked us in."

He grabbed at his heart. "Oh, you wound me. You could have at least played along and boosted my ego."

"I don't think you need that, Carson. I have a *feeling* you've got ego to spare." I tilted my head to the side.

"If you insist on dissing me, I may just have to show

you the real me—lonely and scared." He made an insecure face and looked at his feet.

This guy was funny. I liked him, and as much as I wanted to continue our friendly banter, I wanted to focus on the girls. From the audio feed in my ear, I could tell they were together, running now. Where could they be heading?

I laughed and pushed his shoulder. "I know and you know that person doesn't exist, and even if he really did, I'd have to delay our meeting. You see, nature calls." I whipped my head in the direction of the bathroom. It was quiet in there, which would make it easier to hear the girls.

The deejay's voice filled the room. "Time to line up, boys and girls. The first of three line dances will start in twenty seconds."

"Is he serious?" I asked, jaw on the floor. They did country line dances here?

"Totally."

"What, do they change types of songs every five that are played?" I scoffed, disbelief taking over.

"No, but this guy loves to do a set of line dances whenever he comes here. It's kinda fun," he said, completely serious.

"No way." I stared at him, sure my eyes were the size of pancakes. I took note of the three boys lining up to dance.

"We can't just focus on our studies because we need a well-rounded experience here at Bell Academy." He changed his voice to sound like the principal of the school, Mrs. Chatworth.

"We better hurry," he said, grabbing my hand and

looking pointedly at a group of kids hurrying onto the floor. "We want to be in the second row so that you can learn the steps."

Before I could protest, he pulled me to the closest end of the line, making it just in time. I realized that while he was helping me a great deal with my cover, ditching him wouldn't be easy. Country twang blared out of the speakers, and I followed along, watching the group in front of us to know what to do. Only one of the target boys remained. In the commotion of learning the dance, two had left. How long had they been gone?

I kept going the wrong way, bumping into Carson. He laughed every time. At least he was a good sport. It was hard to concentrate because all I could think about was the mission. I needed to get away for a minute to make sure the team knew exactly who had left. By the end of the second song, I found myself at the end of the line. Carson was turned, talking to the girl on his other side. I slipped off into the bathroom, counting everyone before I entered. Six of the seven kids were missing. Could the other two I'd seen and not been able to identify not be here tonight, or would they leave with the last of the three boys?

I was very much alone in the bathroom and went straight for the window, away from the booming music. I checked my watch monitor for Gina and turned up my earpiece to listen for Karina. The purple dot indicated that Gina wasn't very far away, probably less than a few blocks. I pulled up the location. A parking garage. I gave the team a quick rundown on what I knew via text message, just to make sure they were up to speed.

Halluis was probably already following them.

Hopefully, he'd have enough time to get the trackers on the cars before the girls were able to get them started. He'd have to be super fast once they climbed into the cars to hotwire them. I thought he had the hardest job on this operation.

"I can't get it to start," Karina's voice whined in my ear. "It's not like the one in the shop."

"It has to be, Karina," Gina whispered. "Try again."

"You try, Gina. I can't do it."

I wanted to go help them. I could reach them in less than five minutes, and I had clothes to change into just outside the bathroom door in my go bag. I took a deep breath, fighting the urge to forget about watching for new thieves and tracking the ones we knew about. I mentally sent out good vibes to the girls in hopes it would help them be successful. I glanced up at the window. No. I would stay here. Stay on target. A couple of whispering girls came into the bathroom. I guessed the last country line dance was over. I stepped up to the sink and washed my hands at a snail's pace.

All the while, I listened as Gina tried to get the car to start. No car sounds filled the air, only Gina's grunting and Karina's whining.

"Let's forget this Camry. They must've done something to it. Let's try the next one on the list," Karina said.

I imagined them at a Camry, working to get it started. I knew Halluis was there, somewhere, watching them work and waiting for the right moment to place the tracker. I wondered if he also wanted to jump in and help them. I could imagine the stale oil and gas smells that most assuredly filled the air around them.

The two girls who'd entered the bathroom stepped up to the sinks and washed their hands, still whispering and not paying me any attention. I dried my hands as they dried theirs. Four more girls came in and made their way to the mirrors, primping and preening. I moved to a stall, acting as if I'd just entered the room before them. The two girls from earlier left out the door.

I wiped down the toilet and after putting a shield of TP on the toilet, I sat. The four girls' squeals made it hard to hear. I looked up in the direction of the window. Maybe I should climb out for a little bit so that I could hear better. Finally, the girls left, and I had quiet again. I stayed where I was, not willing to chance getting caught climbing out the window.

"Seriously," Karina said. "Let's try the Accord. Maybe we'll have better luck." Moments later, there was the click of a lock giving way and the sound of a car door opening. Whew! They were in. But no sounds of the car starting came through the com. *Not again. Come on girls.*

"We never should've said we'd do this, Gina." Karina started to cry. "S-Dub is going to kill us or something." Sobs filled my earpiece, and my chest suddenly ached.

"No, he won't," Gina said. I could imagine her putting her arms around Karina. "We'll just explain to him that we couldn't do it. He'll understand. It's our first time, and we've only trained for a few days."

"Amber?" A female voice called. I furrowed my brow. "Amber, are you in here?"

I bit the side of my lip. I'd been gone too long and someone had noticed. That someone had to be Carson.

Good grief.

I stood up and pretended to fix my skirt. Without meaning to it was easy to catch glimpses of people in the stalls, and me sitting still on the toilet without my skirt hiked would definitely be suspect. "Yeah?" I called out, before flushing the toilet, making sure the TP wasn't stuck to me anywhere. I saw a shadow fall over the gap as I listened to the girls in the garage. I stepped out of the stall.

"It's been two weeks, but no!" Karina screeched. "He won't. He's the biggest jerk in the universe. You heard what he said about that person who was looking through the window yesterday. He said he'd kill anyone interfering with his operation, and I believe him."

"Sorry," the girl checking up on me said. "Carson was worried about you and sent me to check on you. Are you feeling all right?"

"He didn't mean *kill*," Gina said. "He just meant hurt. We just won't get paid this time. It'll be okay, you'll see."

I knew I had to answer, but I didn't want to miss anything from the parking garage.

"What about the money? We need that!" Karina was in complete hysterics, and I wanted desperately to swoop in and save the day. I could play it off as a chance meeting. It would be so easy. But I couldn't. The mission came first. In truth, I'd be putting myself and the girls in a lot of danger, and things could go very wrong. There was a pause in the conversation, so I took it.

"I think so." The pause had been super long. "I felt a bit sick and needed to get out of there. It was getting so hot."

"No kidding. We really should have a bigger venue."

I made my way to the sink. She waited. I would have to go back out to the dance. How would I hear what was happening to the girls? I groaned inwardly as I washed and dried my hands. Blast that Carson. At any other moment, I would have praised his actions, but not today.

As I threw the wad of paper towel away, something came over the com. "What are you two doing?" I recognized the husky voice right off. It was Jericho. "You need to shut it. You want to wake up the whole area or something?"

I smiled at the girl who'd been sent to check on me. "Thanks for checking on me."

"No problem. I'm Kirsten." She wasn't going to leave me. I really was going to have to go back to the dance. In anticipation, I used my phone to up the volume in my com as we walked out. Booming music hit my ears, but I focused on my com, mindlessly following Kirsten.

I nodded as I listened to the action in the garage. "What's the problem?" It was Mikado. "We expected you fifteen minutes ago. S-Dub sent us to see what was taking so long."

Four of the six car thieves were together. One was here. I spotted him at the far end of the dance floor. A twisted fear squeezed my gut. Were the girls safe? I counted everyone in the room. No one new had left. I guessed I wouldn't be uncovering the two mystery thieves tonight. "We couldn't get the cars to start," Gina said. "They must have some anti-theft mechanism we haven't learned about, yet." I heard feet shuffling.

A car started. "I don't know what you're talking about." Jericho spit the words at them. I wondered if the girls were cowering or standing their ground. Most likely cowering.

Kirsten and I wove our way through the people dancing.

"What other car were you supposed to lift?" Mikado asked.

"That black Camry," Gina said. I could imagine her pointing in the direction of the other car, her finger shaking.

We made it to Carson, who was dancing with a crowd of kids. "Ah, you are alive." He smiled, and without a shred of explanation, I joined the dance, hoping it was an extended version of the song so that I could focus on the girls and not on conversation with anyone.

"Take the Honda to the drop off point, and hurry." Jericho's voice was menacing. "Somebody has probably already noticed your absence. This was sloppy work, you two." The sound of a slap, a cry, and a gasp flew to my ears. I cringed and couldn't hold back my own gasp, which I hid behind a fake cough as I covered my mouth. "Don't ever let me catch you crying again."

One of the girls sucked in a ragged breath. Had it been Jericho or Mikado who had hit one of them? Anger welled up inside me. They were worse than bullies. I wanted to go teach them a lesson. I had to consciously hold myself back from jumping out the window and going after them. The quiet hum of a car met my ears. The girls must have climbed into the Accord. I heard the engine get louder. They must have

68

been leaving the garage. Quiet sobs broke through the hum. I could imagine Jericho and Mikado were right behind them in the black Camry.

I pretended to get a text and pulled out my phone. I texted the team that the cars were on the move. I hoped they were able to pick up on the feed from the girls, but just in case, I wanted to make sure they knew so they could follow them to their destination—the chop shop or the pier or wherever—even if the trackers failed again. The girls hadn't mentioned anyone getting near the cars, so I assumed Halluis had been successful. I hoped he'd been able to get the trackers on. I wanted someone to watch out for those girls. What would Shareweather do to them?

When I'd finished my text, I yelled out to a questioning Carson, "Parents! They drive me crazy sometimes!"

"I hear ya!"

The song ended, and we moved toward the refreshment table. The sound of the slap repeated itself over and over in my mind. Apparently, someone, most likely Jericho, liked to pick on the weak. The nauseating feeling hit me that I would need to become buddy-buddy with him sooner or later. All his actions screamed sociopath, and I wanted to stay away from him at all costs. However, the truth hung before my face. If I hoped to get anywhere with this group, I couldn't remain with the peons; I needed to be with the upper-level workers. I needed to unravel the hierarchy of this car-theft gang.

I tried to focus on the girls in the car, but it was getting increasingly more difficult.

Karina still cried, and Gina shushed her over and over again. "You can't let him see you're weak. Be strong."

She blubbered over and over again, "We'll be cigged."

I figured I didn't want to know what that meant.

"Karina," Gina said, her voice firm. "Remember when that boy was trying to hurt you?"

Karina just continued to cry.

"You know, back home, out in the gardens?"

I could imagine Karina nodding.

"Remember how I ran and got Laron, and we made it so that boy'd never be able to hurt you? Well, this is one of those times again. You need to listen to me. Stop crying, and I will protect you. Haven't I always protected you?"

Carson gave me a cup of punch, and I drank it in a slow, even manner, hoping to be able to hear more from Karina and Gina. A tremor quaked through me. S-Dub had better not do anything more to those girls. My entire body stiffened. The connection started to cut out the farther away they got from me. Jeremy and Ace would continue to listen in once I couldn't. Karina was taking deep, long breaths when the feed cut out completely. I glanced at my go bag, wishing I could use it to follow the girls. Karina had listened to Gina. Maybe they would be okay. I had to hope.

Chapter 8

My cup was empty, and Carson took it and began to refill it without a word.

"Do you think doing nice things like getting me punch is going to put you in my good graces or something? You should know that I'm very hard to please."

"You? No way." He held the newly filled cup in front of me.

I chuckled and took the plastic red cup from him, bringing it to my lips and counting everyone once again. We moved away from the table as other kids approached. I glanced toward the door Karina had gone out and then to the bathroom door, hoping the girls would suddenly appear or I would hear something in my earpiece. But I knew it would still be a while before they could realistically show up. No one new had left the dance. I was beginning to think the phantom two guys were just that, phantoms.

"So. You were hiding?"

"Hiding?" I said, turning my body away from him. "I

haven't been hiding."

"I lost track of you some time in the second country line dance. I couldn't see you anywhere."

"What are you, my own personal body guard?" The comment came out a lot harsher than I'd intended, and he leaned back but quickly recovered and played it off. I took a deep breath, trying to push away the worry I felt for Karina and Gina.

"Of course not. I only want to make sure you have fun tonight."

"Sorry. I didn't mean it in a bad way. I've had fun tonight because of you." I made myself smile.

"Really?" One corner of his mouth turned up, and his eyes seemed to shine.

"Absolutely." I patted his upper arm. I needed something to distract me. I took it as a good sign that I hadn't heard from Halluis or Ace. I figured that could only mean one thing, the com on the girls was still live. They were simply too far away still for me to hear anything.

A strange old slow song played—like ballroom dance music. It didn't matter. I could keep track of who was there as we turned in a small circle. "It looks like we're about to start another grand dancing adventure." I walked purposefully to the dance floor. "You up for it?" I glanced over my shoulder at him.

He was grinning. "Of course. We'll make dancing history." He caught my arm and led me onto the dance floor. "Get it, history?"

Carson grabbed my hand with one of his and my waist with the other, effectively positioning us to slow dance the old-fashioned way or maybe even waltz.

Once the music started though, he put the hand he was holding up on his shoulder, and his hand fell to my waist.

"I won't even try to fake you out that I know how to dance to such Pride and Prejudice music, but I hope not to embarrass myself."

Apparently they'd just finished a Pride and Prejudice unit in English and had held a ball of sorts last week. I bet it had been a laugh. We didn't just move in a little circle, he added a somewhat sassy style to the dance that fit his personality. I couldn't help but give him a truly genuine smile before starting my recount of the guests.

"Do you mock me, Miss Amber?" His pressed smile showed his dimples. "Something is distracting you."

"I would never mock you." I played along with his Darcy-esque tone, pulling out my best Lizzy Bennett impression. "But a girl must be allowed to have secrets, Mr. Carson. Otherwise, the world would be boring and static." I winked and then glanced quickly toward the restroom door for the girls. It was kind of fun to pretend to be of another age, even in a tiny way like speaking.

He broke formation long enough to throw his head back and feign a laugh. He then quickly put his lips to my ear and said, "Caution, now. You threaten to win me over in a single night." When he pulled back, his rough cheek brushed my skin, his lips only a whisper from mine.

My heart sped up, and I felt my face burn. I tipped my head down in hopes of hiding it from him. Stupid physical response! It had been too long since I'd felt someone's lips on mine, and a part of me longed to feel it again. I pushed my mind to the girls and scanned the room in vain for them again. Still, no one else had returned yet.

Once the song ended, he escorted me off the dance floor. He bowed and walked away. Someone touched my arm from behind me. I turned, thinking it was one of the other Ambassadors, but it wasn't. It was Jericho. Jericho was back? I searched the room for the girls in one wide sweep of my head. That's when I noticed all three of the guys from the auto shop were missing. I found Mikado, but no girls. They were nowhere. My heart rumbled in my chest. Where were they? Were they being cigged, whatever that meant?

"Looking for anyone in particular?" Jericho's husky voice called my attention back to him. "Maybe I can find him for you and introduce you." There was laughter in his voice as he captured my hand in his. "But until then, how about we dance?"

Without waiting for an answer, he moved me onto the floor and gently placed his hand on my waist. Yet again, a song from another era played. His breath was minty, and his fresh-smelling cologne caught me off guard. This guy had just slapped a tiny girl across the face. How could he now seem so normal, so likeable? I resisted the urge to pull away from him.

"No. I was just wondering where the bathroom was." I smiled at him. "I think I drank too much punch that last break. Maybe we can dance later."

"It's to your left," he said, pulling me crisply to him. "I'll take you there after this dance. That is, if you can wait that long."

"I think I'll manage," I said as the music started. This was my in with Jericho, and I thought I had better take it, despite the heavy feeling in my gut. He was an incredible dancer, his execution flawless, hitting every step. No circles for him. When the music stopped, he held me in our last pose for the requisite three seconds, he pulled me out to his side, as if he had been dancing for a crowd, and he bowed, first to the imagined crowd and then to me, still holding onto the tips of my fingers as he did. I didn't know professional ballroom dance etiquette, but it seemed I should bow back, so I did.

He stared at me, like he was waiting for me to congratulate him. I wouldn't give him the satisfaction. I extracted my hand from his and said, "Thanks for the dance," before turning to go to the bathroom.

He seized my hand as it fell to my side. "Didn't you enjoy the dance?" he asked, his eyes probing mine.

I felt my hand turn slick with sweat. "Of course," I said. "I always love a good dance." I was careful not to give him one ounce of praise for his dancing ability, even though it had been exceptional. I tried to extricate my hand, but he held tighter. The music started to play.

"Let's try this again," he said, pulling me to him.

I didn't try to hide my distaste of his forcefulness. I yanked my hand from his. "I'll have to catch you another time. I have a date with the bathroom, remember?"

He cocked his head to the side. "I seem to remember you saying you could wait."

I put my tongue in my cheek, rolled my eyes, and looked away from Jericho. He grabbed my hand and my waist with a suaveness bordering on surreal and gracefully led me about the floor. If I thought there was an ounce of genuineness in this guy, I'd have been tempted to fall for him. But I knew him. I'd seen who he truly was. He was a wolf in sheep's clothing.

Once again, at the end of the dance, he bowed to the non-existent crowd and then to me. I did a deep curtsey. His face was flushed from exertion, and he looked at me expectantly once again.

"Thank you for the lovely dance," I said. "Now, may I go to the ladies room? I'm afraid I simply can't wait a moment longer."

He moved in close. "Most girls would wait for me."

I moved in closer, my lips next to his ear. "I am not *most* girls." I whispered it, my heart hammering in my chest. His arrogance offended me, and I needed a moment to collect myself before I hit him. I knew I needed to get close to him, but I wanted it on my terms. And I really wanted to get in touch with the crew to find out about the girls.

He chuckled before I could move away from him. "No, you most certainly aren't." A look of curiosity played across his face. The music went back to popular rock music. This deejay loved to do sets of music in threes. As I moved, I thought I heard crying on my earpiece. I focused on it as I walked, picking up speed.

I pushed my way to the edge of the dancers and into the serenity of the bathroom, hoping for some quiet so that I could hear. Three laughing girls exited a stall, the smell of alcohol wafting around them. Before leaving the room, the clank of a glass bottle hitting the bottom of the garbage can sounded in the room. I took a deep breath and said in a quiet whisper, "Stupid. Stupid. You cannot make Jericho your enemy." At that very moment, I noticed Gina, standing over Karina in front of one of the sinks.

Without a thought, I rushed over. "What happened?"

"She just fainted and hit her head on the sink. I tried to grab her, but she fell too fast."

I had a choice. I could try to smuggle her out, which would have to happen through the bathroom window, or I'd have to have someone create a distraction so that I could whisk her away through some side doors.

"I'll go get help," I said, standing and hurrying to the door. I scanned the room, considering my options—I could go to a teacher, but it would probably create a scene and quite likely cause serious trouble for both girls. I couldn't risk it. My eyes fell on Carson. Would he help me create a diversion? Could I trust him? He raised an eyebrow at me from the dance floor. I would have to chance it. I didn't think Gina and I could get Karina out of the window without hurting her more than she already was. I waved him over. By this time, Karina was propped up against the wall, looking haggard. I texted Jeremy that I needed a car.

Carson came right over after apologizing to his group.

"What's up?"

"Can I trust you?" I tilted my head to the side.

"Of course." He moved in closer and leaned against the wall just outside the bathroom.

"I need you to cause a distraction so that I can get a girl out of the school without anyone noticing."

"A distraction? Why?"

"Let's just say that the administration wouldn't be very happy if they saw this girl, and she really needs her scholarship."

"Oh, I get it." He made a sign that he thought that the girl'd been drinking.

"Can you help? I thought I'd sneak her out that door."

"It's locked, remember?"

"Don't worry about that." I raised an eyebrow.

"Ah. You are a girl with skills. Nice!" He nodded his head in appreciation. "I know just the thing." A glint shone in his eye.

"Thanks." I grabbed his hand and squeezed it. "And could you cover for us if anyone asks about us and then sign us all out? I don't want anyone to find out we left before the dance was over." I gave him their names, and he nodded.

"Give me five minutes. When you hear everyone start singing Happy Birthday, the way should be clear."

"Got it. Happy Birthday song."

I went back into the bathroom. Karina's chin looked like it would need stitches, and a bruise was blossoming on her cheek. I moved in close. Had Jericho caused that cut or someone else? Did S-Dub hit her, too? I felt my eyes narrow, and I wanted blood. I hated that I couldn't get it. The least I could do was help this girl.

"We have our diversion." I looked at Gina. "Now, Gina, we need to get her up and nearer the door. When we hear the Happy Birthday song, it's time to move. We'll go out the doors by the punch table."

She nodded.

I consulted my watch. Two more minutes. We moved Karina nearer the door. When the song broke out, we helped Karina walk out. The entire student body and all the teachers were at the opposite side of the gym singing to the principal. How had Carson known? Maybe they'd announced it at the beginning of school before I got there. Karina was light, and I could have helped her to the door on my own, but once at the door, I handed her over to Gina and took a bobby pin and opened the door in a few seconds flat. The students and faculty were still singing when we slipped through the door.

As we approached my clunker car, which Jeremy had dropped off for me, I said, "I know it's a beauty, but don't worry, you can't hurt it." I chuckled just a little when I saw the piece of paper that read, *Belgian Waffles or Bust* under the windshield wiper. There was no question it was the right car.

"At least you have a car." Gina sighed.

The two girls climbed into the backseat together. I guessed I'd be the chauffeur to the hospital. That's when I remembered Laron. What would he do when he showed up at the school and they weren't there?

I pulled out my cell phone. "You guys want to call someone?" They shook their heads an adamant refusal.

I parked in front of the emergency room doors and turned the car off.

"Oh, you don't need to come inside with us. We'll be just fine." Gina reached for the door and opened it.

"No. It's okay. I'll stay. I want to." I opened my door. "And don't worry about getting back to the dance to sign out. Carson is taking care of that."

"Really? Thanks for that. But, seriously, we'll feel bad if you stay. Go." She started to climb out. "And we do need to get back. My uncle is picking us up outside the school, and he'll kill us if we don't show."

"But how will you get back in time? I'll wait."

She didn't miss a beat. "There's a hole just around the corner, and we'll hurry and make it back. We couldn't impose. Besides, we don't know how long we'll be here. Go. Really."

"Emergency rooms take forever. You might want to call your uncle." I held out my phone.

She pulled one out of a little purse and waved it. "I've got it covered, and if it looks like they are going to take forever, I'll call him."

"I don't know." I pictured the subway entrance they were talking about. It was safe enough, I guessed. I had helped Karina get the care she needed, but had I also made the deeper connection with the girls that I'd hoped for? Would staying with them create a greater bond or weaken it? That was the question.

She gave me a look that said *stay put* as she helped Karina out of the car and said, "Thanks. We really appreciate it. Drive safe."

Her look told me it all. They didn't want me to go with them. I hoped they wouldn't just leave and not get medical attention. It was out of my hands, and I'd done my best. What would Laron say? They'd never make it back to the school in time. Emergency care was anything but quick. Anxious to find out what really had happened to the girls after they drove away in the stolen car, I sped away to the brownstone. It occurred to me as I drove home that I could no longer hear anything the girls said. Had the bug somehow been damaged or had it been turned off?

Chapter 9

Jeremy and Ace were waiting for me in the kitchen when I got back to the brownstone. Ace had his laptop out and was typing away, but Jeremy was just sitting there, staring thoughtfully out the window.

"So what did you find out? What happened?" I asked, taking a seat.

Jeremy turned to me slowly, seeming reluctant to let go of whatever he had been thinking about. He cleared his throat. "They drove the cars to two different locations," he said. "Just on the street—right out there for anyone to see. Of course, no one but our agents was around. A couple of professionals were there to meet them, and once the kids jumped out and headed for the subway, the guys whipped through the cars, swapping out the VIN numbers and license plates and, I'm assuming, putting fake documents in the glove box. And searching for trackers. They found the one Halluis put on the Camry and removed it. I stuck around the girls, listening to their feed. Would you like to listen to it?"

"Of course," I said.

"We got a conversation between Jericho and whoever is calling the shots. It wasn't S-Dub. We didn't get an ID on the guy, but we need to get to him," Jeremy continued.

"Let's hear it," I said.

Jeremy looked at Ace, who had angled his eyes up to the team leader for direction. Jeremy nodded at him, and Ace started the playback.

"Yes, sir. We did all the cars, but we had a problem with the girls. I'm not sure they're going to cut it. Do you want me to continue with them?"

"I don't have time to worry about new recruits. If you have to spend all day with them to get them properly trained, you do that. It's your responsibility. Make it happen."

"Yes, sir."

The man hung up, and Jericho did too. He swore colorfully.

"Let's listen from the beginning now." Jeremy's hands briefly clenched as he uncrossed his arms and put his fingers on the edge of the table. Ace started the recording from the time the girls couldn't get the cars started, and we all listened.

I flinched, listening to S-Dub hit Karina after they'd delivered the cars. "I should give you a little lesson, too, but someone might ask questions if you're both a bit banged up."

I assumed he'd been talking to Gina.

"Come by the shop at 5:30 to get some more practice in. Idiot girls. I don't know why he insisted I bring you on."

There was some silence on the line until it sounded like they climbed into a car and started to drive.

Jericho swore every other word, calling the girls all sorts of horrible names. "If you embarrass me like that again, I'll have to really hurt you. If you think what happened today was harsh punishment, you haven't seen anything, yet. After school, I'll need to see you in the shop. Be ready to work and no more excuses."

"Was Mikado still there?" I asked.

"He was," Jeremy said.

"So we lost the car again?" I leaned back in my chair.

"Actually, thanks to Halluis's sweet shadowing ability, he stayed with them on his motorcycle." Ace leaned back in his chair as if he were responsible for Halluis's greatness. "Followed them all the way to a shop in Sunset Park."

"Where's Halluis now?" I asked.

"Last we heard, he'd done a perimeter check, and the place didn't seem big enough to hold a bunch of cars. But they could be underground. He was going to try to find a way inside. He should check in soon, and then we'll know more. I'm betting he finds the car, drives the thing out of there, and we can be done with this whole business."

"That would be sweet. I really don't want to be anywhere near Jericho again if it can be helped."

That's when Jeremy's phone rang. "Yes?" After a minute of him listening intently, he sighed and said, "All right, come on back, then." He hung up.

"That was Halluis," he said, rubbing his hand over his tired face. "There wasn't anything at the shop—just the cars they took tonight. Definitely no Mercedes 300. It's probably a temporary storage location, not where they're keeping all the cars." He bit his cheek and looked at his feet.

Ace grumbled a curse. "So we got nothing tonight?"

"Well, not nothing," I insisted. "We learned a lot about how the gang works, and who's really going to be valuable. I realized tonight that those two girls would get me nowhere. I need to either go after Shareweather or one of the boys. Neither of which is appealing."

Jeremy shook his head slowly. "I don't think Shareweather is the answer. I think he's just a hired hand, a grunt really. He's not the one calling the shots, and he's not likely to lead us to anything really useful. Sure, he's Jericho and Mikado's direct supervisor, but there was someone more important that Jericho was talking to on that recording."

"You're probably right," Ace said, his head down. "When I was looking through Shareweather's financials, it appeared that he makes a significant deposit to his account every four weeks. And it appears he makes an even bigger deposit to an off-shore account that same day each month. They probably pay him per car each month. He may not even know exactly who he is working for."

"Lackeys like him rarely ever meet the important people," Jeremy added. "It stands to reason that if Jericho is able to call this person, whoever it is, he must have an in with the real organization." He pushed through the recording and pulled up the call. The voice on the other end was no one familiar. Certainly no one we'd been tracking at the school. "Ace, could you go to

Division HQ to work on isolating the voice on the phone for us?"

Ace nodded.

"Can we take a break for a second?" I asked. "I'm starving."

"All right," Jeremy agreed. "We should probably wait for Halluis to get back before we move on, anyway."

I stood up and started raiding the fridge for something more substantial than the party fare I'd eaten at the dance. I settled on making myself a giant sandwich and had just finished polishing it off when Halluis arrived. We filled him in on our discussion, and he immediately jumped in with his opinion.

"Unfortunately," Halluis looked at me directly, "it sounds like Jericho is the one you're going to need to get to know. Sure, you still want to see if Shareweather will notice you enough to recruit you, but then you'll just be a peon."

Jeremy turned his head away and stifled a groan that only I seemed to notice.

"Ah," Ace said, setting his elbows on the table and leaning forward. "I think you're on to something. Christy can easily get Jericho's attention as a girlfriend and then weasel her way in from there."

"Easy is a relative term, you know," I said, stiffening. I could probably get him to like me, but I didn't want to. "He's so creepy and disgusting. I've never met anyone as arrogant as he is. You should have seen him at the dance. He—"

"Sounds like you already have caught his attention then," Ace said, grinning. "Our little girl, turning heads and making waves."

I rolled my eyes. I thought about my bad behavior to Jericho and hated the idea of having to eat crow and be nice to him. Maybe I could approach Mikado. He seemed like a more civil option. "What about Mikado?"

"Does that guy ever talk?" Halluis said.

"He's not the one who called that person." Ace yawned. "As much as you hate it, it has to be Jericho."

I put my head in my hands and sighed, resigned.

"I still don't like it," Jeremy said. "I'd rather limit her exposure to that sociopath than increase it, but I see no other option, yet. Halluis, just stick with Christy and give her the protection she needs. And Christy, there's no need to become his girlfriend. Just...get close to him."

"She's already got his attention, why not go full force and get as much from him as she can?" Halluis argued. "She'll be able to get a lot closer to him as his girlfriend than as an acquaintance."

Strain registered on Jeremy's face. An argument ensued, with Halluis trying to shout over Jeremy's concerns. I turned to Ace for some support. Ace gave me an apologetic look, but kept his mouth shut.

Jeremy hit his hand on the table and said, "Enough!" Then he turned to me. "Get in the good graces of Jericho as fast as you can. Not as his girlfriend. At the same time, work hard on Shareweather and see if you can't entice him into taking you on. Then wow him. Not in the unbelievable sense. Fail here and there, but show him you're a quick learner and would be not only a valuable member of the team, but someone he needs to introduce to the higher ups. Do it fast and then get the heck out."

Exasperated sighs sounded from Halluis as he shook his head; he obviously wanted me to forget about Shareweather.

"I think it's best if we put a record out there on you as a known car thief. You can use that as an in." Jeremy tapped one finger slowly on the table. "Ace, could you get on that as well? And we need a better way to track the cars."

Even though I thought Halluis was right, my loyalty to Jeremy made me say, "I like Jeremy's plan. I think it's the safest and most likely the fastest route to the top. I played with Jericho tonight, and I'm not sure if it was the right move—I may have burned some bridges there. If I made the wrong move, that relationship could take a while to sweeten. Jeremy's plan gives me two ways in. I can always abandon one if need be." Jeremy's face softened, and he winked at me. I turned to the other agents. "If for some reason Shareweather doesn't take the bait, I'll be rebuilding the bridge with Jericho." I swallowed hard, trying to get rid of the lump lodged in my throat.

Chapter 10

Once inside the school the next day, I heard a guitar playing and someone singing along. It sounded amazing, and I peeked in the door where the sound was emanating from. Carson sat on a chair in the middle of the room, playing and singing his heart out. I hung onto the doorjamb and listened.

"You like what you're hearing?" a familiar voice whispered into my ear, hot breath tickling my neck.

I started, opened my eyes, and turned to see Jericho grinning at me, carrying a guitar in his hand and passing me by. I suppressed a shudder, took deep breath, and said, "Hey." He sat next to Carson and joined him, their guitars blending to make an even more beautiful sound. It was shocking to hear Jericho add his voice to Carson's and having them complement each other perfectly. Jericho turned to look at me, which must have caught Carson's attention because he turned also.

I felt my eyes round as they both smiled at me. The juxtaposition of the two was mind-blowing. Jericho looked at me like a wolf looks at his prey, while Carson looked at me like he was reuniting with a long-lost friend. It seemed I hadn't ticked Jericho off enough to scare him away. I could move forward with him. I was about to go up and sit with them, but Jeremy's voice rang in my ears. I should get in Jericho's good graces but hit Shareweather hard. Since it seemed Jericho still had me in his sights, I wouldn't need to suck up to him yet.

The five minute warning bell rang, and I realized I'd missed my opportunity to check on the shop and possibly run into S-Dub and let him pull out of me that I needed money. I'd just have to make that happen in shop class. In the interest of mending torn fences, I waved sweetly to the boys and then took off for personal finance class.

I made sure to not only acknowledge, but smile and say hi to both Karina and Gina. If S-Dub asked about me, I wanted the people I knew were on his team to like me. Karina had a bruised-up face with a couple stitches on her chin. My chest heated up when I thought about how Karina had been injured. To think a grown man had hit her hard enough to cut her chin made me want to scream. At least I knew she'd gotten medical attention.

I wondered if the girls had made their schedules around each other. They probably had all the same classes. They sat in the back of the room, however, and the only open seat for me was in the front. Personal finances numbed my mind. Anyone with half a brain would face a comatose state during it. I pretended to listen while I pondered how to get to the guy above S-

Dub in the least amount of time.

I made sure to make it on time for my next class, and much to my surprise, Viktor walked right up to me and said, "Hey, I'm sorry about yesterday. I didn't mean to diss on your friends."

I was so shocked, I couldn't speak.

"So, do you accept my apology or not?"

This was the most menacing way I'd ever seen someone offer an apology. I nodded.

"Good. I was wondering if you'd like to go to dinner with me tonight?" His face changed again, his nice one returning.

Was he kidding? I not only didn't like Viktor, but it would take away time that I needed to work on the case. I'm sure my eyes flashed a bit too much, because his eyes narrowed slightly, and I thought he was about to lash out at me when Carson joined the conversation.

"Hey, Viktor. Any way you could pick me and my date up tonight? My sister has dibs on the car."

Viktor's eyes reluctantly moved to light on Carson.

Carson was going to be there? Carson and Viktor were friends? Had I misjudged Carson?

"Sure, if," Viktor swung his face back to me, "I can talk newbie here into being my date. I can't go to Jericho's senior dinner stag, but I've discovered I just can't stand the thought of going with anyone but Amber. If she says no, I don't know what I'll do." His eyes drilled into mine, something of a warning flickering through them.

At the mention of Jericho's name, my mind changed completely. "You know what? I'd love to." I smiled, unable to keep smugness from entering my eyes. It would be good to spend time with Jericho outside of school.

Viktor stood there, a smirk on his stupid face. Did I see glee in them?

"You'd love to?" Viktor took a step closer to me.

"That's what I said." I smiled up at him, genuineness seeping from me, even though I didn't feel that at all. "I'll have to make sure my parents are okay with it, but yeah, sure."

"Awesome," Carson said, walking away. "See you tonight."

"Where do you live?" Viktor asked me, not suspecting a thing.

"I'll just meet you there."

"It's far, way out on Long Island. We're carpooling out there."

"It's fine. I'll meet you there."

"Why don't you want me to come to your house? Don't you want your parents to meet me?"

"It's not that," I said a bit too quickly.

"What is it, then?"

I was silent.

"Forget it," he said, waving his hand in the air and walking away.

I rolled my eyes and reached out, taking his arm. I hated that I couldn't let him walk away. "Look, I just don't want you to see where I live. Okay?" I bit my lip and brought an embarrassed flush to my cheeks as I leaned on a wall of lockers. If he was friends with Jericho, maybe he could spread the word that I was poor.

He blew air out of his nose and said, "Hmmm." He

eyed me like a cat looking over its prey. "I don't care where you live." I could tell by his tone that he did.

"Why don't we meet at some subway hole or something?"

"All right. Wear something warm—sometimes we play night games when we go to his house."

"Okay," I said. "Wait. Whose house?"

"Jericho's."

This was too good to be true. I would have to let Ace know ASAP that I needed a bunch of bugs. Not only would I be in close proximity to Jericho, I'd have access to his house.

"I'm gonna be late. See you tonight." His dress shoes clacked on the shiny tile floor as he walked away. He had a strut that I'm sure brought girls to their knees. Something about the way he walked was familiar, but I couldn't place it—it gave me an eerie feeling, like there was something I should remember about it, but I couldn't think what. Maybe it was just the generally creeped out feeling I got around Viktor—my insides felt like they were full of worms. I so didn't want to be "close" to Viktor at all. I wished it'd been Carson that had invited me. I shook my body, trying to rid it of the awful feelings that guy gave me. He had an aura of danger around him. Good thing I was who I was. I could handle him.

I heard a lot of kids talking about the party at Jericho's house and felt a bit of comfort in knowing it wouldn't be an intimate group. I texted a coded message to Ace at the brownstone to work on getting me some techie gadgets for my date and let everyone know of the lucky turn of events.

Jeremy texted back. *It's a school night. You could refuse. We could refuse.*

I laughed. *It's at Jericho's.* That should make him excited to get some real traction on this case.

He texted back. *Even more reason for you not to go.*

I gritted my teeth. We'd been over this. Jeremy was my handler, so I was glad he was looking out for my safety, but he also needed to trust me. I tucked the phone away. There was no point arguing about it anymore—we both knew I had to go.

I slid into P.E. and took a seat just as the teacher, Mrs. Moore, walked into the studio from her office.

"Lucky," Carson whispered and sat down next to me. I guessed we were both lucky not to be late.

I hadn't noticed that he was in my P.E. class until that moment.

He leaned over to me, whispering. "Did everything work out...you know, with your friend last night? I was worried about it all night."

"Yes, thanks to you! I got her to the hospital. She's going to be fine."

He smiled slightly. "So, I uh, I didn't realize you and Viktor—"

"Don't worry, darling," I said, in a tart tone, reminiscent of the dance. "He was in a pinch and needed a date. I didn't have one, so I obliged. Too bad you didn't think to ask me before he did." I raised an eyebrow at him, smirking. I couldn't help but think about his whispered words at the dance. I had to turn things around and help him see me as a friend only.

The teacher, Mrs. Moore, cleared her throat. "I must say that I am extremely pleased with your efforts at the dance yesterday. Many of you tried some of the dances out. Yes, it was me who forced the deejay to play them. You were very brave. Most of you, however, didn't try. Just so that we are clear, I must see steady improvement over the next three weeks before the practical exam. Jensen, I need you, Michelle, and Danica to work with me. We've got a long way to go. Now, Shelly and Aman, please demonstrate the correct way to samba."

Shelly and Aman stood without a second's pause and moved to the open floor of the studio while Mrs. Moore started the music. I hoped I wouldn't still be at the school in three weeks and had a hard time paying attention. All I could think about was going to Jericho's house and what luck I'd had in securing an invitation. After the demonstration, Mrs. Moore started the class in on clapping. After a good thirty seconds of applause, Mrs. Moore, said. "Now, it is your turn. You all need to work on looking like Shelly and Aman." She clapped her hands and said, "Up, up. Everyone up."

"I, too," Carson said, offering me his hand, "wish you had been here two weeks ago when I asked Laura to be my date."

Had he been thinking about my comment that whole time? I had to do something to make him see where we had to stand.

"I would have taken you in a heartbeat." He pulled me into standing position and then up tight to him. I had to lean my head back to prevent it from smacking into his. I cleared my throat.

"Listen, Carson. I need—"

The music started, and he grinned before putting us

into samba starting position. "Can we talk after this?"

I knew this class was important to him. I'm sure he didn't want to get in trouble because of me. I'd have the talk with him after we danced. I nodded.

"Let's knock 'em dead." I thought I might die trying to keep up with him. In fact, Mrs. Moore stopped us and gave me a quick private lesson on swinging my hips and arms in the most unnatural ways to make us look like we were dancing the same dance. I couldn't imagine ever being at an event where I would actually dance this suggestive of a dance, but as I looked around, I noticed that all twenty in the class took it very seriously, though only a few were actually able to do it. It seemed most of these boys had never danced any ballroom before and, while I had, with this dance, I felt as they probably did.

I let out a sigh of relief once the song ended. "Sorry I was such a lame partner. I've never learned the samba before. I felt like an idiot." I breathed hard and brushed my arm across my forehead.

"We can't be perfect at everything, but one thing's for sure, no one was critiquing your abilities," he said, pulling me close to him. "I just like having you in my arms." I saw a flash of his perfectly straight white teeth before he pushed away from me, his hand sliding down my arm to my hand. "Let's get a drink." I followed him, my mind whirring with questions about this guy.

Could he get me closer to Jericho and if so, how? Was he a player like Viktor, just smoother so that he didn't seem like a parasite? He grabbed a clean hand towel from a stack next to the sink and wiped his neck and face. I followed suit, but only dabbed at my sweat. I took a long draw on the water shooting out of the drinking fountain, and Carson did, too. I hadn't noticed his beautifully bronzed skin until I saw him in the light of that room. His muscled arms looked like they could wrap around a girl and keep her safe. Too bad we lived totally different lives. Too bad I didn't feel for him what he apparently felt for me. I pulled him away from everyone.

"Listen, Carson. You and me?" I moved my hands toward him and back to me several times. "It would never work."

"What are you talking about?" He frowned.

I'd have to be totally clear and leave no ambiguity. "I think of you as a friend. Nothing more. I mean, I see you in my life as a very good friend or best friend, just not as a boyfriend." I bit my lip waiting for his response.

"You like someone else?" He leaned back.

I did, so I nodded. "Are we okay, then?" I raised my eyebrows.

He curled his top lip over his teeth and then, sighing, said, "Yes." He nodded a few times. "I don't like it, but yes."

I grinned. "Good, because you make me laugh, and I love to laugh." I grabbed his arm and led him back to the dance floor for more practicing.

I was bushed when class was over, but I didn't want to miss the chance of asking Carson what I could expect at Jericho's.

"So, Jericho lives out on Long Island. Is he one of the super rich in one of those amazing mansions out there?" I laughed quietly.

"Actually, yes."

"You're kidding?"

"Nope. They own something like sixty acres. You can't even see the neighbors from his house. It's crazy gargantuan. I've been there a lot, and I don't think I've even seen all the grounds. They even own a private island. It's crazy."

"Wow! And you'd never know it."

"Uh. Have you met the same Jericho I know?"

"I mean, he's not that different is he?"

"Trust me, he is. No one can have a bedroom the size of most people's houses and be normal."

"If you don't like him, why do you go to his parties?"

"He didn't used to be as psycho as he is now. We grew up together. Not that we lived near him. We just happened to go to the same preschool and have been in the same schools ever since. I probably wouldn't go to this party if it was a regular one, but this is the senior bash. I wouldn't miss it, even if it is held at Jericho's family mansion."

I wanted to ask about it being the senior bash, but I had to stay on target. I needed more info on Jericho before tonight. "So he has a huge room huh?" Carson nodded. "So I'm assuming he has servants and all that jazz, too?"

"At least a hundred of them. All at his beck and call."

"Well—"

He didn't let me finish. "I'd love to keep chatting, really, but I have guitar lessons in fifteen minutes, and it's twenty minutes away."

"Oh, sorry," I said, giving him an exaggerated frown.

"Call me later. We can chat, *as friends*, as long as

you'd like." He ran off.

The halls were practically empty. With no one to hit up for information on Jericho, I headed for the nearest hole.

***

I didn't have a chance to rest when I got back to our brownstone.

I found Ace in the back room on a computer.

"Ace! I thought I was all alone. Where is everyone?"

"Jeremy's at headquarters, and Halluis is working with a team on getting the repeaters that we need to set up from Long Island to get the feed from these little babies." He pointed to a bunch of little items on his desk. "Your wish is my command."

"I guess it's safe to say that Jericho's life is about to be invaded. His secrets are our secrets."

"You got it." Ace taught me how to use the devices he'd created, and we practiced different things I could do to gain access to Jericho's room and what to do if I got caught—one of which included me sailing onto his bed and pretending I wanted to hook up with him. I didn't even give that option a second thought.

"The best thing would be for you to get this little guy into his phone." He held up a little metal disk. "This is the one thing that would really give us all his secrets. However, you have to open the phone back and set the disk on top of the SIM card, which also requires removal of the battery. And yes, if he opens the phone and removes the battery, he will see it. It is the most risky bug to place, but also the most valuable."

To get Jericho's phone from his pocket, I'd have to be very close to him. I'd also have to have an extended amount of time with the phone in order to pull it off. That required me getting close to him twice. Very close. Had I the time, I'd practice on his exact phone until it became second nature to me, but time was one thing I didn't have. I needed to meet Viktor in an hour at a subway entrance half an hour away.

"Jeremy wants you to stay close to your phone so you can alert us if there's any trouble. But, you know, don't get in any trouble, okay? It's just you and me tonight, which means you're basically on your own." His forehead knit slightly, and I was surprised to feel a rush of warmth at his worry. Why was it that Ace worrying about me was charming, and Jeremy worrying about me was irritating as heck?

"It's going to be fine, Ace. I've got this under control," I said, patting him on his tattooed arm.

He nodded and said, "I've got Jericho's house plans upstairs if you want to take a look." I followed him up.

"I don't have a lot of time, but I'll look really quick."

"It'll be good for you to have a general feel for the layout. Of course, we don't know which bedroom is Jericho's, but you'll be able to see where all the bedrooms are. And get this, there are twenty-five, not including the guest and servant houses. He lives in a real mansion. It's totally sick."

I glanced through the mansion plans, immediately having them in my memory. I'd sift through them on the drive out there. I thanked Ace and rushed to my room to find something to wear.

The phone in my pocket vibrated. It was a text from Viktor. *You almost ready?*

I responded. *Getting there. My dad is driving me*

nuts about tonight. He's ticked you didn't come meet him. I got the feeling it would be useful if Viktor knew Amber had someone big and strong waiting for her to come home safe and sound.

Parents really can suck. I hope you're up for a really great night. Jericho puts on the best parties.

I'm excited.

When are you heading for the subway?

I'll leave in about half an hour. I've got to get ready. See you soon.

Can't wait.

I dressed in layers so that I could easily peel off what I wouldn't need. I definitely didn't want to get a chill during the night. I didn't want any excuses for Viktor to feel the need to pull me in close. I did, however, need to look hot to get Jericho's attention. If I knew anything about him, it was clear that he liked hot girls. The layers were also a convenient bonus when trying to hide a bunch of surveillance equipment. The cameras were the bulkiest of all, but still only the width of a pencil. I put the most precious bug, the phone bug, into my pocket, taping it to the lining. If the opportunity arose to place it, I needed easy access to it.

As I was heading out the door to catch the subway, my phone vibrated. It was Viktor.

Be ready in ten and don't go to the subway. I'm picking you up at your house.

What? I texted back.

I'm almost there. Be ready.

Chapter 11

I cursed silently. This couldn't be happening. I'd texted Viktor about my dad wanting to meet him—it would seem strange now if there was no dad at all. I didn't want anything to blow my cover, and even something as small as this could cast suspicion on me later. I needed a dad, and I needed one quick.

I shoved my phone into my pocket and ran up the stairs after Ace. I burst into his room, and he looked up from his computer in alarm.

"Ace—I need you."

"Wha—what's going on?" Ace sputtered as I raced past him to his closet. I flung it open, then let out a groan of dismay when I found the hangers bare and all the clothes on the floor. I dropped to my knees and pushed through the pile, finding half a dozen pairs of ratty jeans, about ten snarky T-shirts, and three or four knit beanies.

"Dangit, Ace, don't you have any adult clothes?" I growled, leaping to my feet and heading out of his room, toward Jeremy's.

"Christy, what are you doing?" Ace laughed, shocked by my strange behavior. "What's wrong with my clothes? Will you please tell me what's going on?"

I pulled open Jeremy's closet and felt a surge of relief. Of course, Jeremy would have suitable attire. I pulled out a long-sleeve plaid oxford shirt and a pair of khaki slacks then thrust them toward Ace, who'd followed me into Jeremy's room, a look of baffled amusement on his face.

"Put these on," I said. "I need you to be my dad."

The half-smile disappeared, and his skin turned white. "Christy, please tell me you're joking—"

"Viktor is going to be here in," I consulted my phone. "Six minutes. He's expecting to meet Amber's dad."

"But Christy, I can't—"

"You said it yourself—it's just you and me tonight. There's no one else. I need you, Ace." I held out Jeremy's clothes. "Please?"

He swallowed visibly, then held out a shaky hand for the clothes.

I gave them to him and then gripped his arms. "Thank you, Ace. I know you can do this. I'll do my best to get Viktor in and out, super quick I promise. You don't even have to say anything. All you have to do is stand there and look scary."

I ran downstairs and heard muttered curses behind me as Ace changed into Jeremy's clothes. This had to work. I cringed, remembering Ace's pale face and wide eyes. If he couldn't pull this off, I'd have a lot of explaining to do. I paced the floor. The minutes waiting for Viktor to show up dragged on like hours.

Finally, the doorbell rang, and at the same time Ace appeared at the top of the stairs. I was momentarily frozen, staring up at him, the change was so shocking. The plaid shirt covered his tattoos completely, and he'd cinched the slacks up at his waist just enough to indicate maturity without looking ridiculous. He'd also added a blue sweater vest to the ensemble, and it was the perfect touch. His scruffy facial hair was gone, and his hair was slicked down in a nerdy, greasy way that emphasized the slight gray streaks at his temples. He looked ten years older, like he could actually be my dad.

To top it all off, he carried a rifle in his right hand. The change was so over the top, I had to put my hand up to my mouth to stop the laughter bubbling up inside me. He nodded at me, no trace of his earlier fear anywhere on his face. I took a deep breath to get rid of my laughter and steady my nerves and turned to the door.

Ace descended the stairs and came up behind me as I opened the door to find a cleaned up and nicely dressed Viktor standing on the stoop.

I shook my head at Viktor, "How did you find me?"

"The school has a directory. Not difficult."

I took in a deep breath and glanced back at Ace, who crossed his arms over his chest, making sure Viktor noticed the rifle. A bit over the top maybe, but I had told him to look scary. I'd also promised him I'd keep it short. Well, Viktor had seen my dad; that was all we needed. Time to get out of there.

"All right, well, I guess we'd better be going."

Viktor nodded, but Ace put a hand on my arm. "Just

a minute there, young lady. Why don't you invite the young man in?" His voice was subtly deeper than I'd ever heard it, and it resonated with confidence.

My jaw almost dropped in total shock, but I managed to turn it into an annoyed teenagerly scowl at the last second. "Dad," I practically growled, shaking his hand off my arm. "What are you doing? Don't embarrass me in front of Viktor."

He ignored me and opened the door wider, stepping close enough to Viktor to make him visibly uncomfortable. Viktor shifted on his feet, but didn't back up.

"So. You're Viktor?" Ace said. He let his eyes travel over Viktor's entire body, making it obvious he was judging every last inch of him.

Viktor swallowed hard then nodded, "Yes, sir. Viktor Megolovic." His eyes flicked to the gun. "Nice to meet you, sir." Viktor held out his hand.

Ace deliberately set the rifle down against the doorjamb, then took Viktor's hand firmly in his. Viktor's eyes rounded as Ace gripped his hand so hard it turned white. Ace pulled him just slightly closer and said, "I just want you to know I'm a certified expert marksman." He paused a moment to let that sink in before adding, "And I love my daughter." Then he winked and made a sucking sound out of one side of his mouth and nodded his head before releasing Viktor's hand.

As it fell to his side, Viktor shook his hand lightly. "Of course, sir. I'll take good care of her. I promise." He smiled stiffly at Ace, who nodded gravely.

I fought down the laugh that threatened to burst out

of me. I kept up the embarrassed teen act and hurriedly said, "Okay, Dad. I think that's enough. Viktor, you ready?"

"Yeah," Viktor said. "My car's just right down the street." He pointed toward a large Cadillac Escalade parked in front of a fire hydrant with its hazard lights flashing.

"Bye, Dad. See you around midnight."

"I expect you to be on your best behavior tonight, Amber. I'll be waiting up, so check in with me when you get home."

"I will. Don't worry. I won't be late."

Viktor led me to the passenger side door. I wondered if he was making a show for my dad. After I climbed in, he walked around to his side, opened the door and waved. The windows were tinted, so I got my first glance of the passengers after watching Viktor get in.

He turned the car on, his face a mask of calm. He waved once more as we pulled out into the street, and then he let his true colors show, swearing colorfully. "Amber, could your dad be any worse?"

I hid my face, acting embarrassed. "I doubt it."

"What happened, Vik? We couldn't hear. Don't hold back." The voice was unfamiliar. I craned my neck to see. Carson and his date sat on the seat directly behind us, along with Mikado and his date, squished together. A boy with a shock of platinum blonde hair and deep blue eyes sat in the seat at the back with a pretty girl with a mass of silky red hair.

The platinum-haired boy was still snickering after asking the question.

Viktor recounted the whole encounter, adding all sorts of belligerent cuss words. Then he turned to me and said, "No wonder you didn't want me to pick you up at your house."

I shrugged and gave my best told-you-so look.

"I don't blame the guy," Carson said. "If he knew anything about you, he'd never have allowed his precious daughter to go anywhere with you."

Viktor laughed like Carson had just given him the biggest compliment, ever—further confirmation that I had reason to be wary.

The boy in the back high-fived Carson and said, "That's right. Parents watch out, Viktor's in the house." He and his date laughed it up. "Precious cargo..."

"Hey, I warned you. I wanted to meet you at the subway hole. You should have listened to me."

"Well, I'm glad that's over. That dude is psycho."

"Hey!" I protested. "He is my dad!"

"All I have to say is you better be worth it," he winked at me, sending another wave of revulsion through me. "I'm done talking about parents now—let's get this party started!" He cranked up the music, and everyone started screaming along to the songs and throwing their arms in the air, rocking the truck. I played along. I had no doubt my "dad" was a passing memory. So much for the protection I'd hoped to gain. I was on my own.

Chapter 12

It was a good hour and a half to get to Jericho's house on Long Island because of the terrible traffic. It surprised me on one level that New York, with all its millions of residents, didn't have wider streets to accommodate more cars, or at least double-decker streets. The subways were packed, the streets were packed. There had to be a better way. With all the people in the city, they should have a better handle on it. Real estate was too expensive to widen the streets, and the truth was the subway was the way to get around the city. Unfortunately, the best way to move around Long Island was in a car.

I never thought I'd find New York as cool as I had. The food was to die for, and there was never a dull moment with all the interesting people and places to see, not to mention all the cool street artists. While I did find a lot of it confusing, it was interesting, and I once again thanked Heaven for my job that took me to such amazing places

My mouth dropped as we drove up the long

driveway to Jericho's. This boy's family had money and a lot of it. I knew from the house plans that the place would be big, but I had no idea how stately it would appear. Well-placed lights lit up the exterior stone walls and accents, accentuating the grace and grandeur of the mansion. According to information I'd read on Long Island, most of the mansions out here were built between 1890 and 1930. Of the 1200 built by the extremely wealthy of their eras, only about half still remained. This one smacked of Tudor style, and I fell immediately in love with the extravagant estate.

We arrived at approximately the same time as six other cars, all pulling into the forever-long circular drive right after us. Kids tumbled out, shrieking with delight to be there as the drivers handed valets dressed in black and white suits their keys. The cars disappeared off to the side of the property. Fountains, lavish balconies, and gazebos spotted the well-manicured landscape around us. A sculpture of a beautiful woman, which looked suspiciously like one I'd seen in a garden in Belgium, caught my eye as we walked up the majestic steps to the front door.

Once our feet hit the landing, one of the tall, wide sections of door opened, and we followed another man in the same type of black suit through a chandeliered and marbled grand foyer and into a large reception area. The mission and Viktor and Jericho all flew out of my mind as I entered the lavish building.

We left the shiny, hard marble to step on one of many ornate rugs that seemed to divide varying sections of the room. We'd come upon a large seating area complete with elegant furniture. I ran my hand over the wood of one of the pieces. Although nothing was modern, it felt comfortable and welcoming in the room. Large hot fires raged in all six of the fireplaces around the room. The walls were completely trimmed up with warm wood, not a speck of plastered or sheet-rocked walls to be seen.

Viktor motioned for me to take a seat, and I marveled at the shiny, well-placed chandeliers and lighting that graced the room. Viktor walked right up to the lavish bar and returned with two glasses of some type of cola. I took it with a smile, "Thanks, Viktor, you knew just what I needed." I pretended to take a drink and then set it on a glass coaster on the side table next to us.

"Hold on there." He looked around the room before picking my glass up. "Let's sweeten the pot a little." He held the glass close to his chest and pulled out a flask from his pocket, splashing some of the liquid into my Coke. That was all it took to bring me back to reality.

"There." He handed it to me and then did the same to his drink. He clanked his glass against mine and then chugged the Coke, now laced with some type of hard liquor. I pretended to take a few swallows. He leaned into me and whispered, "Jericho's parents don't supply the good stuff, but they also don't forbid it." He laughed.

"So who's driving us home?" I said, tapping my fingernail on the side of my glass as I scanned the room for Jericho.

"Me." He knocked his glass into his chest.

"I don't think so. Not if you're going to be drinking." I set my drink back on the coaster.

"We're here for four hours. I'll only drink until this flask is out, and then I'll sober up. I do it all the time." His face scrunched up in irritation. "Besides, maybe it will loosen you up a bit." He sat next to me and put his arm around me as he took another few swallows of his alcohol-laden drink.

I did worry. If he was impaired in any way when we left, it would be me driving, not him. "I'm pretty sure it will be me driving at the end of the night, and no *loosening up* is going to be happening. I barely know you."

"But you will after tonight," he said, putting his face directly in front of mine, an understated smirk showing on his face. I turned my head away from him and rubbed my hand over the sparkling wood hand rest.

His hand landed on my thigh, and I resisted the urge to pull it away immediately. I couldn't have him making a scene. I needed to be here. I turned to him, an eyebrow raised. "Look, if you want me to think of you as anything other than a friend, you need to slow down and show me why I'd want that."

His hand left my knee, and he stood up and flashed his hands in front of his chest. "All you need to know is this." He took another long haul from his drink and headed back to the bar.

I pulled out my phone and texted a coded message to Ace. *These kids are probably going to need someone to drive them home. Find someone from HQ to act as my mom by the time I get back.*

The wood in the room sparkled with a luster I'd never seen before—polished to more than just a shine. If I'd wanted to, I was sure I'd be able to see my face perfectly. No mirror needed. I wondered if the bugs would even stick to the slick surface. And if I were lucky enough to have them stick, how long would it be before the staff polished them away? I'd have to be smart in my placement of the bugs for sure. I'd have to put them somewhere the servants wouldn't accidentally come upon.

I found it curious that the various seating areas each offered a slightly different feel—from bold to sedate and relaxing. Even with thirty kids sitting and standing about, the room felt spacious. My spidey senses were calm. That realization left me to wonder about Jericho's family. Were they good people, and he was the rotten apple on the tree? Was it possible to be truly good parents and have a sociopath son or daughter? Viktor stood talking to a thin, blond boy. Viktor postured, as always, but the boy seemed relaxed and calm.

How was I going to get into Jericho's room with the wait staff around? I counted twenty in this room alone. Several moved about the room with tiny hors d'oeuvres while others stood about waiting for someone to help, and still others worked behind the bar.

Viktor summoned me over to him, and I reluctantly walked over. He immediately pulled me to him and introduced me; his breath already stank of the alcohol. They continued to chitchat while I scoped out the room and the people in it.

More teens crashed into the room over the next twenty minutes, adding to the loud chatter all around us, yet still no Jericho. I had to find a way to turn the conversation to things that would help me get to know

Jericho and this house better. I pulled slightly away from Viktor so that I could join the conversation.

"So, Jericho's parents set this party up?" I asked.

"Yep. This is his annual senior dinner. He invites all the seniors from the Academy to come. So glad I'm a senior this year. I mean, Jericho has parties out here, but this is the one everyone looks forward to their whole time at the academy."

"That's very generous of them."

Kyle, the boy standing with us, leaned in and said, "It's like a drop in the bucket for these people. If they wanted to be generous, they'd pay for all of us to go to college."

Viktor punched him in the arm, and he swayed. "You got that right." They laughed, and then Kyle sort of pulled away from us. He massaged his arm as he walked to another group of people.

Just as I was about to ask more questions, someone grabbed Viktor by the arm, and he turned and talked to the boy for a minute or two before turning back to me. "That was Johnson. I can't stand him. Thinks he's better than everyone else, and you watch, when Jericho's parents show up, he'll be all up in their faces, groveling."

"Why?"

"Look around you. Jericho's family is loaded. Johnson wants a piece of it and is willing to grovel for it. I hate groveling. If you want something, go for it. Kinda like I'm going for you." He winked. Oh, brother.

"So what? Does Jericho have his own wing in this place?"

"Just about. His room is about the size of my entire

house. You could get lost in there."

"Seriously? That seems so over the top."

"Everything is over the top here. But don't worry. I'm here to protect you. Let's move over there." He motioned with his head toward a group of about ten kids standing by a large window draped with rich, creamy fabric. I noticed that Viktor wasn't the only one putting a little something in his drink. I'd seen four others do the same thing in a matter of minutes. I stopped looking for it, resigning myself to the fact that, despite the glamorous surroundings, it was still going to be a typical party and that I'd have to work around all the craziness and unpredictability of drunk teenagers.

"Hey, Stewart," Viktor said to a boy walking toward us. "I didn't know your mug was coming tonight."

"Viktor," the boy said, pulling his gorgeous date toward us, "this is Melanie. She goes to Our St. Catherine's."

Viktor stood, "Nice to meet you, Melanie." I'd only been at the school for a day and had already overheard several kids talk about the girls that went to that school. They had a definite reputation. Viktor shook her hand and then turned to me. "This is the beautiful Amber. She just started at Bell this week and is already bringing the school to its knees."

I looked at Viktor and when his eyes met mine, I felt my cheeks turn crimson, which was so odd, so I turned to Stewart and Melanie. "Nice to meet you." Both shook my hand. The greeting seemed so formal. Was it the house, the furniture, the men in black suits that made us say things like *nice to meet you* instead of *hey* or *hi?*

We made small talk with the couples near us, but I was much more focused on imagining Jericho's phone and how to disassemble it and attach the bug in the shortest amount of time. A hum spread through the room, and I looked to see what the fuss was about. Jericho stood in an entryway to the room with a knock-your-socks-off bombshell blonde on his arm.

"Dinner is served," he announced, a flashy grin on his face. Behind him I saw a man and a woman, elegantly dressed and stiff looking. His parents? Jericho's eyes met mine. Did they linger a bit long? What was Jericho doing with the car thieves? Money was definitely not his motivation. Everyone followed him out of the room and into a massive dining hall with three long tables set in a very formal fashion—all in white and crystal. A team of waiters, also all in white, descended on the room once everyone was seated. Great. More people to have to watch out for. Jericho stayed standing and then tapped on his glass, bringing everyone's attention to him.

"Everyone, these are my parents. I wanted to thank them for arranging for such a nice evening. Thanks, Mom and Dad." He hugged them both, and then his dad spoke.

"We're glad you all could come. We love A.G. Bell Academy and are excited to have its scholars here with us tonight. Enjoy your evening."

It just hit me what Viktor had said earlier that Jericho's parents had this dinner every year, not just for his son and his classmates. "Why do they do this every year?" I asked Viktor in a quiet voice.

Viktor leaned over to me as Jericho's parents left the

room. "His parents own a company made up of engineers that regularly come up with the new best thing. His dad owns thousands of patents and adds to his collection daily. He has a huge stake in the school."

I nodded. When he'd told me about that kid Johnson brown-nosing, I guessed it wasn't for the money, but for the work opportunities it would provide.

I thought about what I'd seen as we were led into the dining area. We'd passed through a great hall with statues and busts of historical people lining it. At the end of the hall were stairs that led to what the plans listed as living quarters. The problem was that there were four areas listed like that, and all were at very different parts of the mansion. I needed to narrow it down.

The waiters set a bowl of clam chowder and a small salad in front of each person. Like they were practiced in the art of manners, all the guests waited until everyone had received their food to begin to eat. The room filled with talk about the latest cool stuff on Pinterest and Facebook and some totally crazy Vines. Phones were passed from person to person and laughter pealed through the air. I looked on my phone too, pretending to be just as involved with the same things, but I was searching for any recent pictures Jericho's friends might have posted of his house and room. There were a lot, but most gave me no clues because they were close-up selfies or photos of groups of kids that filled the entire frame. I'd have to ask questions to get my answers.

It may have been my imagination or my fears taking

over, but it seemed that every time I looked in Jericho's direction that he was looking at me.

I leaned over to Viktor. "Is this where they eat every day?"

"Nah. When I've spent the night, we eat in a room near the back of the house. I think this is only used when big groups come."

So this room would not be a good spot for a bug.

"I was thinking maybe they all ordered up room service."

"Right?" He nodded. "If it were me, I would. Guaranteed."

"Yeah. If I had to walk a mile for breakfast, I'd eat in bed." I was hoping he'd give me a clue as to where Jericho's room was.

"You got that right."

Backfire. How could I ask without it sounding too nosy or like I was interested in Jericho? I bit the bullet and said, "Do you think it would be weird if I asked him to see his room? I'd like to see this big-as-a-house room. I'll probably, no, I definitely will never have another chance to."

He waggled his eyebrows. "You don't need to ask. I'll take you up there myself later tonight."

Double. No, triple backfire.

I sighed and turned to the girl sitting next to me.

The first course was followed by lobster tail, and then dessert. I managed to choke down enough bites to not appear rude, but it was difficult. I hated seafood.

"Hey, do you know where there's a bathroom?" I asked the girl sitting next to me, since Viktor was talking to a guy across the table.

"I'm not exactly sure, but you can ask the dude at the door. I'm sure he knows." She pointed to a guy standing as sentinel near one of the closed six sets of doors around the room.

"Okay."

I stood and headed for the guy. Viktor grabbed my hand.

"Where are you going?"

"To the restroom. I feel a bit sick."

"Ah, yeah. I think there's one right outside the room." He gestured to a door.

"Thanks."

Instead of asking the guy at the door, I took the door Viktor had indicated. That would give me an excuse to explore a little. Besides, because I had the house plans in my head, I knew exactly where a bathroom was. My goal was to cross one of the four living quarters off the list of possibilities of being Jericho's room. Just as I got to the first landing of the wide, marble staircase, a man in one of the black suits at the bottom of the steps stopped me.

"Miss. Are you looking for a restroom?"

I turned slowly. "Yes! Is there one up here in Jericho's room I could use?"

"I think you've got your bearings mixed up. That staircase leads to his parent's wing. But there's no reason for you to go all the way to Jericho's room. There are several lavatories on the main floor. I'll show you the way."

"Oh! Great! It would be just like me to go the complete opposite direction I'd intended." I expected him to negate or verify what I'd said, but he said nothing besides, "Right this way." At least I'd eliminated one possibility.

After dinner, we put our coats on and made our way outside to the expansive gardens, and we bunched up together right below the wide steps leading down from the enormous columned patio leading out to amazing grounds. Pools of water were inset into a long walkway, some with beautiful, lavish fountains. It appeared to go all the way to Long Island Sound. Bare trees and bushes lined the sides. I could make out three swimming pools and wrought iron gazebos, and dormant rose gardens dotted the property.

Jericho remained, elevated on the cement patio before us, and said, "All right. The game tonight is kick the can."

Shouts of *All right, Right on,* and *Wahoo* sounded all around us, and kids high fived or pushed each other a bit in celebration.

Viktor looked at me and grinned. "This will be fun."

I had to work hard not to shrink away from him. An involuntary shiver raced through me as he bumped into my shoulder.

"This version of kick the can," Jericho continued, "has special rules. The object of the game is to get to the can and kick it." He pointed at the big can in the middle of a grassy area next to us. "Of course, the person who's *it* will try and prevent you from kicking the can. If he or she touches you before you kick it, you're out and have to go sit in jail, over there." He pointed to a far section of the deck.

"The person who's *it* is trying to capture as many people as he can in the shortest amount of time." He motioned to a huge whiteboard, which had all our names on it, on the far side of the grassy area where the can lay. A man in jeans and a black winter coat stood next to the board. "Jeremiah, there, will keep track of the score. Whoever gets the highest score will win whatever is in that mystery box." A large box stood next to the scoreboard on the ground. "And believe me, you want it." He flashed his teeth again.

"There are a couple of twists, of course."

The place erupted like everyone had won a car. They were obviously expecting this.

"Take advantage of whatever ones you like. Here are the rules for hiding from the person that is *it*: the first round will be singles. Everyone has five minutes to hide on their own. No one can share the same hiding place. After ten minutes, Mr. Heyer, here," he indicated a tall man with dark hair and eyes, "will let off a flare, letting you know it's time to double up. You will have three minutes to merge with someone else. If you can't find anyone to pair up with, you have to go for the can, and anyone who gets caught without kicking the can first has to drink a shot." He looked back toward the house as if someone might be within hearing distance and could scold him for it.

Someone shouted out, "Here, here!"

"What you do in that ten minutes is your own business, but be sure to share later." He chuckled. "After another ten minutes, the flare will go off again, and you'll have three minutes to triple up. Just imagine what can happen with a threesome."

Cat calls sounded all around us and then bursts of laughter.

"After that last ten minutes, he will fire the last flare to end the game. If, of course, you can't find anyone to merge with when the flare is shot, you must go for the can. Anyone who doesn't kick the can loses. You will get negative five points. But as we all know, there are some things that are better than winning. Very few, but there are some. To sweeten the pot, I have another twist. There are ten pristine bottles of Appleton rum out there." He swept his arm out over the gardens. "Feel free to drink as much as you'd like while in that hiding spot."

"Does anyone have any questions? Oh, yeah, those of you who are never *it* get the chance to win, too. The sooner you kick the can, the more points you get. Of course, if you get caught, you lose ten points. And the person who is *it* must be outside the red line during the hunt."

I noticed the large area on the ground around the can marked off with red tape. It was obvious that this game was meant to tempt the participants with either great make-out sessions, alcohol, or some mystery prize. There was something for everyone. I'm sure most everybody would be taking advantage of at least two. I didn't want to be anyone's prize, but I also needed time to go explore the house. I needed to plant the bugs and cameras. An entire game would take thirty minutes, but I'd never have that full time. Maybe I'd have twenty minutes max. I'd have to hang out near the patio pretending that I was trying to win by kicking the can. Others would be choosing that option too, so I wouldn't look suspicious

Chapter 13

I decided the best plan of action would be to hide close to the house and sneak in, but I needed some more direction as to where Jericho's room was. I turned to the girl next to me, who happened to be Jericho's date, and said, "Gosh, I can't imagine living in this house. It's bigger than a hotel. I bet Jericho gets lost on his way to his room." I watched her carefully.

Her eyes flicked to the west wing of the house before she said, "He never gets lost, but I have a few times." She smiled, her face thoughtful.

I wondered how often she'd been in his room. Jericho came down and pushed his way between us, his hand sliding down my arm. I stood firm, but his date moved to the side to let him in. He didn't look at her first; his gaze settled on me.

"I hope you liked dinner."

"It was great," I said, forcing myself to be nice.

"What are you talking about? You barely ate anything—you looked like you were being forced to eat sand or something," Viktor said.

I punched him, feeling heat in my cheeks. "Not cool. He didn't need to know that."

Jericho chuckled. "Sorry about that. I could have my chef make you something. I can't have you starve." He winked at me.

"Seriously. I'm fine."

He leaned in close and whispered, "I'll come looking for you. Look for me." He moved away from us with his date on his arm. Jericho was definitely not upset with me. Despite my revulsion for him, I considered trying to find him for half a second, but knew the more important thing for tonight was placing the bugs in his room. If I had the chance, I'd go for his phone. Maybe I'd get to do both.

I narrowed my eyes in his direction as he disappeared into the crowd.

"Where should we hide?" Viktor asked, having no clue what Jericho had just said. "I say we hurry from place to place until we find one of the jackpots."

I swung my head around to look at him. "I thought we were supposed to hide separately."

"We are, but we need to know where each other will be, so we can partner up. We'll run parallel to each other until we find the booze and then hide right by each other."

"Maybe I intend on winning the prize." I waggled my eyebrows.

"There are better things to be had in this game." He gave me a seductive glance.

"Maybe for you, but for someone like me, expensive prizes look pretty enticing. And I can get drinks from you any time I want." I looked toward his coat pocket, pretending not to know what he was really insinuating.

He raised his eyebrows. "I have something better than even this." He patted his pocket.

Since he didn't let it go, I said, "Like I said, I want what's in the box more."

"I'll have to prove you wrong. Give me the chance." He moved in, his nose just to the side of mine, his soft breath sending a whisper on my cheek and lips.

"I'm not that kind of girl," I said, my lips grazing his as they moved before I jerked away. The flare went up. I took off, pretending I was headed away from the house, and disappeared into the crazy crowds looking for a place to hide. I made my way west, checking for Viktor every minute or so, and then headed in the direction of the house. I hid in some tall bushes near a door leading inside.

I watched as the boy who was *it* headed out in the opposite direction, looking for players to catch. I didn't hesitate. I started up toward the house—then someone grabbed me. I resisted the urge to hurt whoever it was, reminding myself that we were playing a game. I knew it couldn't be the boy who was *it*, he was all the way on the other side of the building. It couldn't be Viktor, could it? Why hadn't I noticed him following me? I held the scream that had lodged itself in my throat and turned abruptly around, ready to take the necessary steps to get away from him, but it wasn't Viktor. It was Carson.

"Shhh!" he whispered, pulling me close to him. I could feel his heart pound against my chest and his shallow breath on my neck. Heat permeated through me. Once I gained my senses, I said, "Sorry, this spot is already taken." I had to get into the mansion, alone.

He pulled back and looked at me. "I thought you were vacating it."

My face reddened. "I had already chosen this spot, but realized I needed to use the bathroom, so I was going to try to make it inside and back in time for a sneak win. Seriously, the guy is so far from the can, anyone could beat him there."

"You think you can beat Austin until you find out how fast he is. He's the wide receiver for a rec football team. They nicknamed him Wind."

I totally wanted to take him up on the implied challenge, the competitive part of me burning to win, but I knew it would make it more difficult for me to complete my mission tonight. I had to stick with the bathroom excuse.

I looked him straight in the eye and said, "Maybe I'll give him a run for his money when I get back."

His firm grip on me relaxed. I crouched down, and he followed suit.

"Cross your fingers for me."

"Maybe I should go with you," he said.

"How embarrassing would that be? No, just wait here. When you see me next, I'll be kicking the can in victory."

He let go. I turned, and after checking the area again, I slunk up next to the house, slid along the exterior stones and through the door. I kept it slightly ajar and moved quickly to the west wing and up the stairs, not running into a soul. I could hear clanging of dishes and muted voices coming from the dining hall as I passed, but I thought it interesting that no one stood guard anywhere like earlier. A place like this called for security guards, didn't it? That's when I realized I must be on camera.

I changed my whole demeanor, acting like I belonged, relaxed and calm. I looked all around and murmured, "I should have asked where the bathroom was. Maybe up here." I started up the stairs, running my hand over the intricately carved wood of the banister and singing a popular song under my breath, hoping that helped turn away the attention of the security guy who was sure to be following my progress. *Please let me find the bedrooms camera free.*

I tried the first door to my right. Locked. Then I tried the next one, and it was locked, too. All the while, I scanned the area for cameras and found no hint of any, but I proceeded as if there were some. I crossed the hall to the door I hoped led to Jericho's room and turned the knob. *Voilà*—it opened. I pushed my way in.

The room was like a huge, open apartment. Viktor had been right. I spotted the bathroom right away and used it, just to keep up pretenses in case there were cameras in the room. I used the opportunity to get the bugs ready so that I could easily place them. I made my way to Jericho's windows and looked out over the game. I couldn't see much because it was so dark, but occasionally I saw someone move here or there. I was walking a fine line. I didn't want security to be suspicious about what I was doing in his room, but I thought it would be more realistic if I acted as if I was in awe of everything. I brushed my hand over things, planting several of the listening bugs that way—on his couch, his lampshade, by his door, all in places the staff would be unlikely to accidentally come upon.

Then I went back to the window, took one last look and headed over to the door. It cracked open. I hurried under the bed in a panic. Only then did it occur to me that it would cast suspicion on me. I felt like a total idiot and was going to climb out, ready with an explanation that I was looking for an earring, when the bed bounced above me. Whoever it was had just jumped on the bed. It couldn't be the guards, could it?

Then I heard the giggles and knew it must be a few kids hooking up. I rolled my eyes and shimmied toward the end of the bed to escape. I thought I'd have to crawl along the floor to prevent notice, but I quickly discovered the two people in the bed wouldn't notice me if I were a train barreling through the room. I stood up and walked out the door, carefully shutting it behind me. Maybe there weren't any cameras anywhere. Or perhaps security turned a blind eye during parties. It felt off somehow.

I turned to walk down the hall and bumped right into Viktor. "Ugh," I said as air pushed out of my lungs. He didn't move, just stood there like a solid wall, smiling at me.

"Not that kind of girl, huh?" He raised his eyebrows and pushed me into the door.

Chapter 14

I made myself be rational. "I had to take my chance and get a look at his room. I decided to use the bathroom while here and when I came out, I had company." It felt good to think of showing him. At least he couldn't use the room as he'd intended. I reached behind me and opened the door. When I stumbled in, I was surprised to see the couple look up at us. The two said, "Already taken, Viktor. Find your own room."

He chuckled behind me and pulled me out of the room saying, "Have fun. Sorry to have disturbed you." Then he turned to me. "No. I think you had your mind on something else." He took me to the next door—one I hadn't tried to open earlier. I hoped it was locked. He tugged on the handle, pushing on the latch. The door didn't budge.

Thank heavens.

He swore. "We'll find somewhere else."

I was about ready to yank my arm away from his grasp when I heard Carson's voice.

"There you are. I was starting to wonder if you fell in."

I chuckled quietly as Viktor let go of my arm. Carson deserved a huge kiss.

"Shouldn't you be worrying about your own date?" Viktor snarled.

"I couldn't find her. I've been waiting for Amber to get back from the bathroom so I could see Wind kick her butt in the race for the can."

I took a step toward him. "I think you might be in for the shock of your life." I took advantage of being free of Viktor's hold and walked quickly toward Carson. I could see a mischievous look in his eye that told me he knew he was saving me, just like a good friend should. I could hear Viktor stalk up behind me and didn't let him get close enough to grab me. I bounded down the hall and stairs, the boys following behind. I heard them talking, and the tone was not nice.

I didn't even try to make it back to my hiding spot. When I opened the door, I high-tailed it for the can. Carson had been right. Out of nowhere, I saw Wind speeding for the can. Lucky for me, I was faster. Thank you Division training. I picked up my speed a notch, not enough to make me appear weirdly fast, but fast enough to beat him by a few seconds. He was mad, too. He stomped his feet and glared at me. I turned my attention to the boys on the steps, who stood there, opened mouthed, staring at me. I grinned a big toothy grin, then bent over and pretended to breathe hard as Wind marched up the steps and snagged both boys, hustling them into the losers' section of the yard, which now held about twenty kids. I watched as the boys drank their shots. The large group of kids laughed loudly. So much for their squabble. I stood alone in the winner's section.

The man wrote our scores down on the grid on the board. I was the only one with a positive number besides Wind. His score was double mine already. I was hoping to be *it* next so that it would be easier to win the whole shebang. If I could win the big prize, it would bring me up close and personal with Jericho, who would most definitely give out the prize. The funny thing was I hadn't seen him come in this round of play. By the time the last flare shot into the air, all but ten had been caught, and I still stood by myself. Winning was definitely not the real prize in this game. I looked back at the losers and several were taking more shots. Alcohol was the prize for sure. I spent the time searching for Jericho.

Wind got credit for conquering the ones who didn't even try to come in, too. They slowly meandered in, all looking a bit disheveled and definitely off balance. The crowd cheered, whistled, and catcalled as they came in. While Carson seemed a bit tipsy, Viktor was full-on drunk already. I would definitely be driving home. In fact, most of the kids couldn't run a straight line by the end of play. When all was said and done, Wind beat my socks off, but I was the only other person in positive digits. I made a super sad face while Wind opened the big box after Jericho appeared and gave it to him. It was a laptop, and a nice one at that.

Wind turned to me in a very dramatic fashion, bowed, and handed it over to me. "She beat me. She wins."

Lots in the crowd guffawed, and others said, "No way."

I let myself be as grateful as was humanly possible, screaming out and jumping up and down. Then I hugged him, hard. Only a slight smell of alcohol was on his breath. His smile was huge. Now was my moment with Jericho. I turned to him and said, "Thank you, Jericho. There is no way in the world I thought I'd ever have something as cool as this." I moved toward him, cringing inwardly at the thought of having to hug him, but hoping I'd get his phone in the process. "Thank you so much." My arms wrapped around him and he shifted, changing the hug to a grossly inappropriate one. I wiggled out, just barely refraining from stomping on his foot and kneeing him in the groin. *I am Amber. I am Amber.*

I had the phone.

"I'm not that grateful. Down boy." I backed up down the stairs, my hands up under my coat working on opening the battery compartment of his phone. Whatever happened, I couldn't get caught.

"I was just showing you how grateful I was that you were grateful."

His smile creeped me out. I took another step back, bowing my head down to hide the revulsion I felt. "Point taken," I said.

As I held the open phone in one hand still under my coat, I used the other to reach for the bug in my pocket. Someone bumped me from behind, and I lost my balance and control of the phone. The battery cover flipped through the air and landed on the step next to Jericho.

I stifled an anguished cry and as if on instinct, I flew myself forward, slamming into Jericho and bringing him down with me. I let his phone fall to the ground and in a flash, let mine drop too, forcing the battery cover off as I grabbed it from my pocket. The bug remained taped to the interior of my pants pocket. Useless.

"Oh, my gosh," I said trying to get up and off of Jericho. "I'm so sorry. Someone bumped me and—"

He pulled me close. "I know what you were doing."

I froze.

"You do?" I blurted.

"I do." His hot, breathy whisper hit my ear like a muggy night in Memphis.

I'd been compromised, and my phone was disabled. By me. I had no way of signaling the guys that I needed an extraction. How had I messed this up so quickly? I readied myself to spring up and run for all I was worth. I may have screwed up this mission, but I wasn't going to give myself to him to torture.

His tongue licked the outer edge of my ear, and he said, "Meet me in the theater later, and we can get things going. You don't need to play games to get me. I'm more than willing." Then he licked my ear once more.

"I just might," I whispered. I pushed off him, sickened and yet very, very relieved. I stood up, and he rolled over to his knees before standing which gave him the perfect view of one of the broken phones.

"Ah, crap. My phone!" He picked up the phone and then glanced at me before searching for the battery and back of it. "Wait. Here's another one." He held up another backless phone.

"Is that mine?" I shrieked. "Oh, please don't be

broken. Please. My parents will absolutely kill me, and I'll be phoneless." I snatched it from him and winced noticeably. "It is!" I got to my knees and searched for the battery and back. Everyone started looking around, and two other kids brought us the parts. I quickly put mine back together and then sat on the steps to try it out. Jericho was doing the same thing, but Viktor took the opportunity to sit between us. Territorial swine. I turned my body away from him. Jericho's date asked him a question, and they started talking.

Jericho's phone rang as I put my phone up to my ear. He laughed when he saw it was me. Ace had programmed all the kids' numbers into my phone.

"What are you doing, hot stuff?"

I played along. "Nothing. Just at a lame party at this really lame guy's house."

"Well, I'm going to the movies tonight. Why not ditch the party and come to me?"

"Really?"

"Yep. I'll be waiting."

He then stood up and walked back inside with his date in tow. Viktor stood and held out his hand to help me up. I took it, and we walked back inside.

I'd dodged a big one, and all I wanted to do was get back to the brownstone as fast as I could. It wasn't to be. I needed to shake Viktor so I could spend some time with Jericho and give his phone a second try. That meant we couldn't go to the movie. We'd have to go for the dancing. And being with Viktor in the theater was a bad move all around. No. I'd dance with Viktor, take a chance to get away from him and then get the bug into Jericho's phone. A bad feeling settled in my gut, and I thought better of the plan. While it would have given me a second opportunity to get the bug into Jericho's phone, I figured if he were to find a bug in his phone after tonight, he'd have to suspect me. I couldn't risk it. No. I would not be getting close to Jericho today. Dancing it was. Safety in numbers—and no couches or recliners.

We moved toward the room. Viktor followed behind and placed his hands on my hips. I lurched forward. It was an involuntary motion like my body was rejecting his very touch, and I smashed right into a guy in front of us.

"Sorry," I said. "I tripped."

He laughed and stumbled to the side. "You've been doing that a lot tonight." Viktor had consumed a ton of alcohol, but he seemed to still be able to control himself. I took that to mean he drank often. Most of the songs were fast ones, making it harder for Viktor to misbehave. I had to be on my guard for every slow dance. For most of them, I conveniently needed a drink, the bathroom, or some fresh air.

Viktor had run out of his own liquor and was taking it off everyone else. He would try to get me to drink too. "You're no fun, Amber. Come on." The longer the night wore on, the more frustrated he got with me.

I would say two words, "designated driver," each and every time. I kept one eye on Jericho. He would disappear and reappear. Sometimes with his date and sometimes without. I wondered what he was doing.

Everyone thanked Jericho as we left the house. He gave me a truly inappropriate hug that made me blush. When Viktor's car pulled up, the valet turned to me and said, "Your laptop is in the trunk."

"Thanks."

He opened the driver's side door, and I climbed in. I hoped they didn't allow anyone to drive home smashed.

"That was pretty cool that Wind gave you that laptop. He was basically saying you're the queen of speed." Viktor gave me a creepy smile. "One day I'll test that speed." I shook my head and closed the driver's side door.

There was a lot of chatter in the car for about fifteen minutes, and then it got quieter and quieter until everyone fell asleep. Out of nowhere, Viktor reached over and took one of my hands from the steering wheel, holding it in his. He looked behind him and then looked at me. Carson and his date were in the far back, and Mikado and his date along with the boy with platinum hair and his date were directly behind us.

"Uhh," I murmured, and tried to pull my hand away from his. "I'm driving." He squeezed tighter and talked low.

He slid over to me, way too close. "I want to tell you about something I think you'll love." He looked behind him again. "Looks like we've lost everyone."

I peered behind us in the rearview mirror to see everyone leaning on their dates, mouths open in unflattering ways. I pushed air out of my nose and tried to pull away, but I was already pushed up against the door. He held tighter still.

"Seriously. You'll like what I have to say." He relaxed his hold on my hand, but not enough that I could easily pull it away. "I know a fairly easy way for you to make some money, and you won't have to play any games."

I narrowed my eyes. "I don't think so," I said, totally misinterpreting what he was saying and not knowing it. I yanked my hand out of his.

He laughed. "You'll be perfect for this. Seriously. Hear me out. It has nothing to do with selling your body." He laughed again. "Man, you're so suspicious. I know someone who gives great jobs to teens who need them. You'll make awesome money, and it's fun."

"What is it?"

"I can't tell you here." He peeked behind him and then back to me before looking at the road again. "It's not easy, but it's lucrative. After watching how fast you are, I think you'll love it. Meet me for an early dinner tomorrow, and I'll tell you about it."

"Dinner, huh?" What was he talking about? What kind of business was he running on the side? And what did my speed have to do with it?

He smiled. "All your money troubles will disappear."

After that, he slept too. I thought back on my first day at Bell, watching the kids in the auto outbuilding with S-Dub. I looked over at Viktor. Had he been one of the mentors I'd seen? I remembered the niggling feeling I'd had as he'd walked away from me that day in the cafeteria. That's what I'd been trying to recall—I hadn't seen his face in the auto theft class, just his back, the way he walked. Now that I was putting the two together, it seemed obvious. I had seen Viktor in Shareweather's class that morning. His strut was unmistakable.

My mind spun, trying to process the implications. Maybe I wouldn't have to make nice with Jericho after all, seeing as I already had a very strong in with Viktor.

Of course, he could be just another peon. Still, it was another option. The only question was, was it any better?

I pulled up to the brownstone and put the car in park. I shook Viktor awake. He wiped a string of drool from his mouth then reached his hand out for the keys, making an obvious move to try for a kiss at the same time.

Classy.

I pulled the keys out of his reach, and my lips as well. "Nice try," I said. "But my mom is going to drive you guys home."

"What the hell, Amber? They'll know we've been drinking!" I was pleased to see that his face paled a bit. Maybe Ace's threat had had an impact after all.

"They'd rather everyone be safe than judge. I know my dad came on pretty strong, but as long as I tell him you were good to me, he won't shoot you." I couldn't resist adding, "Much."

Viktor swore and made a grab for the keys again, but he didn't have a chance to do anything else—Ace and a female agent I'd never met opened the door to the brownstone and quickly approached the car.

I got out, and so did Viktor. "My wife will drive you to the subway station," Ace said in his dad voice. "I'll follow behind and drive her home once we see you safely on the train. You can get your car tomorrow."

"Thank you, Mr. Smith," Viktor said awkwardly. "We're really just a little tipsy—nothing too extreme, I promise."

"Well, I won't call the cops on you, if that's what you're worried about. Just go straight home, and there won't be any problem." He paused for a minute, then growled at Viktor, "Were you a gentleman tonight?"

"I was, sir," he said. I had stepped out of the road. "I'm sure Amber will verify that."

"He was, Dad. Please don't embarrass me any more."

"All right, then," Ace said, and headed toward another car parked on the street—it must have been the one the female agent had come in. The agent was already in the driver's seat of Viktor's Escalade.

"Good night, Viktor." I gave him a hug and turned to go into the brownstone. I couldn't wait to take a shower and get Viktor's smell off me. Then Viktor called out.

"Wait. You forgot your laptop. I'll grab it for you." He got back in the car and popped the trunk, but instead of getting out himself, he sent Mikado out. He handed me the computer, then leaned in close. "Whatever you do, don't meet with Viktor tomorrow. I can't say more than that. Just trust me."

He got back in the car as if nothing had happened, and they all drove off, leaving me standing, completely shocked, in the middle of the sidewalk.

Chapter 15

I showered, scrubbing Viktor off me. I lay on the couch, waiting for my team to get back and thinking through everything that had happened. I fell into a fitful sleep. Viktor and Jericho kept invading my dreams, and whenever I woke up, Mikado's warning echoed eerily through my thoughts. When Ace woke me, I grabbed his wrist and nearly pulled his arm out of the socket. He slammed into the coffee table and swore.

"Oh, my gosh. I'm so sorry! I thought... I thought..." I shook my head.

"Remind me not to ever wake you up." He scowled at me.

I sat up. "I'm sorry. I just hardly slept, and when I did, I dreamt of Viktor, Jericho, and Mikado. They make for terrible dreams. I need to take another shower before school. I think I can still smell his cologne on me. Maybe that's triggering the dreams."

Ace's scowl deepened, but this time it wasn't for me. "I get it. To be honest, playing your dad last night has made me feel a little more paternal toward you. I don't like the idea of you getting involved with those guys any more than Jeremy does."

I sighed. "That makes three of us."

"Four," Halluis said from the doorway.

I squinted over at his silhouette. "What is this, a morning pow-wow?"

A look passed between Ace and Halluis, then Ace spoke. "Look, we just want you to know we have your back in this mission. I mean, not that we didn't before, er, of course, you know—"

"What Ace is so eloquently trying to say is," Halluis cut in, "you're our girl, Christy. We won't let anything happen to you."

I started to speak, then had to cough and rub my eyes, feigning residual sleepiness to mask the tears welling up. They seemed to get what I was trying to say, and Ace patted my shoulder awkwardly before they both vacated the room.

"Thanks," I whispered to the empty room. They were my team. I was their girl. Now if only I knew where I stood with Jeremy.

I rushed up to shower again. Sure I'd scrubbed every trace of Viktor off me, I headed down to get a bite to eat. When I saw Jeremy setting fresh bagels on the table I felt the urge to run to him and let him wrap his arms around me. The thought brought a flush of heat to my cheeks. Obviously some part of me was still Christy the mouse, searching for a protector—I'd thought I'd left her far behind. Great, Hadden, I thought. That's a perfect way to prove to Jeremy how capable you are—run to him like a scared little girl. I ducked my head, trying to hide the embarrassing thought from Jeremy and the rest of the team, already seated around the table. Luckily, they were deep in conversation, and no one noticed my discomfort.

I pulled my phone out of my pocket, and Jeremy looked at me sharply. "Any word from Viktor?"

I nodded. "He's sent me a few texts already. I'm to meet him at five at a restaurant called Mishka's."

Jeremy's jaw tightened, and he shook his head, but then he just sighed and bit back whatever argument he wanted to make.

"Well, if we're moving forward with this," he said, shooting Halluis a dirty look, "then I want you to be prepared. Come on, let's run through a few scenarios before we send you off to school."

I sighed inwardly, though I didn't let my face show anything but patient compliance. Why wouldn't he just trust me?

For the next hour, he drilled me on different scenarios, going over and over again what I should do, what I should say, how I should look. Finally, Halluis cut in.

"Look, Jeremy," Halluis said. "There's no way we can discuss every eventuality. It's likely that nothing we talked about will happen. Christy is more than capable. She'll be able to figure it out."

I turned to him and said, "Why, thank you, Halluis. Jeremy seems to always beat things into the ground." I shot Jeremy an exasperated look, but then felt bad for encouraging the division between the two men. Still, it felt good to know he had my back—and that he believed in me, too.

"I just want to help her be ready for the most likely

problems. That's all."

Jeremy's phone chimed. "That's my cue to leave. I've got some stuff to do before the dinner."

***

I had a hard time focusing on keeping up my cover during the school day—I was so preoccupied with my upcoming dinner with Viktor that I barely even registered a word any of my teachers said. At least I had Jericho's party to excuse my lack of concentration. Every other kid who'd gone was fighting to stay awake all day, so the teachers, though frustrated, didn't seem particularly suspicious.

At lunch, I bypassed the tables with all the popular kids like Mikado, Viktor, and Jericho to sit with Hank and his friends. Carson was nowhere to be found once again. Much to my surprise, both Gina and Karina joined us at lunch. If anything lasting was to come from my stay at Bell, I hoped Gina and Karina would find some friends. Hank and his gang swept them into their group and didn't look back.

Finally, the tedium of the school day was over, and I headed back to the brownstone. As I changed, I gave myself a pep talk that Viktor wasn't creepy at all and that I could handle him. Someone knocked on my door right after I got dressed. I opened it to find Jeremy standing there.

"Hi," I said, somewhat awkwardly. We hadn't had a one-on-one conversation since the night of the dance, and it felt odd to be alone with him. The urge to pull him in for a hug was strong, and to fight it, I shoved my hands into my pockets. "Did you need something?"

He leaned up against the doorjamb. "I just wanted

to talk to you about this dinner tonight. I want you to be really careful. This guy Viktor—I don't like what I've been hearing on the audio feeds."

I shuddered. "I know. I wish it wasn't necessary—he's such a creep. But the more I learn about him, the more I think he's probably involved. He could be the one to lead us to the car. I can't pass up that chance."

Jeremy sighed and ran his hand over his face. "You know, Christy—I'm not sure it's worth the risks you're taking."

"What do you mean?" I turned away from him and moved into my room to sit on the bed, hoping he'd come, too, and explain to me what was on his mind. But he stayed leaning against the doorjamb.

"It's…" he started, but then shook his head. "It's nothing. I just want you to be cautious. Extra cautious. There's no reason to put yourself in any extra danger."

I felt a little heat rise up in my chest, and I couldn't keep the irritation out of my voice. "Jeremy, how many times do I have to tell you, I signed up for danger? I knew what I was getting into. Can you just please trust me to handle myself?"

He grimaced. "Of course. But you have a team for a reason. Halluis will be shadowing you, and he's going to put surveillance in Viktor's car so we can follow and listen in. We'll also try to get a tap on his phone. We haven't been able to get into Jericho's yet, but cross your fingers Viktor's will be easier.

"I wish we could bug you, but I don't want to chance that anyone would discover you were wired. That would be disastrous." He tipped his head back to me. "Halluis will be close at hand, but it will have to be up to him to step in if you're in danger. You can't signal him or call out to him in any way. It would ruin the mission if they discovered someone was watching you."

"You think?" I said, fighting back the urge to roll my eyes. To shake off my irritation, I got off the bed and grabbed a pair of raggedy shoes to go with my jeans and T-shirt.

"Do I look like I'm financially challenged?" I threw my hands onto my hips and pushed my bottom lip out. "Really, I'm going for desperate. How'd I do?"

"You always look desperate to me, so..."

I punched him. "Thanks a lot!" I smiled, and he grabbed me into a hug that quickly turned awkward.

With our faces too close, he said, "You're amazing. You'll do just fine."

I pushed away, though it was harder to let go than I expected. "What did you have to do last night?"

"I went to NY Division HQ and worked with the computer guys to make sure your new past was all in place in case someone looks into it."

Halluis had already set up my record—Jeremy was a bit of a micromanager, never satisfied that people actually did what they were supposed to when it came to me and my safety. A rush of frustration flooded me. It was fine for him to be protective of me when I was in witness protection, but I was a full-fledged agent now. Why wouldn't he just let me do my job? I wanted to call him out on his behavior, but I held my tongue, if only barely. He was the mission leader, and things were going to be done his way. If nothing else, I could at least show him that I could follow orders. I'd prove to him I was every bit an agent, and not a little girl needing to be saved.

"And everything's in order?" A sense of calm settled over me before he even spoke.

"Yep, and it will definitely stand up to any test anyone throws at it." His face held a satisfied expression.

"Perfect. We better get downstairs."

He gave me a quick nod and opened the door for me to go through.

Once downstairs, Jeremy had us run through the plan one last time so that they would know my whereabouts.

Ace said, "We'll be here listening in on Jericho. Good luck, Christy. Oh, and Halluis was able to get into his Gramercy Park condo and bug his landline. How would it be to have a mansion on Long Island for the weekend and a luxury condo while at school during the week?"

"Yeah, he lives a hard life. And I bet those aren't the only houses his family owns." I took the car keys and headed out. Jeremy left out the back door—as always.

***

Once at the restaurant, I told the hostess I was meeting someone, and she directed me to the table where Viktor sat. He was alone. It surprised me. It made me wonder if he was not only a recruiter, but the boss. There was a spooky feel in the restaurant. The lights were kept low, and the décor was all in black and deep red fabrics. I couldn't see all the way across the room. Creepy, just like him.

I walked hesitantly up to the table, and Viktor stood as the waiter slid my seat back. I sat, and he helped me move closer to the table. I smiled, easily slipping into my alias of Amber. The waiter poured me water and then asked what I'd like to drink. I glanced over at Viktor. He was already drinking what looked like Coke.

"Could you just bring me some lemon for my water? I'd love that."

The waiter nodded.

One side of Viktor's mouth shot up and he huffed a bit, but said nothing.

I kept folding and unfolding my hands like I was nervous. He kept looking at them. He reached across the table and put his hands on mine when I placed them, folded, on my plate for the fiftieth time.

"Just relax. We're two friends sharing dinner together." His eyes lingered on mine, and I felt heat enter my cheeks. He was handsome in an angular way. His eyes seemed to probe mine. It was a shame he was so ugly inside. I took it as a good sign that he was sitting across from me. Maybe we were entering a more business-like relationship now. I could only hope. His warm hands on mine sent a terrible jitter up my spine. My spidey senses were raging. Real danger was here. I wondered if it was him or someone else in the restaurant. I would have to wait it out to see.

"I couldn't believe how fast you were last night. I've never, and I mean never, seen anyone beat Wind in a foot race, even when he was twice the distance away from the goal."

I pulled gently on my hands, to let him know I was okay. I clasped them in my lap. He smiled.

"I'm really great with a keyboard, too. Fastest fingers in the east." I laughed, but the joke fell on deaf ears because the waiter came up with a nice salad and asparagus and asked what we would like for our meal. We had no menus, so I looked at Viktor with a question on my face.

"You like steak, don't you, Amber?"

"I love it, actually."

"Great. Get us two filets, please, and some garlic potatoes on the side." He turned to me. "I hope that sounds good to you."

"Sounds great. Thanks." I licked my lips, lifted my napkin, and whispered. "But I don't have any money to pay for it." I wanted to drill in the fact that I needed money.

He smiled. After sending the waiter away, he said, "I got this. No worries."

"Oh, good, cause this place is screaming money."

"My parents own it."

I looked around, letting my mouth turn into a frown. "Wow! This place is great."

He nodded.

"You didn't tell me you were a richie, too." I took a big bite of salad.

"Just because my parents are rich doesn't mean I am. And yeah, they have a lot of money, but nothing like Jericho's parents."

After swallowing the salad, I said, "Sorry. Do they make you work here?"

"I used to, but now that I can drive, I have a much better job."

"Oh. Am I going to need a car for this job, because my parents—" I wanted him to tell me more without censoring what he wanted to say.

He put up his hand and waved it back and forth while shaking his head. "No business during dinner."

I stared at him, open mouthed, wanting to look a bit silly.

"Okay?"

"All right."

"So, tell me about your parents." The question was direct and demanded an answer.

We then went into a long conversation about my life. I was glad that Jeremy had made me go over everything a thousand times, it truly felt real as I told him about it.

"They're teachers." I made my voice monotone, uninterested. "They work at Helman's Academy for the Blind. They feel it's important to give back to a distressed community. My summers are all spent in other countries, doing some sort of service project."

"I get it. Your family isn't poor. They just choose to spend their money on others instead of you." He raised an eyebrow.

I looked down at my empty bowl of salad and half-eaten plate of asparagus, trying to look like that really bugged me.

Our main course came, and we ate and talked until the last bite left the fork. He told me freely about his family and his past. He didn't live a charmed life like I'd thought. While he revered his father, I could tell there was tension there. When he told about his father forcing him to kneel with bare knees on rice for ten times the duration of his lateness, no matter the excuse, to show him the importance of keeping his word—no matter what—I couldn't help but soften toward him, but that didn't mean I condoned his choices. No matter his past, he could choose for himself who he wanted to be. What surprised me was that he agreed with his father's methods after having to endure them.

My stories of woe didn't come close, but he seemed to bury the true feelings he had for those encounters and create a wall, thick and rough to keep people back. No wonder he was so awful, he'd been denied love and acceptance in exchange for discipline and loyalty his whole life.

"Why don't we switch gears now?" Viktor wiped his mouth with the cloth napkin.

"Did you just say switch gears?" I smirked.

"Do you have a problem with that?"

"No, it just not normal teen speak, that's all."

He glowered at me, a look of distaste spread across his face.

"I mean, are you really a teenager? Seriously?"

He seemed to suddenly find it all very funny and laughed outright. "Do I seem like the kind of person who would return to high school after he left it?"

I chuckled. "No, but your choice of words was odd. It's funny."

"Are you doubting me?"

"Maybe. I mean, the way you're beating around the bush, I think you're going to ask me to do something illegal or something."

"Are you opposed to doing something illegal?"

"Well," I stuttered, "of course. It's *illegal*." I looked around, eyes wide like I was afraid someone would overhear. "Are you for real? You really want me to do something illegal?" I didn't want to seem too eager to join his little gang. I thought showing some scruples would be a good thing.

"Whoa! Whoa! Just calm down." He held his hands out in front of him, moving them up and down like he was telling everyone in a choir to sit down.

I took a deep breath and eyed him.

In a low voice, he said, "Tell me about your arrest."

I let my eyes shoot open and brought my hands to my lap, rocking a couple of times. "Who told you I'd been arrested?" No wonder he felt he could be so out in the open about doing illegal things.

"I have connections. I'll leave it at that." That terrible grin spread across his face. "Just tell me about it."

"What? Did you do a background check on me or something?" I appeared totally indignant. I wanted him to work for me so that he would feel like he'd really done something amazing by hooking me.

"Or something." He pulled in one corner of his lip and bit on it.

"You can't just go around looking into people's lives without their consent. Can you? Come on. How did you even have time for that?"

He leaned forward, his forearms resting on the now almost empty table, his head moving toward mine.

"Why did you break into that car? I think it's so funny." He echoed my earlier words.

"You wouldn't think it was very funny if you had no car to get anywhere. It's not like I stole the cars or anything. I just borrowed them. If I needed to be somewhere, I'd hotwire the nearest car, go where I needed to go, and then return it. No harm, no foul. I'd

Cindy M. Hogan

even leave money for gas."

"Them?"

I covered my mouth, like I'd said something I shouldn't have, but then smiled, like I was really proud of my accomplishments and excited to talk about it. It was time to let him know I wasn't really opposed to illegal activities.

"So, it wasn't just once. Even better. Ingenious. I knew there must be a reason behind your criminal behavior. Seriously, the way you hold yourself, no one would ever know." He had been looking at his fork, but his eyes flicked to mine when he said the last sentence. He liked the idea of me being totally incognito.

"But you found out. How did you find out? The records are supposed to be sealed."

"Like I said, I have connections." He tilted his head to the side and fingered the fork he'd been eyeing.

"What, do you want me to steal cars?" I chuckled. Right after I said the words, something inside me felt strange. Was I afraid? Maybe I wasn't supposed to get mixed up in this mess after all. Maybe I should have gotten the heck out and let someone else finish the operation or maybe I should have done it from afar and not get directly involved. I tapped my foot, trying to get rid of the odd feeling.

"Yes." He said it completely matter-of-factly.

Instinctively, my eyes flitted toward the exit, and I couldn't ignore the fact that a massive, tall, and unbelievably tan man stood between me and the exit. He must have had to have his clothes custom made for him; there was no way his biceps would ever fit into any shirts I'd ever seen. Would I stand a chance against

150

him if I had to? I suddenly wished I had my knife in my boot and my gun on my thigh.

I turned my head very slowly back to Viktor. "Hmm. Interesting. I never would have thought..."

"So, you ready to join us?"

I let my true feeling of nerves manifest on my face in the form of a flush, but managed to make it seem as though I was excited, though scared. I leaned forward, letting my body indicate eagerness.

"I'll admit I've missed the thrill—but I've already been caught for this. I could get in a lot of trouble. I could lose my chance at a future."

"Or this could be the best chance you've ever been handed." He looked extremely self-satisfied. I could tell he thought I should be overcome with gratitude to him. "Now, just sit there nicely, and I'll fill you in on all the details before my uncle gets here."

"Your uncle?"

"Alexander Molgilevich to you. He'll serve as the witness to our agreement. How many cars have you stolen?"

"I just told you, I didn't steal any. I just borrowed them." I laughed. Was Alexander the man Jericho had called? My heart raced at the prospect of meeting him.

"How many cars have you borrowed, then?" He leaned back in his seat.

"This doesn't leave this table?" I leaned forward and spoke low.

"Of course not." Behind his eyes he was laughing.

"A hundred and two."

His jaw slackened for an almost imperceptible second, and then he recovered. I'd obviously wowed him.

"And how did you learn to do that?"

"The Internet. I learned all the ins and outs and then tried it. I guess I have a knack for it. Knack is also a word normal people don't use any more, but I like the sound of it." I grinned, raising an eyebrow.

He shook his head. "Whatever, Word Girl. What types of cars were you able to get into?"

"Most older makes and models. I don't own a smart key. That would be awesome you know, to have a smart key and be able to get into almost any car you wanted."

"If you were given a smart key, could you bypass the keypad on doors?"

I gave an exaggerated frown. "Maybe, if I got to try it a few times. The Internet makes it look easy." I brushed my hands across the table linen.

"It's not." He looked at his phone and appeared to be reading something. He nodded and then punched something into his phone.

"Consider the next twenty minutes your job interview. There's a green Camry, license plate BKJ 4521 in the third row of cars across the street. Go get it. Drive it into our garage, and come back up here."

Chapter 16

He slid a bag across the table to me. Tools of the trade, I was sure.

I looked at him, awestruck. These guys didn't mess around.

"Your time has already started."

I stood up, and the man blocking the exit moved out of my way. "No problem," I said before I hurried past him.

Viktor call out after me, "And don't be late."

Once outside, I ran across the street, past the parking lot and then doubled back, weaving my way through the cars, pretending I belonged. I spotted the Camry without a hitch and immediately went to work on it, using the tools Viktor had given me. I felt eyes on me. Was it Halluis or possibly someone from Viktor's gang? I hated being watched. I couldn't help but notice that a smart key was included in the packet. It only took me two seconds to unlock an old car like the Camry. Another thirty seconds to hotwire it and five minutes to pull out into traffic, make a left turn, and circle back around to the restaurant's garage.

I made my way up the escalator and into the restaurant. I took a moment to compose myself before heading in. I brushed my hands down my wrinkled shirt and over my outdated pants and then took a deep breath.

The man had moved in to stand behind my seat, blocking my view of Viktor. When I got in a position to see around him, I noticed Viktor was no longer alone. His uncle, Alexander, had arrived. The sharp angles of his face caused deep shadows to form just beneath the ridges of his cheekbones, giving him a truly spooky appearance—almost vampire-like. I moved in, triumphant.

I sat in my seat, and his uncle stood and took my hand and kissed it. "Amber. Nice to meet you. I am Alexander." His Russian accent was thick and smoky.

"Nice to meet you, too." I made sure to make my hand tremble in his.

"No need to be nervous. You did an amazing job just then."

I pulled the pouch of tools out of my pocket and slid it across the table to them. The uncle pushed it back toward me. "That is yours to keep." He raised his nose in the air, like a dog sniffing for something, and took a deep breath in. "I think we've seen enough. Don't you, Viktor?"

Viktor gave an exaggerated nod. "For sure, Uncle."

"You got us a good one here, I can feel it." He smacked his lips.

Danger seeped from their every pore, but a great sense of satisfaction overcame me. I was in.

"One thing," he said, leaning toward me as he stood

to leave. "You cross us, and I will not only kill you in the most painful way possible, but I will also slowly cut up your mother right in front of your eyes. Then I will hang your father over her cut-up body." He held out his hand to me. "Again. Nice to have met you. You will be a definite asset to our little business."

This man was pure evil. I had to find a way to end his reign of terror. No one would have to suffer under his hand ever again. I forced myself to continue to look scared while inside a phoenix was rising.

He turned to Viktor. "Give her all the details. I need her ready to go Thursday night." He gave me a pressed smile before walking away. Four men surrounded him as he moved to the front door.

I memorized every line of his face and body. I could see the faint bulge of a weapon at his hip. We would find out who he was and bury him.

Among other things, Viktor told me to be in Mr. Shareweather's class by six sharp on Thursday to get a bit of instruction from the master. I bet I could school the engineering teacher on a few moves. Then again, when I saw Jericho and Mikado in action the other day, they'd been amazingly fast. It seemed I did have a few things to learn.

I had my marching orders, and I stood from the table to leave when Viktor grabbed my hand and moved next to me. I had to reach deep to look him in the eye. He smiled. "You know, a big part of me wanted you to fail the background."

I furrowed my brow in confusion.

He nodded, his eyes seductive. "You see, I'm not sure my uncle will approve of the relationship we are

155

about to have."

Burning ice flashed through my veins. I had to be quick. "He doesn't seem like a man we'd want to anger. And if you think he wouldn't approve, then we shouldn't begin one."

He clucked his tongue and rubbed his thumb over the back of my hand, which he still held. "I disagree. We can always ask for forgiveness later." He squeezed my hand and leaned in and kissed my cheek, lingering over-long. I suppressed a shudder and managed an ambiguous smile. As much as I hated it, I needed to keep my options open—if I needed to get closer to Viktor to further my mission, I couldn't close that door by acting too disinterested. I'd have to leave him with a little hope, at least.

Chapter 17

Once back at the brownstone, Halluis drew a picture of the uncle as I described him. He faxed the scarily accurate depiction to Division, who got back to us in less than thirty minutes. This dude was bad with a capital B. He'd been indicted for money laundering, murder, espionage, and racketeering, to name only a few of the charges listed on his two-page criminal history. So, why hadn't he been put away a long time ago? He always got off on some technicality, or it appeared in some cases that he was helped by dirty judges. Everything indicated that Alexander Molgilevich was a high-ranking member of the Russian mafia.

Each new development added a wrinkle to Jeremy's forehead. I didn't dare tell him what Viktor had said at the end of the evening. I believed that if he thought he had cause, like a sociopath wanting to be my boyfriend, he would find a way to get me off the case. I couldn't allow that. I would not fail any assignment given me, and more than that, I had to help put an end to Alexander's reign.

"The Russian mafia," he growled. "We've run smack dab into one of the most ruthless crime families out there."

The four of us sat staring bleakly at each other in silence.

"So, where do we go next?" I asked.

"Nowhere," Jeremy insisted. "This mission just got way deeper than a simple car-theft ring. We need to call this off."

"Hold on there a moment," Halluis cut in. "You don't have the authority to call off the mission. There is no way I am going to go whining to the director and tell him that things got too hard so we're backing out."

"If that's what you think I'm doing—"

"That's exactly what you're doing! You've been trying to get out of this mission from day one—"

"You have no idea what you're talking about—"

I couldn't let this go on. I slammed my fist on the table, rising to stand as I did. "Hey!" I shouted. "Everyone, shut up!"

To my surprise, they did. They stared at me, blinking in shock.

Ace held up a hand tentatively. "For the record, I wasn't saying anything."

I whirled on him. "Well, maybe it's about time you did. Halluis is right about one thing, we have a mission to accomplish, and you standing on the sidelines isn't helping anything. I've seen what you can do, and I'm not going to accept this 'glorified tech support' excuse of yours a second longer. Get in the game, Ace." Ace looked chagrined but didn't argue.

"And as for you two," I said, turning to Jeremy and

Halluis. "There's no point arguing until we know more. We don't even know if this car-theft ring has anything to do with the mafia. It could be something Alexander is doing on his own. We just don't know. We need to gather more information before we make any decision."

Halluis opened his mouth, but then shut it and simply nodded.

Jeremy sighed. "You're right." He paused only a second longer before adding, "I may know someone undercover in the Russian mafia, an FBI agent. If I can get ahold of him safely, we may be able to get some answers."

Now that my big scene was over, I felt a bit awkward standing over the three of them, so I slowly settled back into my seat. "Okay, then. Let's get on that."

***

Two hours later, Jeremy and I met up with the hulking Agent Kozlov at a Division safe house for a whirlwind thirty-minute rundown of the Russian mafia, known to insiders as the bratva—the brotherhood. His speech was clipped and heavily accented but deep and gruff at the same time. I had to concentrate to understand him, and there were moments I wished he'd just speak in Russian.

"We thought for a long time that old structure, including the *vory* had gone away, but now it's back with a vengeance. From what you say, I think they are trying to enter Christy into the bratva as a *vory*, one step up from the lowest rank, *shestyorka*."

The most annoying part of the meeting was how Agent Kozlov tended to only look at Jeremy like I wasn't even there. I tried to ignore it, figuring it was a

Russian thing. "Seriously?" I tried not to sound too indignant.

"Don't take it as an insult."

I wasn't. I was still trying to internalize the fact that the mafia was alive and well.

"*Vory* are middle management, in charge of the grunts—the *shestyorka*. *Shestyorka* are worker bees, very common in this outfit. The girls you saw—typical *shestyorka*. They do all the small stuff and lots of it. You identified eight kids so far? For certain, there are more you didn't see, working just under this Shareweather person. He is for sure a *vory*, in charge of maybe twenty *shestyorka*. It takes most *shestyorka* ten or more years, from age twelve, to make it as a *vory* or be rejected."

"By rejected, you mean killed?" Jeremy said.

Agent Kozlov nodded and pursed his lips.

That was the wrong thing for Jeremy to hear.

Kozlov continued. "Non-Russians have a hard time getting past *shestyorka* rank, almost never get past *vory* rank. Viktor's uncle, Alexander Mogilevich is a brigadier. Christy will be joining his brigade of *vory* and *shestyorka*."

"But the car thefts—they're definitely part of the bratva's operations? Not some side project of Alexander's?" Jeremy asked.

Kozlov nodded. "It's a major source of income for the bratva. This cell you found deals with cars, money laundering, and arms dealing."

"So, we've hit upon a support group, then?" I asked as something else dawned on me. "What about Viktor, Mikado, and Jericho? Are they *shestyorka*?"

"These are most likely *vory* in training, working under Shareweather but with direct contact to the brigadier. Jericho and Viktor, at least. Mikado could be just *shestyorka*. Viktor, as brigadier's nephew, probably has some sort of special place in Alexander's ranks. I'm not sure about the other two. Any link to Russia?"

"Not that we have found, but both are extremely wealthy."

"Interesting. But this is not just a support group. It's one of two main groups under this *Pakhan,* the Godfather figure. But there's no guarantee you're in, yet." His gaze was sharp, almost cruel. "So please, do us all a favor and get out while you can. You're jeopardizing everything I've worked for, and you have no chance of getting that car before it ships to West Africa."

I bristled at his dismissiveness. "No chance? I'd say I'm well on my way."

He snorted. "You think they'd ever trust you with the location of the shipping yard? It's on a need-to-know basis. I don't even know the site of my shipment, yet. I've been in five years, and I'm Russian. How long do you think it will take you, an outsider, to earn trust I haven't even gotten yet?"

I spoke the next sentence in Russian, "I'm not here for a long-term stay. All I need to do is find a car."

He leaned back and actually looked at me. "Impressive," he answered in Russian. "But how will you explain how you know Russian so well?"

I switched back to English. "I don't want them to know I speak Russian. I'll use it to eavesdrop on their conversations…. So," I said, mentally pulling up the information I'd gotten from the Bresen Spy Academy, Module 81.10, about the structure of various mafias. "So, are you one of the two spies then?"

"Actually, no. I'm one of the bulls, the *byki*, more like bodyguards. I protect the Councilor."

"Do you have any information that could help us locate the car we're looking for? You say you don't have the address of the shipping yard for your shipment, but do you know where they hold the cars before they ship?"

Kozlov shook his head. "Look, even if I did know, I don't think I would tell you. To have you Division guys barging in to rescue one car could destroy everything I've worked for these last five years. Do you know what I've had to give up, what I've had to become?" He locked eyes with Jeremy, and I could see that he was haunted.

"In one year, I'll have enough to bring down the whole bratva. Don't ask me to do anything to endanger that." He stood up. "I've told you what I can, and I can't stay any longer. What you do now is up to you."

Jeremy and I watched him go. I knew what he was thinking without him having to say it. He wanted to abandon the project. Before he could derail it, I would have to try to convince him that we should stay on it.

"We can't give up on this, Jeremy. Seriously, there must be something really important about this car that we don't know about, or Division wouldn't have sent us after it. If you think about it, it's really not only about the one car, it's about all of them. We find it, and the whole car theft ring will be exposed. Once it's exposed, the FBI or whoever, can shut it down. Think of the impact we could have...how many people we could help."

He looked at me with a calm patience that made me feel a bit frantic. He didn't interrupt me or even twitch as I talked. I was going to lose this battle. "Jeremy?"

"Normally, I would agree with you, but in this case, there are too many variables, too much danger, too many unanswered questions. Every time I go to the director with my concerns, he ignores them and basically strong arms me into getting to work instead of getting to the bottom of things. It's just not safe. The mafia? Hello! The four of us cannot take that organization on and expect a good result. I'm certain that when the Director hears what we have to tell him, he will take us off the case immediately and turn it over to the FBI and CIA so they can mount an appropriate operation to bring them down."

"But think about this. What if being a four-man team worked to our advantage? The mafia would have no idea we were coming. No one could leak information, and we could get in and out without a lot of hassle. Don't you think it would be the greatest challenge ever?"

"But," Jeremy said, raising an eyebrow, "what if what we did exposed Kozlov and ruined all the work he's done to bring down the entire network? Would it be worth it to save one car when in a year all the cars, weapons, people, and drugs could be saved?"

I sighed.

"We have to consider the big picture. Our pride can't get in the way of the greater good."

What could I say to that? He was right, really. I had no way to counter what he was saying. The risk was too great. "You're right. We better get to headquarters."

Jeremy gave me a sad look and immediately asked for covert entrance into Division Headquarters, giving instructions that we needed Director Skriloff to be present. I stewed the whole way there, still trying to think of a reason why we should stay on the case, but the writing was on the wall. It was simply too dangerous for us to continue without more specialized training about the mafia, and it would be a silly move that would jeopardize everything Kozlov had worked for. The car-theft gang would fall if he were successful, along with the entire structure from the *Pakhan* to the *shestyorka*. I had to concede to a defeat beyond my control.

***

Even in the middle of the night, Division was hopping. Sure, not every desk was full, but the night shift was at least half-staff. The director, however, worked about a ten-hour day and then went home. He'd be getting out of bed to come meet with us. I hoped that wouldn't make him less approachable. We made our way through the cubicles in central command and down a long hallway to a conference room. It shocked me a little to see Director Skriloff already sitting at the head of the oval table with a smile on his stern face. He wore a crisp suit that hung perfectly on his moderately toned body. He'd even taken the time to slick down his graying black hair. That's when it occurred to me what he thought we were going to say. He thought he was about to report to whoever had hired us that we had retrieved the car. He was about to be one very upset man.

"I didn't think you would succeed in such quick order. Is the car in the garage now? Was there any damage?" His broad smile hitched his glasses up a bit on his nose, giving him a comical look.

"I'm sorry, sir," Jeremy said. "We haven't uncovered its whereabouts as yet, and it doesn't look like we'll be able to."

The director's face fell, and he rubbed at his clean-shaven chin. "I don't understand."

"It would seem that this is not a small-time theft operation after all. It is an arm of the Russian mafia, shipping cars to West Africa."

The director shifted his head to the side, an abrupt, short movement. "Did you say the Russian mafia?"

Jeremy nodded with one slow motion. He explained what we had learned from Agent Kozlov, though I noticed he didn't mention any names.

A look of complete dejection spread across the director's face. "No wonder. I guess nothing can be as simple as it seems on the outset." He bit the corner of his lip. Silence filled the room while the director seemed to be thinking. His eyes darted from one side of the room to the other, and then he closed them and took in a deep breath. Finally he spoke, "But I'm afraid we can't abandon this mission."

Jeremy raised an eyebrow, and his jaw dropped. I believe I shared the same reaction. "Sir," Jeremy said. "I don't mean to challenge you, but there is no way one car could be worth risking bringing down the entire Russian mafia."

"I am your director, and I am telling you that it is worth it." He spoke in a clipped, irritated voice. Somewhere on the edges, I thought I recognized a bit of a challenge.

Jeremy's jaw tightened, and I knew he was doing everything to stay calm. "Surely, Director Skriloff, we should be working with the FBI to make sure we aren't jeopardizing the undercover agent's life or his operation—

"Let the FBI worry about the FBI. And on that note, you were given strict instructions not to share information between agencies, and yet you defied that order."

"Sir, I—"

"I don't want to hear any excuses," Skriloff barked. "Your actions will be noted in your record. I suggest you follow orders with more integrity in the future if you want to stay in the field."

Jeremy's face flamed red. I knew Director Skriloff's attack on his integrity must hurt.

"Director," I said carefully. "It was my idea to go to the FBI agent—and we did learn some valuable information from him that we wouldn't have been able to get otherwise. And honestly, sir, after what we learned I don't think we can in good conscience continue this mission."

Director Skriloff turned to glare at me. "Who authorized you to speak? A second-year agent, and you think you have any right to lecture me on what missions we can or cannot continue? I am your director. I am privy to information that you—for very good reasons—are not. It is not your place to question the ethics of the mission. It *is* your place to trust your superiors and follow orders." Anger boiled just beneath his words, and his face turned red as he delivered his diatribe.

"Your mission remains the same. Retrieve the car by any means necessary before it is shipped off, never to be found again." He rubbed the back of his neck. "I expect you to use your training to infiltrate the mafia and uncover the location of the vehicle. Once you have the location, you are to retrieve the car and bring it here. Do you have any questions?"

"Is there something you aren't telling us?" I blurted.

Director Skriloff's eyes bugged out in barely contained rage. "Of course there's something I'm not telling you. I've told you exactly what you need to know to *do your job* and nothing more. Now go do it." He turned away for a moment and when he turned back, his face was a mask of calm. "I am anxious to receive your report that you have located the vehicle."

***

Jeremy and I didn't speak on the way home from headquarters. For my part, my mind was spinning with everything we'd learned, and I didn't trust anything coherent to come out of my mouth.

For better or for worse, we were back on the case. Only now there was an extra element of danger. I had to find a way to retrieve this mysteriously important car without endangering myself, Agent Kozlov, or the FBI's efforts to bring down the bratva. The pressure made it a little difficult to breathe, and more than a little difficult to sleep that night

Chapter 18

I got to the school five minutes before Mr. Shareweather. Without a word, he opened the back shop door and let me inside. Watching him up close like I now was, I couldn't help but notice how he had the look of a Russian—the prominent, round cheekbones, gray-blue eyes, thin lips, and a strong jawline. Could he be of Russian ancestry and was trying to hide it with the ridiculous name of Shareweather?

He unlocked some cupboards and pulled out two small tablets, handing me one. "I understand you're quite proficient in stealing cars without high-tech security systems." His voice was flat, devoid of humor.

"I guess so."

"Either you are or you aren't. This is no time for being modest."

I nodded. "Then, yes."

"I am, by some miracle, supposed to make you proficient with these high-tech systems in one and a half hours. You appear to be someone with some intelligence."

"Yes." I did not look away.

"Then, we work."

He was forceful and impatient throughout his instruction. Luckily, I had watched several videos provided to me by Division about the process, and there were only a few differences between what I'd already learned and what Shareweather was demonstrating—it seemed the Russians had found a slightly faster way to get in with the program they had. The tablet also had a jammer function that prevented GPS from locating the car once they'd stolen it. The process was slick, actually. By the time school started, I had my time down to four minutes.

"I am rarely surprised by the kids Viktor sends me." S-Dub's voice was flat and gruff. He left it like that, just short of a compliment. I chose to take it as one. Inside, however, I wanted to spend more time on it so that I could get closer to Mikado and Jericho's time of three minutes. Then again, there were two of them. Maybe paired with someone skilled, I'd be at three minutes, too. But did they plan to pair me with anyone?

Viktor was standing just outside the shop as I exited it. He leaned in and took my hand. "How'd it go?"

"Excellent, I think, but S-Dub is pretty short on compliments." I frowned.

"Ah, S-Dub has had a rough life. He expects a lot of his protégés. You'll learn to appreciate him over time." I couldn't help but notice how perfectly Viktor's short beard, mustache and eyebrows were trimmed. He took great care of himself.

"Do you hire someone to keep you looking like a GQ model, or do you do it yourself?"

He pushed a quick puff of air out his nose and stroked his chin. "This is all me, baby. All me."

I tilted my head and gave him a look that said, tell me another one.

"Okay, okay. I might have someone help me out a couple times a week."

I chuckled. "I thought so." I didn't want to compliment him, but it seemed like the right thing to do. "They do a *great* job." I nodded several times.

He pressed his lips together and raised his chin. "Thanks. I want to look perfect for you."

I knew the truth of the matter was that he wanted to look perfect for himself, but a girlfriend would coo at such a statement, so I did.

"Should we go in?" He gestured toward the doors to the school and started to pull me that way.

I tugged back, the feeling that I should show some vulnerability hitting me pretty hard. "I just don't want to let you down."

He turned back to me and took both my hands this time, putting his chin on his chest. "Ah, Amber, this is not the time to feel unsure. You can do this. I know it."

I let my head loll forward. "You know what? You're right! I can do this."

"That's my girl. Just wow Alexander tonight, and you're in."

That wasn't anything new. What I needed to do was get him to invite me to his uncle's house somehow. If I could manage that, I might be able to find some information on where they were shipping from. "What if I don't, though? What then? He'll hate me, won't he?"

"Once you know him better, you'll see, he's pretty

great."

Now that I had my foot in, and he was thinking about me getting to know his uncle better, I would leave it and get back to it later. "I hope so. I'd really like to get this to work." Now it was time to play a little hard to get with him. I looked pointedly at his hands holding mine. "I also don't know you well enough to be holding your hands. No fair taking advantage of my vulnerability."

He smiled and brought one of my hands to his lips. "A little vulnerability looks good on you." He raised one eyebrow. "But only a little. In time, you'll come to trust me, too." He led me inside and school started as usual.

On my way to second period, I ran into Carson. His face was clean-shaven, and he had his guitar slung over his shoulder.

"Hey."

"Hey, yourself." I smiled.

"Did I see you with Viktor this morning?" His blue eyes narrowed slightly.

"You did." I wanted to ask him why he was Viktor's friend, but thought better of it. I had no idea if he was involved in the car theft gang or not.

He pulled me off to the side, away from all the traffic in the hall. "Be careful. He's dangerous."

"Dangerous?"

"Let's just say I've had a few run-ins with him, and it wasn't pretty." He kept his voice low as we walked down the hall, leaning close together.

"But I thought you were his friend."

"I play my part well, then."

"Seriously? You hang out with him, but you don't

like him?"

He nodded. "His family—"

"Amber!" Jericho interrupted. "You enjoying your new laptop?" He tapped my forearm.

Carson took a step back from me, and my eyes flicked from him to Jericho. "Are you kidding? It's fabulous. Thank you again." Why had Carson stepped back like that?

"I'm not the one you should be thanking. It was Wind who gave it to you." Despite his words, I could see he totally wanted to claim the credit. "Come on, Carson. We don't want to be late for calculus." He motioned with his head in the direction of their class.

Carson pressed his lips together before saying, "We'll finish this discussion later." He smiled and then mouthed. "Be careful."

What did he know? I couldn't imagine him being a part of the gang, but who would think Karina or Gina would be, either? I looked around the students rushing through the hall and wondered how many of the student body were somehow involved with the thefts. Had Kozlov been right that there were at least twenty kids under S-Dub roaming the halls of this school?

I rushed to class so I wouldn't be late. At lunch, Viktor tried to get me to sit with him, but I chose to sit with Karina, Gina, Hank, and the nerdy boys who had saved me from social suicide instead. I kept hoping Carson would come to me and finish what he'd started, but I didn't even see him in the lunchroom.

"I think they look great, Hank." Karina smiled widely, and while her teeth weren't perfectly straight, Hank's were, and his braces were gone.

"Wow, Hank. Your teeth look great. Feel a bit slimy?" I'd never forget that first day after getting my braces off and how slick and slimy my teeth felt for a few days.

"Yep! But I don't care. It's awesome having them off." He leaned in toward the middle of the table. "Do you think Kara will go out with me now?" When he said her name, he looked toward a table to our left where I assumed she was sitting.

"Which one is she?" I asked.

"The one with the long black hair and sun-kissed skin."

I smiled. She was a beauty, her oriental heritage gifting her all good things. "Has she turned you down before?"

"No," he admitted. "But I figured a girl like that wouldn't want to date a brace-face."

"I bet she's dying to go out with you," I said. I noticed a slight scowl cross Karina's face. Was she hoping he'd ask her out?

"I can't wait to get braces. I hate my teeth." Karina's hands flew to her mouth.

"When are you getting them?" Hank asked.

"Well, our insurance won't pay for them, and my parents don't have the money, so I got a job to pay for them. Hopefully I'll have enough by the end of the year."

"Man. That's harsh, Karina. I can't believe you have to pay for them yourself. If you want my opinion, though, I don't think you need them." Hank patted her hand.

"Really?" She blushed slightly.

"Really."

"Oh, I don't know. This one overlaps that one, and it bugs me." She pointed to a pair of teeth that were crowded.

"Well, if it bugs you that much, I might know someone who would give you a good deal, considering you're earning the money yourself. He's super nice. I'll talk to him."

"Seriously? That would be great, Hank. Thank you."

"No problem."

They smiled at each other and moved on to another topic. In just a few short days, I'd found Hank to be completely genuine and kind-hearted. It was a relief to be around him—he had nothing to do with the mafia, and he was just a purely good kid. It was nice to have that respite from the darkness of my mission. Maybe his goodness would rub off on Karina and pull her away from the path she was heading down.

I stared at Karina. Had she started with the mafia to pay for her braces? My heart broke a little for her at that moment. I noticed Gina staring at me. She gave me the stink eye, I'm sure wondering why I'd been staring at Karina. So, I spoke up. "I don't think she needs braces, either. What do you think, Gina?"

"I think she's perfect how she is."

"I agree." I loved that new friendships were forming. I looked at Hank. It was all thanks to him. The world could be changed if we could put one of him in every school in America.

Viktor met me after school, and when he looped his arm through mine, he slipped something in my pocket. I pretended not to notice. "You ready for tonight?" He spoke with a quiet voice.

"I think so." I answered, matching his volume.

"Good. Don't worry. Everything will be okay. I've given you a cell phone that you'll need to keep on you all the time during lifting periods."

I put my hand in my pocket and looked up at him like I was startled. "How did you get that in there?"

He pushed a sharp breath out of his nose, pressing his lips tight together in a show of what he thought was cool. "I'm good at things like that. You'll have to either sneak out or tell your parents you have a study session or something. You'll get a text with a time, place, and a particular vehicle for you to lift. It will also have a link that you press once you start the lift. You'll then follow the directions the phone gives you to the drop off. Mikado will be there to assist you today in case there's a problem."

"Mikado? Like the Mikado here at school?" I had to play along, and a good part of me was glad I hadn't been given Jericho as my partner. The bad part was that Mikado had tried to warn me away from this, and I'd not listened. He'd probably be upset about it.

"Yes. However, you won't treat him like a friend here at school. You can't let it seem like you two work together or even see each other outside of school."

I nodded.

"It's very important that you don't give yourself away or anyone else on our team."

"I understand."

"Do you?" He squeezed my arm, hard.

"Ouch!" I jerked my arm away.

"Sorry," he said. "I just have to be certain you

understand this is not a game, and there are strict rules that must be followed."

I looked at my shoes and then up at him. "I don't want to let you down, Viktor, but I'm new at this, what if something goes wrong? Am I out then?"

"It's not going to happen. It can't. Alexander is my uncle, and anything you do reflects on me now. Don't make any mistakes." He leaned toward me, his face reddening.

Not the right move on my part to play the underdog. He wanted someone who would make him look good, like a Ferrari or Mustang. I'd have to be more direct. "I do know what I'm doing. I guess I'll be okay. Are you sure your uncle will like me? Maybe if I could spend some time with him, he wouldn't scare me so much." If I was to be a Ferrari, then he'd want to show me off to everyone. It was time he did just that.

"Don't get ahead of yourself. Succeed tonight and maybe, just maybe I can arrange to have you to dinner or something." His green eyes flashed.

I smiled and leaned on him. The thought of dinner with Alexander Molgilevich sent my heart racing. If I could get into his house, possibly sneak a peek at his files, his paperwork, it could tell us a lot. This could be the break we needed. "I'd like that," I said.

"Now, can I take you out for a treat? It can be our second date."

"And when was our first?" I angled my head up toward his face. My arm still ached from him pinching it.

"Certainly you haven't forgotten our dinner at my family's restaurant." He pulled away from me.

"I thought that was business." I suppressed a laugh.

"After dinner was business."

I tilted my head to the side to question the statement.

"All right. We won't count that. Our first date can start right now. No business."

"I don't know. You said yourself that your uncle wouldn't approve. I don't want to upset him." I chuckled and punched his arm.

"You're such a tease."

"No, I'm not. I've told you straight up that I wanted to get to know you better before there could be anything between us. And besides, I just don't know if it's smart for me to start work with the score in the negative for me simply because we're going out. I want to be amazing at this job."

"Leave my uncle to me." His face was resolute. "I've no doubt you'll wow him."

I stepped away from him. A gust of cold wind whipped my hair around, and I pulled my hoodie on. "I'll do my best."

"Well, what if...what if I told him how I felt about you first and got his blessing?"

"Could you? That would really settle my mind." I shoved my hands deep into my pockets.

He chewed on his lip. "Perhaps if I brought you to family dinner on Sunday..."

"Seriously? Oh, you don't think he'd think we were railroading him, do you? I'd hate for it to backfire." Heat spread through my chest in anticipation of truly getting an invitation even if I had to be that Ferrari.

"Nah! Yes. That's what we'll do. You'll amaze him

tonight, and I'll bring you to dinner on Sunday. Not only will that ease his mind, but hopefully yours too." He smiled. "I'm anxious to get to know you better."

"Me, too." I leaned on his shoulder. He wanted to get to know me better? What happened to the guy who tried to force me into a bedroom at Jericho's? "Without anyone getting bent out of shape because of it." Inside, part of me was celebrating while the other half cringed in fear.

"A rain check on our first date, then? Sunday at six? I'll have to get you around five. He lives in Brooklyn."

"All right, then. It's a plan."

"Just wow him tonight." Agitation scored his face again.

"I'll do my best."

"Good. See you at school tomorrow, and be amazing!"

I hurried into the subway hole with a marked spring in my step, and he headed for his car, whistling as he went. It shocked me to run into Carson at the bottom of the stairs leading to the platform.

Chapter 19

"Carson? You're not taking the subway today, are you? Did something happen to your car?"

Carson was one of the last people I thought I'd ever see going into the subway. I waited for his answer. "Actually, no. I mean, my car is fine and no, I don't intend to take the subway. I wanted to talk to you." He looked around and then took my arm and led me to the platform. "Let's talk down here, though."

"I looked for you at lunch."

"Yeah," he said. "I had some things I had to do." Once on the platform, he took me to a bench, and we sat. "I wanted to finish telling you about Viktor. He's not what he seems." My heartbeat quickened at the thought of getting some inside information on Viktor and his family.

"You mean he's not a self-centered, egotistical boy?"

He chuckled. "No. He is that. But his family—they aren't the best of people. And it seems that people who get caught up with him end up either disappearing or turning into sullen, mean, angry people."

I turned quickly to him. "You're not suggesting that he's some kind of sociopath are you?"

He leaned closer to me and licked his lips. "Maybe. I don't know. I only know that people who get tangled up with him come out with problems or never come out."

"And you? How have you avoided his influence?"

He swallowed hard. "I haven't."

Chills ran up my arms, but I had to play it cool. "Ah, Carson. You're the nicest boy I've met at school. If you're a product of his friendship, then I have nothing to worry about."

"I'm serious. I wish I could tell you more, but I can't. Please. I don't want to see you get hurt." His shoulders curled, and his eyes appeared wet.

I could hear the train coming. Why was everyone always trying to save me? I wanted to scream at him and tell him I was a very capable girl and could take care of myself. Instead, I held my anger inside and spit, "Thank you for the warning, but I can take care of myself." Did every great guy on the planet see me as some weak thing who needed his protection? Ugh.

He looked as if he wanted to argue more, but I cut him off, not wanting to lose it right there.

"I think my train is coming. Really, Carson. You don't have to worry about me."

We stood, and he hugged me goodbye.

I was dying to find out if he worked for Viktor in some capacity. I would find out. It would be difficult if I didn't get an assignment that put me working with him directly, but I would find out.

***

Back at the brownstone, I told the team about

Carson's warning, and my suspicion that he was somehow involved with the bratva. Jeremy pulled up Carson's file to see what we knew about him. Discovering it wasn't much, he sent Halluis to comb through the audio recordings from the school and Ace to find out anything he could on Carson's family.

"We need to know exactly what he knows—or thinks he knows."

The two agents disappeared upstairs, and I looked expectantly at Jeremy.

"You, study up on the felony you're about to commit."

"Isn't there something more useful I could be doing?"

"The best thing you can do is make an impression tonight, so even though you might think you know this stuff, you'd better put a little more study time in."

I bit back an argument, nodded, and pulled out one of the team's laptops, hunkering down to study hotwiring, the docks and container ships. Jeremy disappeared into the kitchen and, I assumed, out the back door.

The sensation of waiting—for more information on Carson, for Viktor to call, for Jeremy to come back—was enough to drive me insane. I couldn't concentrate at all on the videos I was watching, and my mind kept drifting, and strangely enough it kept landing on Jeremy.

A few hours later, Jeremy returned with a large pizza, and we ate in near silence. Halluis and Ace hadn't found anything to connect Carson with the bratva, and Jeremy said nothing about where he'd been. The only thing to disturb the tense quiet of the evening was a brief argument about trackers. Halluis thought I should carry some with me tonight and place them on the cars I would be stealing. Jeremy disagreed.

"They've been able to find and disable every tracker we've attempted to place. If Christy puts trackers on her cars, and they find them, they'll have reason to suspect her."

"But if they don't find them, the trackers will lead us right to the cars. *Voilà, mission accomplie.*"

"If it were that easy, we'd have done it by now. The trackers are no use to us. Whatever tech the bratva is using to detect them, it's nothing we've seen before. They've outsmarted us in that arena. We have to find the cars through other means."

"But your FBI friend—what was his name, Karloff?"

"Kozlov."

"Kozlov, then. He said himself that they would never reveal the whereabouts of the shipping yard to a low-level member. If we don't risk the tracker, we may not find the car before it is too late."

Jeremy said nothing, just stared back at Halluis.

Before the argument could escalate, it was interrupted by the chime of my cell phone, announcing a text message.

It was time. I was to be at a particular restaurant at nine sharp to lift a very nice vintage Mercedes. It had been retrofitted with the latest security advances. The bratva must have a very specific buyer who wouldn't be showing it about for a long time. There were only three of this car left on the planet.

"I've got to leave now if I'm going to make it on

time," I said apologetically, not sure to whom I was apologizing.

Halluis pursed his lips. "Very well, no trackers, then. Off you go, mademoiselle. Know that I will be there—in the shadows."

***

I met Mikado at a small park near the restaurant. He looked upset to see me coming toward him.

"I thought I told you to avoid dinner." He only looked at me for a second then looked past me.

"You did. And your words only made me that much more curious." I fingered the charm on my necklace, and I stomped on some dirty, crunchy snow.

He gave me an exasperated look. "You'll regret it."

"Maybe. But it's hard to tell just yet." I bent my knees and then straightened them, looking out at the frozen park and wishing spring were already here. I wanted to see New York with color. The drabness of winter with the leafless trees and brown grass echoed my feelings of gloom.

He shook his head. "Don't come running to me when things get hard. This is awful work."

"Why not stop, then?"

He rolled his eyes. "You don't get it." He grabbed my upper arm. "There is no out. Once you're in, you're in until you die."

"I don't get it. It's just a job."

"Oh, I see. Let me guess, Viktor told you what a good job this was to get you through college. And what exactly do you want to do with your life?" He was speaking through his teeth with forced restraint, and I cowered slightly under the pressure of his touch. If I hadn't been wearing a coat, his nails would most likely have broken the skin. "I'm going to be the head engineer for BMW."

He laughed, a wretched sound in the darkness. "And I was going to be a lawyer." He started to pace, his fists balled at his sides.

"So—be a lawyer."

"No. They won't allow it. Or if they do, I'll just be their lawyer, doing all their dirty work. No. The only way you or I will be engineers or lawyers is if the *Pakhan* needs us to be. And even then, he'll choose exactly what we do with our studies, and he'll own us. Forever."

I let my eyes go wide and said, "You're exaggerating."

"Not one bit. I tried to tell you. Why didn't you listen to me?"

"Say what you want. I'm not scared." I jutted my chin out.

"You should be. Let's go." He pressed his lips together and shook his head, a deep sadness shadowing his face.

Our phones beeped. Mikado said, "We're on."

It turned out that Mikado and I were quite the pair. It only took us three minutes and twenty seconds to get me in the driver's seat.

"Impressive, Amber. Now, press your finger on the button on the last message and follow the directions."

"Aren't you coming with me?"

"I have another car to pick up." His eyes darted away from me. "I'll see you at school tomorrow, but act as we always have. We are not friends." He walked away. I drove out of the parking lot.

Once on the main road, I followed the directions as they were spoken to me from the phone. I was led to a semi with its back doors open and a ramp attached. Two men stood on either side of the ramp. I drove straight in, turned the car off, and hurried out.

Once I was out, they lifted the ramp, and the truck rumbled away. One of the men pointed to a subway hole, and without a word, I walked toward it. To my surprise, I got another text that sent me to another location. I guessed Mikado and I weren't finished with each other after all. As I rounded the corner to arrive at my assigned location, I took a stutter step. Mikado wasn't standing there; it was Jericho. He spotted me and moved toward me.

"Guess you were expecting someone else?" He had a smirk on his face.

I braced myself for his pompousness. "No. I mean, yes. I was just with Mikado and figured—"

"Never assume anything, and *never* talk about prior or future assignments with anyone. Maybe I was here for some other purpose."

"Sorry. I—"

"Don't be sorry. It's a rookie mistake. I'm here to make sure you don't make any more of those."

His soft demeanor and voice surprised me.

"What is the code message they gave you at the bottom of the text? That's what you'll say to anyone you think is the contact you're supposed to meet."

I pulled the phone out and scrolled through the message. Sure enough, at the bottom of the text was the statement, *Crazy how there aren't any stars out tonight.* And then another, presumably the reply, *Only in this neck of the woods.*

So, I repeated the first phrase to him, and he responded with the other phrase. "At that point you'll move into position for the lift without another word passing between you."

I scanned the area for the car listed and spotted it right away. It helped that Jericho was headed for it already. I walked purposefully, but without haste. No one was around. No one. The bratva had an amazing handle on their operations.

Once in the car, driving it to the pickup location, he spoke again. "Do you always play hard to get or just with me?"

I had a choice, I could own up to it or pretend with a bit of sass that I didn't know what he was talking about. I went with my gut, which told me he liked sass. "I don't know what you're talking about. If I thought someone like you would want little ol' me, don't you think I'd jump at the chance?" I spoke in monotone and looked him straight on.

"I think you and I are going to get along just fine." He nodded. "Definitely."

I snickered. Definitely a sass kind of guy.

We drove the car inside a truck. This time the two guys standing near the ramp jumped inside when we exited. They raised the ramp, and the doors to the truck shut behind them.

"Why are they staying inside this time?" I asked as we walked to our next lift.

"They'll relocate for the next car. While they wait, they'll reassign the VIN number, remove the plates, and put the new title information in the glove box. Great, efficient system, don't you think?" He raised his eyebrows.

I nodded, trying to look contemplative, which wasn't hard because I was processing everything he was saying. They probably sent *vory* to hit up the local junkyards to get VIN numbers from cars that were similar to the ones they were stealing. As far as a forged title, that was another matter.

"Now, let's talk about how you hook up to the computer system. You're wasting about ten seconds doing it the way you are." He then went on to explain how he shaved off that ten seconds.

"I guess you're the man I'm supposed to ask if I have any questions. Are you the official trainer?"

He chuckled. "You could call me that."

"Well, I don't want to call you anything that you really aren't." I turned pointedly to him. "What are you exactly?"

"Someone you want on your side." His voice was serious, deadly.

We'd only walked a block when he said, "Now, try to do what I told you to do when hooking up the computer this time."

I'd been a little lost in my thoughts and hadn't noticed we'd arrived at our next lift. It turned out that we completed eight lifts together within a mile radius, and we were inching up on that three-minute miracle he and Mikado had pulled off the other day. The competitive side of me wanted to beat it.

After we loaded the last car, he hopped out of the semi with a definite happiness that wasn't there when

I'd first met with him. We headed into the subway and, once on the platform, he picked me up and swung me around while he hollered out. He set me down and said, "That was awesome. We are quite the team." His hands gripped my upper arms, but he let go in a rush as his eyes fell on something behind us. I readied myself to take a hold of the knife in my shoe as I turned around. Jericho stepped back and chewed on his bottom lip.

Viktor stood not ten feet from us, his face stony, cold.

He took a few steps forward, his head cocked to the side. "I agree, *Jericho*. You two did make a great team." He enunciated *Jericho* in a way that negated whatever words followed it. Did they not like each other? If not, why did Jericho invite him to his party? My question was answered when Viktor stepped forward and took my hand in his. "Do you agree, Amber? Were you two quite the team?" The malice in his voice sent a bold shiver to my chest.

I wanted to remove my hand from his, but something close to a deep fear, along with the plan I knew I had to follow, kept me from it. I couldn't risk alienating Viktor. Not now. Truth be told, I didn't want to be near either one. "I did shave forty seconds off my time with him today. He's a decent teacher."

Jericho clenched his jaw for a split second. I was sure he was hoping I'd give him a glowing review, and the word *decent* made him want to hit someone. He gave a curt nod. The train roared in, and I had the feeling I was at a shoot-out between the two of them.

The train's doors opened with a whoosh. Viktor broke the staring match. "Isn't that your train,

Jericho?"

"It is."

"And it's mine, too."

Viktor pulled me close to him. "I'll take you home. There's no telling what kind of creeps you might run into on the subway this time of night. But you," he looked at Jericho. "You better hurry."

Jericho glanced at me and then rushed to the train, barely slipping inside as the doors shut.

Viktor pulled me around to face him. "Was he bothering you tonight?"

There was obviously some kind of power struggle between the two of them. Not sure if he wanted a yes or a no, I decided on the truth. "Actually, no. He was super helpful, like I said. I'll be a pro in no time if I continue to learn from him." I made sure not to say work with him, in hopes Viktor wouldn't think about the time I would have to spend with him. It didn't really matter though. In less than a month, they'd both just be a memory. In the meantime, it was Viktor I had to keep close. He had the most direct link to Alexander. I gazed up into his eyes, smiling slightly.

His features softened.

"Thanks for saving me from another nasty ride on the subway." I gave him a bigger smile, and he pulled me into a deep hug.

He spoke to the top of my head. "You were amazing tonight. Nine T-cars in under three hours. My uncle is really impressed."

"T-cars?"

"Top cars. You know, ones that cost big bucks."

"Oh. I get it." I pulled back slightly and then wished

I hadn't because he didn't loosen his grip much. It made it so that my face was only inches from his. Even though I wanted to turn to the side, I feared it would make him see that he repulsed me. I forced myself to hold my position. His eyes dilated and then fell on my lips. Before he could make his move, I said, "Surely, you don't want our first kiss to happen in the subway." I raised a single eyebrow.

He closed his eyes and took a deep breath into his nose, holding it for an extra second before releasing it. He pulled me in for another hug and then released me. "No, I don't." He growled and then ran his hands down my arms to my hands, shaking them lightly before letting one of his hands remain in mine. He pulled me, almost running, up the steps and into the late night air.

He didn't slow once we made it out. Instead, he jogged, dragging me along behind, to a nearby parkway. He pulled me under a tree and then stopped, his eyes glistening in the lamplight and his breaths coming out hard and ragged. With one hand still in mine, he ran the back of his fingers over my fingers, along my jaw, and rested them under my chin, raising my lips to his. They fluttered across mine, and I took a sharp breath in. His lips became hungry against mine.

I managed to stop myself from pulling away and slapping him just in time. The instinct to run was strong—Viktor was the last person on earth I'd want exploring my mouth with his, but I couldn't risk putting him off. He needed to believe I was just as into him as he was into me. He needed a strong incentive to bring me closer into his confidences.

Unbidden, thoughts of Jeremy sprang into my mind.

Somehow, thinking of him made it easier to quell the revulsion I felt with each press of Viktor's lips. I told myself I wasn't imagining they were Jeremy's—that would be impossible. It was just that remembering Jeremy let me remember that I was getting us all one step closer to our goal. That was it.

Finally, when the kiss had gone on just long enough to encourage him, but not so long that he would take it as permission to go further, I pulled away and sighed.

Viktor groaned and leaned his forehead against mine, but I just smiled and settled my head into his chest.

I pocket texted Ace to come out of the apartment to save me. I wanted to give Ace an opportunity to get a tracker on Viktor's phone. While it wouldn't be as good as a listening device, it would let us know where he was at all times. That would give us the opportunity to get into his phone to put the listening device in there.

"You know, Viktor. There's one thing that is going to ruin all your plans for me."

"Yes, and what is that?" he said, seduction thick in his voice.

"My parents."

His head jerked to me. "Your parents? There's always a way around parents."

"I'm surprised you're saying that after meeting my dad the other night."

"We can handle them."

"Fifty bucks says they're waiting for me on the stoop."

"It's one in the morning. They—"

"They have a strict curfew on school nights. Eleven

o'clock. I haven't been answering their trillion texts. They'll be on the porch."

"I can handle them."

"Well, you'd really better get me home. I'm going to be grounded for a year."

He grabbed my hand, looking agitated. "I said I would handle them. Trust me." He squeezed my hand a bit too hard.

"You don't know my parents," I insisted. A part of me wanted him to be afraid or at least respect my parents. I hoped it would help him keep boundaries with me.

"Parents love me. I've never met parents I couldn't conquer." He spoke with a sharp tone that smacked of impatience.

Looking at his green eyes, exuding charm, I had no doubt it was true. "Whatever you say." I rolled my eyes and chuckled. "I'm just thinking this was the shortest relationship I've ever been in."

Chapter 20

We pulled up in front of the brownstone, and he double parked. I couldn't see Ace anywhere. I would have to kill him for sleeping and making it possible for Viktor to attack me yet again.

He must've noticed the absence of my parents, too, because he said, "And did I mention that I am the luckiest dude ever? Fifty bucks richer!" He jumped out and opened my door, then led me up to the brownstone entrance. At least, that's where he thought he was leading me. Out of the dark shadows, Ace jumped in front us before we could touch the first step. His striped oxford was undone at the neck and untucked from his gray slacks, and his tie, still tied around his neck, was a bit loosened. He looked for all the world like a distraught father who'd been waiting on his daughter for hours. He lunged toward Viktor, looking punch-drunk from exhaustion, the rifle still in his hand.

"Well, hello. Nice of you to bring my daughter home so... so...early."

He bumped into Viktor, where I'm sure he tagged his phone, and then moved between me and Viktor. I hoped he got a bug and a tracker and not just a tracker.

"Where have you been?" He shot Viktor a look that could kill and then focused back on me. "You get in that house right now. You better have a very good reason for your lapse in judgment, young lady."

I started up the stairs, impressed and a bit in shock over Ace's acting abilities, but Viktor didn't let go of my hand. I pulled, hoping he'd let go.

"Mr. Smith, please. I'm so sorry. Don't punish Amber for something that was my fault. You see, we were working on our English presentation on early twentieth century life and fiction. I convinced her that in order to immerse ourselves in that time frame, we couldn't have our cell phones anywhere near us. We lost track of time—," he looked down in mock humility. "We were researching the manners and customs, and I just knew we'd never fully understand if we didn't experience it."

He opened his eyes wide, like he wanted me to expand on what he'd said. He was good. "It was really amazing, Dad," I said. "I learned so much. He had his parents convert part of their restaurant to immerse our study group in the time period. Viktor rented period-appropriate clothes and everything. I just got so swept up in it all—you know, in everything I was learning. I'm so sorry, I had no idea how much time had passed by the time we finished. Then it was so late, I figured you two had gone to bed, and I didn't want to bother you."

He tipped his head to the side like he didn't buy it.

"Okay, you got me. I figured you wouldn't be as mad if you slept on it first. I knew you would be livid, but there was a good reason."

Viktor broke in. "Would you like to talk to my parents? They wanted to call you, but I told them to wait until tomorrow so they wouldn't wake you. I'm sure they're still up." He pulled out his phone and pushed a button.

"No," Ace said after looking at me raising my eyebrows. "No reason any of us should be up any later than we already have been. Just have them call us tomorrow."

Ace pulled the rifle up and aimed it at Viktor. "And I hope for your sake that they corroborate your story."

"Dad," I said, "Do you think you could stop pointing that at him? And where is Mom?"

He quirked up one side of his mouth and lowered the gun. "She wore herself out crying. Fell asleep a good thirty minutes ago. We'll need to be careful not to disturb her when we go inside."

"Thanks, Dad. Thanks for worrying about me. Honestly, it would have made me feel pretty bad if I had found you in bed when I got here. I love that you care enough about me to wait up." I hugged Ace and then skipped up a couple of steps. "You're the best dad a girl could ever have." I winked at him when Viktor couldn't see.

"And you didn't tell us anything about this social experiment. Had we known where exactly you were, things could have been very different."

"I promise to give you all the information you want from now on. And I didn't know until I got there what the study session entailed this time. We won't make that mistake again."

"You better not," Ace said, his tone serious.

"You have my word, Mr. Smith. We will keep you informed."

"I want to be able to trust you," he said to me.

"I know, Dad. I'm sorry for worrying you. Let's go in. Believe it or not, I'd really like to climb into bed. Tomorrow morning will come way too quickly."

"Good idea," Ace said. "Thank you for bringing her home. That shows some good judgment, at least. Some."

We headed in, and Viktor went to his car. I waved to him and he waved back, a mischievous and arrogant look on his face.

I counted my blessings that I'd avoided another lip-locking session with him.

Ace shut the door behind me. "Period-appropriate clothing and full immersion studying, huh?" He tsked. "The lies you teens come up with these days."

I shrugged. "He's creative, you have to give him that."

"We had eyes on you until you entered the subway. What happened? Where did you go? We worried when you didn't get on the train." We headed for the kitchen. Halluis came in the back door and winked at me, but said nothing. He'd seen the lip-lock, obviously.

"Yeah, well, Viktor had different plans for me. He—" I spotted Jeremy, leaning on one wall in the kitchen. My face flushed as I remembered how his handsome face had filled my mind when Viktor kissed me. For some reason, I found I didn't want to mention the kiss in front of him. "He...was waiting for us when we got to the platform. He, uh, wanted to give me a ride home."

"Thus the text." Ace chuckled. "What's the matter,

don't you want some lip action with that fine young man?" He opened the fridge and pulled out some milk. "Anyone else want some cereal while we debrief?"

"Cereal? Really?" Halluis said. "What is it about you and cereal in the middle of the night?"

"When no pizza is available, cereal hits the late-night spot." He grabbed some cereal and headed for the table.

Halluis grabbed some bowls and spoons. "Well, it's disgusting to listen to someone eat cereal when you aren't. So I guess we're all in. And the ruse to get the bug on his phone was genius. Way to go."

"I'm stuffed," I said. "I'm the one who's got to fill you all in anyway. But yeah, great job on the bug. It'll be nice to know who he's talking to and when. Is it already online?" I leaned my elbows on the table.

Ace pulled out his phone and after punching some keys, he said, "Not yet. I wonder why?"

"Give it a bit, it has a lot of muck to get through." I chuckled.

Jeremy still hadn't said anything. I furrowed my brow. I would have thought congratulations were in order—I'd pulled off the evening with flying colors. Didn't that merit a word of praise from my mission leader?

I related all that had happened, minus the make-out session, and how Viktor was certain he could get me into the family dinner at his uncle's house. "If I can get into his home office, I can find his files, maybe some paperwork. He's likely to keep his paperwork close to him, right?"

"It's a good place to start, in any case," Halluis said.

"We've got to rule the house out, may as well be you that does it since there's no getting in there day or night without some in. It's a well-guarded fortress."

"Good thing you're so great at sneaking around without being caught," Jeremy said.

I bristled. "What does that mean?"

Jeremy shrugged. "You're just good at what you do, that's all I'm saying."

"Oh. Thank you," I said hesitantly. I could have been imagining it, but I thought I'd heard a tone of accusation in his voice. I tried to shake it off—why would Jeremy be upset? I'd done my job, and I'd done it well. It was only my ridiculous imagination that was making me think that he might be jealous. He probably didn't even know about the kiss, and if he did, why should he care? I fought back a flush of embarrassment at the realization that maybe that was exactly what I wanted. For him to care.

"We'll try to get some guards distracted while you work. Fireworks or something. The intel on the uncle tells us that these family dinners last a good hour before they start to break up and head into the sitting room. I think your best opportunity would be twenty minutes into dinner."

Ace pulled up the uncle's house plans. One look and I had the plans memorized. Luckily, the bathroom was only three doors down from Alexander's office. I knew it was a long shot that anything to do with the stolen cars would be there, but Halluis was right, it was the best chance we had and totally necessary to eliminate. I also knew that if I'd refused Viktor's kisses, my chances of getting an invite to the dinner diminished quite a bit.

The plans for the next two days were set, and as my brain became fuzzy and my yawns could no longer be stifled, I headed to bed. This would be another four-hour sleep night. I wouldn't be full force tomorrow. Five hours is what I needed, but I'd make it work.

***

I surprised myself when I beat my alarm waking up. I showed up at the auto shop at the school five minutes early. S-Dub taught me some more bratva insider tricks to steal some of the cars that had supposedly unbeatable alarm systems. I knew from being a part of Division that nothing was unbeatable—I just didn't know other groups proved that point also. When I walked out, I was greeted by an eager Viktor, who scooped me up into a hug, kissing my cheek as he did. I found myself looking around for Carson and Jericho. It was stupid. Did it really matter what they thought?

"You looking for someone?" Viktor asked, no worry in his voice.

"Oh, no, I was just hoping I didn't forget anything after that awesome night last night."

"It's crazy, even though I didn't get a lot of sleep, it wasn't hard to get up at all. Not at all. And I realized why as I drove to school this morning. It's because I knew I'd get to see my girl and get a bit of action."

His breath was minty and he moved in for the kiss, but I turned my head and said, "Yeah, I woke before my alarm clock." Sure, it had nothing to do with him, but the admission fit so nicely into what he'd said, I couldn't resist.

His smile broadened, and he kissed my nose. Some kids walked by us and into the school. I heard whispers and chuckles as they passed. I pulled back from him. "I am really excited to see you—I'm just not a big fan of PDA. I hope you can understand that." I had this terrible thought that he would be holding me and kissing me throughout the day. I couldn't stand that idea. I was dreading Carson and Jericho's reaction to seeing us together. I knew Carson would be terribly disappointed. Mikado, too, for that matter. I shook my head and sighed. What was I doing? These guys would only be in my life for a few weeks. It was silly to think about what they thought. And it was totally not necessary for the mission.

"You shouldn't care what other people think, Amber." Then he kissed me, hard until I pulled back and huffed.

"Viktor. I'm going to have to teach you some manners." I trudged off, and I heard him snigger behind me.

I was invisible to Mikado, as I'd always been, but Carson wasn't about to let me slip through his fingers. He caught up with me between classes.

"You can't seriously be with him. Out of everyone in this school, you choose him? Even after I warned you?"

I had to get him to buy my relationship with Viktor, at least for a few more days, but I wasn't sure what would convince him that I, nice Amber, would choose such a devil as a boyfriend.

"I just don't see it, Carson. You've got him all wrong. Seriously. He's so good to me."

"It's all an act. I'm telling you. Save yourself some grief and end it now before it really begins."

"I like you, Carson. You're a good friend, my best

friend here. It's nice of you to want to protect me, but I'm a big girl, and I can take care of myself."

"That's just it. You are my friend, and I don't want to see you get hurt."

This wasn't working. I was going to have to be mean to the one boy who had been so nice to me and was only trying to help. "Look, Carson." I adopted a stern tone to my voice. "I appreciate you and everything, but I like Viktor." The words were thick in my mouth, and I wondered if they rang true. "And I'm with him. You are going to have to accept that and come to terms with the fact that nothing is going to happen between you and me. I see you like my big brother. Nothing more. I'm sorry."

Just then, a hand grabbed mine. I jerked my head around. It was Viktor. "What would you have to be sorry about?"

"Oh," I said, pushing the fake anger out of my tone. "I got a drink from the fountain and when I turned around, I ran right into Carson and made him drop his stuff. I'm so clumsy."

Carson's face was a mask of hurt. My insides swirled like a tornado.

"You're not clumsy, Amber. I'm sure Carson was to blame. He should have been paying better attention." He looked pointedly at Carson.

"Whatever," Carson said, looking at me, his pained expression turning to indignant anger as he stalked away.

I wanted to reach out to him and take back everything I'd said, but I couldn't. I had to keep Viktor believing I was with him one hundred percent. I needed to get into his uncle's house.

"We better hurry, or we'll be late."

We sprinted to class and stepped inside just as the bell rang. At the end of it, we headed for lunch. "I'm so excited to meet more of your family Sunday."

"About that, I'm not so sure this week would be the best week."

My heart leapt into my throat. "Is your uncle not having the dinner?"

"No, he is. He just suggested we wait until next week. He's got a lot of stuff going on at work this week and wants to be able to give you the attention you deserve."

"Did he really say that?"

"What?"

"That he wants to give me the attention I deserve?"

"Not in those exact words, no."

I sighed. "I guess we'll have to lay off until then. I mean, we really can't be together until he approves our relationship, right? It's going to be terrible to wait for a few weeks to be together again." I looked up at him.

He scrunched up his face in thought. I had him. "I don't think it means that. I mean—"

"You can't tell me that now you think he'd be okay with us. It's been, what, a day? And you think he's changed?" I stood there, exasperation on my face.

"No. I mean...he'll never know."

"Are you kidding? Several people have already congratulated me on snagging you, and I haven't said a word to anyone."

"You're right." He sighed. "I'll see if I can't bring you and then leave right after dinner."

"Yes. Please. Ask him again. I don't want to put things on hold between us." It would be too late if we waited until next Sunday, I just knew it.

"I'll see what I can do."

I flung my arms around him and gave him a kiss on the cheek before saying, "Thank you! Thank you!"

I saw Jericho staring at us, a sour look on his face until he noticed me notice him. Then he smiled at me and walked away.

***

I got a text at eight that night giving me directions to my next lift. Viktor had explained to me that S-Dub would need me every day this weekend in order for him to meet his quota of cars, so I wasn't surprised when the text came in. I walked briskly through the cold, a chill wind numbing my face as I hurried to my destination to meet my lifting partner. However, when I got to the place, I was met by Viktor, not Jericho or Mikado.

"I didn't realize you lifted cars with the rest of us."

"I don't. I wanted to see you for a few minutes tonight at least."

"All that effort, for little old me?" I flirted, though I was cringing inside as he once again led me under a tree and kissed me. This time, Jeremy's face came to mind immediately, and I found myself almost enjoying the kiss, until Viktor's hands began exploring my back, breaking my foolish illusion. I couldn't match Jeremy's face with Viktor's insistent fumbling—his hands inside my jacket, only my shirt keeping them from my skin. He was searching for the hem of my shirt, I was sure, trying to push his way even closer.

I had to find a reasonable way to end this, preferably to make him end it. I had been covertly sniffing for the last minute or so, my nose running thanks to the cold night air. Now, I sniffed hard, allowing a tiny snort to come through. Viktor pulled away, and I made a move toward him as if to kiss him again, then stopped and let out a sneeze. I smiled an apology and reached in my pocket for a tissue.

He pulled back. "Sorry. I guess this wasn't the best idea. You're cold."

I wiped my nose. "I'm not, just my nose is."

He looked at his watch. "Well, we've still got a few minutes, and I'd hate to waste them." He pulled me close and hugged me tight before kissing my nose, which was most certainly red with cold, and then my forehead, my cheek and finally my lips once again. He kept his hands on the outside of my coat this time.

Someone cleared his throat, and I jerked back, but Viktor held me tight. He turned his head in a slow, methodical motion toward the noise. Jericho was standing there. This was why he had done this. He had wanted Jericho to see us kissing. He wanted Jericho to know I was taken. I loathed him even more. "Guess it's time for you to go." He kissed me again, a lingering, hot kiss, given to drive in his point to Jericho. I suppressed a shiver. "Good luck."

I nodded and once I reached Jericho, we headed off to lift our first car that night. He didn't say one word, and the awkward silence dug at me. Finally, after the third car, he twisted his head to me and gave it a little jerk. "Why are you with Viktor when you could have me?"

"Maybe I want him and not you."

"That couldn't be true. Put me against him, and I win every time."

He turned away and covered his mouth, continuing to give me the silent treatment. I'd said the wrong thing. His anger caused us to make a few mistakes along the way, but we were still able to lift the requisite eight cars before midnight. Barely.

I couldn't allow a rift between us, not when I could still need him at some point during the mission. "You can't be mad at me. Viktor came to me before you did. Besides you have a different girl on your arm every few minutes, and I want a steady boyfriend. On top of that, you couldn't handle me."

"Leave him, and be with me." The muscles in his jaw tightened.

"I can't do that."

He pulled the car to the curb and slammed on the breaks. "Why not? I can tell you don't really like him. You seem to tolerate him."

"Oh, and I should like you instead?"

He sat up even straighter, and he bit the corner of his lips before turning to me and giving me strong eye contact. "Me or someone else. Just not him."

I wondered what had fueled this rivalry between them. I pushed a breath of air out of my closed lips. "Come on. You don't really like me. You just like the competition with Viktor."

"As he likes it with me." His eye twitched and then faster than I thought possible, he grabbed me by the neck and pulled me to him. His lips were hard, insistent. I pulled back. He was strong, but I was stronger. I narrowed my eyes at him.

"Don't you ever do that again." I spit each word at him. "If you think that helped your case, you're mistaken." I felt something warm on my lip and yanked the visor down to see a small trickle of blood come from my bottom lip. I brushed it away. "In fact, don't you ever touch me again!" I put every ounce of venom into my words as possible.

He laughed, reminding me of his sociopathic nature. He only wanted me because Viktor had me. I shouldn't have encouraged him.

I had no idea what he thought he would get out of that kiss, and I didn't want to know. He threw the car back into drive, and we put the car away in its semi. I didn't wait for him to go to the subway. I got out of there as fast as I could, and a piece of me even hoped that Viktor would be waiting for me. He wasn't. It wasn't that he could protect me more than I could myself, but I just didn't want to be alone. The creep factor of Jericho was too great. The only solace I had was in knowing my team had their eyes on me.

The train came only seconds after I reached the platform and I watched, hoping Jericho would miss it. As we drove away, I saw Jericho reach the platform but miss the train. I sat, only then noticing my heavy breathing. Only two others were on the subway, and they looked innocuous enough, so I let myself relax. I had twelve minutes to regain my composure.

Chapter 21

Halluis met me at the exit to the subway. I hid my surprise. I'd been hoping to see Jeremy waiting for me. He must not have been able to make it back in time.

Halluis said, "You okay? You look a bit spooked."

"Jericho totally attacked me tonight. I could have taken him down, you know, but I would've had to blow my cover, and that was not an option." I shook my head, trying to clear my brain after days of no sleep. "I really wanted to kill him or at least knock some teeth out, but this mission...ugh!"

"Jericho—major creep. Sorry about that, but seriously, are you okay?"

"I think so. He just really gets to me. I should have known better considering what I've seen him do."

"I hate to say it, because I never thought I would, but I'm glad you had to hook up with Viktor instead of Jericho."

"Yeah. I'm counting my blessings for sure. Has anything good come from the bugs we set in his house?" We started back toward the brownstone.

"Nothing. Except some hot nights with a few different girls. He never talks on a phone in his rooms. We believe he does everything through text. Just like they make you do. We should have made it a priority to get into his phone. We haven't been able to crack it. It's still secure. As is Viktor's."

"But didn't Ace get a bug in his phone?"

"Yes. But it isn't transmitting for whatever reason."

"I should have had Jericho's phone."

"Things happen. You tried and came really close. Honestly, closer than I thought you would get. They must have some seriously ingenious blockers on their phones to keep them secure."

"Like ours are secure?" I said, the irony of the situation hitting me hard. "I can't help but see the similarities between the efficiency and security of the bratva and Division. How can we expect to bring them down if they have the same or better technology than we do?"

He huffed. "Yeah. I know. But we have Ace. He'll figure it out." We entered the brownstone.

I went into the kitchen to get a drink and was a little sad to find Jeremy sitting at the table with Ace. I wished he'd thought to come get me after the horrible night I'd had. They stopped talking when we walked in, and Jeremy barely spared me a glance. I had to find an opportunity to talk to him and find out what was up. After a slight stutter step, I made it to the sink and grabbed a drink. I sat at the table between the two guys, and Halluis sat too.

Business-like, Jeremy asked for a brief on how the night had gone, and after I'd given it, we reviewed what was going to happen Sunday with the dinner, even though I still wasn't sure I'd be going. Jeremy barely looked at me throughout the discussion, and not once did he remark on my performance for the evening. A wave of hurt rushed up inside me. If he thought I wasn't doing my job well, why wouldn't he just come out and say it? Maybe he was just being tactful. Whatever he had to say, he didn't want to bring it up in front of the rest of the team.

The discussion ended, and everyone rose from the table. Instead of hurrying off to bed, I moved over to the sink to work on some dishes, giving Halluis and Ace the chance to head to bed, and giving Jeremy the chance to talk to me alone. If he had something to say, I wanted him to get it over with already.

"You wound up?" Ace asked as he left the room.

"Nah," I said. "I'm dead tired. I'll be right up." I heard their footsteps on the stairs at the same time the back door shut. I stood and ran to the door to catch Jeremy, but he was already gone. I closed my eyes, closed my mouth, and breathed out hard through my nose. I looked at my cell and thought about texting him but decided against it. I wanted to talk face to face. I'd really hoped he'd take the opportunity to talk to me tonight. Maybe I'd be able to catch him alone in the morning and we could have it out. His disapproval, however silently it was expressed, was shaking my confidence. I needed to know what I was doing wrong, so I could fix it and have Jeremy at my back again.

***

He wasn't there in the morning, and I fought back the bitter feeling of disappointment. I decided I'd have to take things into my own hands, so I texted him before going out the door to run. *We need to talk.* I was doing some cross training, so every time I stopped to do a different exercise, I checked my messages, but he never did answer me. I ran through the trails in Tompkins Square Park, weaving through groups of NYU students getting away for a day of sun in the park even though it was still quite chilly. Tall trees and ample bushes shaded parts of the walkways, allowing ice to remain. I dodged them with adept feet.

As I left the park, sweaty and winded, feeling totally rejuvenated and alive, I got a shock from Carson. After I'd dropped to do some pushups, I found him sitting on a bench close by.

"Carson?"

He stood. "Fancy meeting you here."

"Seriously? Don't you live in Brooklyn?"

"Okay, you caught me. I went to your house this morning, and I saw you leave for your workout. I've been sort of following you."

"Following me?"

"Well, I wanted to surprise you and take you out for breakfast, but I barely missed you as you ran out of the house. I couldn't get to you fast enough. I figured you'd most likely pass by here again, so I waited." He pointed to the brownstone in the distance. "And if you didn't, I have a clear shot to your place and would know when you returned."

"All that trouble for me?" He was too sweet. Maybe a bit stalkerish, but sweet, nonetheless. I couldn't help but think about how much he reminded me of Rick, a guy I'd totally fallen for while in D.C. and thought I'd have a future with, but being spies made it impossible.

"So, breakfast?"

"Breakfast sounds great. But I'll need to shower first. You mind waiting?"

"Of course not."

My phone buzzed, alerting me to a text from Viktor. *I have an hour for lunch. Meet me.*

I took a second and answered him after checking the time. *Sure. One-o-clock?*

He named the place, and it was set.

I thought it would be fun to have breakfast with Carson and maybe I could get him to spill that he worked for Viktor in some capacity.

I texted my team that I was about to bring Carson in the house so they could be sure to be gone.

We walked back to the brownstone. My teammates had either gotten my message or they were gone anyway, so I was free to put Carson in the TV room. I flipped the TV on and gave him the remote. I got ready as fast as I could. He sat in the same spot when I returned as he had when I'd left him. He was laughing. His laugh was hearty and fun. I couldn't help but smile. "I'll never get enough of *Modern Family*—so funny." His eyes sparkled like a star.

"My favorite is Gloria. Her accent gets her into so much trouble." I laughed.

He stood up and clicked off the TV. "Yeah, she's hilarious. You look nice."

"Thanks."

He motioned with his hand for me to head to the front door, and we walked to a café not far from where we were. After ordering, he reached across the table and grabbed my hand. I stiffened slightly, but then relaxed. His face had turned serious. "I'm worried about you."

"What are you talking about?"

He looked around at the people surrounding us and then said, "Viktor. And yes, I would love to be the one kissing you, but if I can't be, then you should know he is no good. I wish I could tell you more, but I can't. His family is dangerous. I'm begging you to say goodbye to him and get out now."

"You've got to give me more than that." What did he know? He was acting like he knew Viktor and his family were bratva.

He shook his head. "Seriously, I can't tell you anything. I can only warn you." He moved closer to me. "I've been around him and Jericho almost my whole life. Shoot. Since I was five. I've seen stuff. Heard stuff. Believe me, they are bad news, and if I could get away from them without any consequences, I would."

Our food arrived. He took a deep breath in.

I leaned back in my chair. "You are so confusing. I'm still not sure, but I'll consider what you've told me."

"That's all I can ask for. Thank you." He sat back, letting go of my hands.

"I suppose if you're right, I should be thanking you. I'm lucky to have you as a friend. Anyway, I'm starving." I picked up a fork to dig into my eggs. "I sure like the non-serious you better."

"Really?" He rubbed his hand over his face. "Putting my non-serious self forward."

It was fun hanging out with a normal boy, but I was concerned that I was leading him on. We laughed and

212

talked for the better part of an hour, and then I announced that I had to get back.

"Unfortunately, I've got to get to work, too. My employer is such a beast."

"Oh," I said, excited to start this conversation as we stood to leave. "I didn't know you worked. Where do you work?"

"Be prepared to be underwhelmed—the docks."

I stood up straight, my shoulders tightening and a dizziness seeping into my head. "Really? The docks?" Was this the connection?

"My parents own a shipping company. I help with the books and scheduling. Next week is going to be busy. We have three ships sailing."

We made it to the sidewalk, and an ache rose up in my chest. My intuition was telling me something.

"Wow! People around here don't play around, do they? No one's a captain of a ship at Bell—they gotta own the ship and the captain."

He chuckled. "It's not as glamorous as you might think. The piers stink, and the people who we employ aren't always the best—if you know what I mean."

"Are you telling me you aren't rich?" I laughed.

He put up his hands. "I didn't say that." He gave me a breathy laugh. "I'm just saying it's not the best business to be in. That's all."

I nodded. "You mean you don't want me to come visit you at work?"

He stopped for a second. "You'd want to come see me?"

I hated to lead him on, but if it was his shipping company that was moving the bratva's stolen cars, it would be practical to get closer to him. "I've never been to a real, working pier. I've been to the ones that they've been turning into parks, but that's about it."

"Maybe we can work something out."

"Let's see, you live in Brooklyn. Do you operate out of Red Hook?"

"That's the one."

Tingles spread through my body. Red Hook it was. "No way. Isn't that one of the most dangerous areas in New York?"

He nodded, and we started walking again.

"I'm not sure I want to go there."

He didn't reply.

"But I guess if I had you to protect me, I'd be okay." I squeezed his solid upper arm.

He chuckled. "I'll see what I can do."

We walked in companionable silence until we reached the brownstone. My mind was like a rocket, speeding through the implications of the possible and most probable connection between the bratva and Carson and his family.

I stepped onto the first stair and said, "Thanks for breakfast and the company. I had a great time."

"Thanks for coming. It was fun." He looked at his feet and then back up at me. "I hope I can trust you not to tell Viktor or anyone about our little conversations."

"Of course," I assured him. "If Viktor's the bad guy, we need to keep him in the dark because bad guys do, well, you know, bad things to people who betray them."

He didn't smile. He seemed to go a little pale, though, so I said, "Don't worry, Carson. I would never do that. Ever. You saved me from being a wallflower, remember?" I gave him a sheepish look.

"Thanks...See you on Monday."

"I'll be there with bells on." I watched him get into a BMW across the street. I'd so hoped he had nothing to do with this whole mess, and now it was turning out that he might be smack dab in the middle of it.

Chapter 22

No one was at the brownstone, so I changed to meet with Viktor. I couldn't wait to tell everyone what I'd learned.

Viktor met me outside the café. He leaned in and kissed me, not a quick peck, but a full on, minute-long kiss. My face flushed with a fury.

"You look so cute when you're embarrassed." He stroked my hair and looked around, a look of gloating on his face. He wanted everyone to see him kissing me, owning me.

I looked at my feet then pushed my face into his chest and kept my head down so that he couldn't kiss me again. He chuckled and led me inside. We took a table. "So, do I have plans for dinner Sunday?" I gave him a bright smile.

"You do."

I grinned and threw my hands in the air. "Seriously?"

"Seriously." He leaned in to kiss me, and I shifted so that he kissed my cheek.

"Don't do that again," he said. His eyes darted around the café, making sure no one had seen me diss him.

"What?"

"Dodge my kiss. You are mine, and when I want a kiss, I can have a kiss."

"Remember what I said about manners?"

He huffed.

"I told you PDA was hard for me. Give me a chance to ease into it."

He flared his nostrils and pushed back in his chair.

I pocket texted Jeremy. *It's on.* I couldn't help but bemoan the fact that he hadn't ever responded to my earlier text. I decided to text the other agents too. A hollow feeling covered my chest. I'd never had to wonder if Jeremy would protect me and be there for me before. Why was I worried about that now?

Viktor left as soon as we'd eaten and I had all the information about the next night's dinner.

I found Jeremy, Halluis, and Ace around the kitchen table when I got back. Both Halluis and Ace were eating apples and peanut butter. Jeremy didn't eat any, and I happened to know he loved peanut butter.

"He's picking me up at five. Dinner's at six."

"Do you know if they're expecting you to lift cars tonight?"

"I think so. I haven't heard otherwise. Viktor said I'd be busy all weekend."

"I bet the shipment is going out early next week." Jeremy ran his fingers through his hair. "Christy has been picking up at least eight cars a night, Mikado six, and those two girls have lifted eight since Sunday. On top of that, Viktor said Alexander was busy with work this week. It seems logical to assume that the shipment goes out at the beginning of next week. If we're going to get that car back, I figure Christy is going to have to locate the car by tomorrow, and we'll have to act on whatever information she finds as soon as we get it. We can't let that car leave the country."

"No pressure, Christy," Halluis said.

"We knew it was a long shot from the beginning. If the shipment sails before we get our hands on the car, no one will be able to blame us." Ace rubbed the back of his neck.

"Whoa! Whoa!" I said. "You're all acting like it's already over. It isn't. Not by a long shot. I think I know what pier the ship will sail from. At least we can know it pretty quick."

"What are you talking about?" Halluis asked.

"Carson's family owns a shipping company." I let that sink in. "It uses Red Hook terminal, and three ships are sailing this coming week."

Ace stood and headed for the stairs, calling over his shoulder, "I'll get on it."

"Wait up," Halluis called after him. "I'll go with you." And he, too, disappeared up the stairs.

Jeremy pushed back hard in his seat but didn't challenge me or tell me to be safe or anything. Something was very wrong. He refused to make eye contact with me and tapped his fingers on the table. He acted nervous, upset even.

"We will get the car back," I said. "You'll see."

Jeremy stood and headed for the back door, again without any explanation, but I stopped him, putting my hand on his upper arm.

He shrugged it off and kept moving toward the door.

"Stop, Jeremy, please. We need to talk," I said, a bit louder than I'd intended.

Jeremy sighed and turned halfway toward me, a note of exasperation in the press of his lips. "What about, Christy? I have things to do."

I'd laid out a calm, rational argument in my head, detailing Jeremy's odd behavior and professionally asking for an explanation, but when faced with his show of indifference, I found myself speechless.

Jeremy shook his head and turned again to leave. "There's nothing to talk about. Good luck tomorrow." He left, shutting the door behind him.

I only paused for a second before wrenching the door open and racing down the few steps to Jeremy. I grabbed his arm, but he kept moving toward his car. "What am I doing wrong?" I demanded.

He turned back and faced me, both of us breathing hard, standing just inches apart in the pool of light cast by the porch lamp. "You want to know what you're doing wrong? You're being too reckless, that's what!"

I dropped his arm and took a step back. "Too reckless? What are you talking about?"

"You put yourself in one dangerous position after another, throwing yourself after these psychopaths and criminals without a second thought!"

"Throwing myself after them?"

"Yes! I told you to get close to them—you were not supposed to be kissing them. Do you have any idea how reckless, how dangerous that was?"

"You're treating me like some inexperienced kid—

you've been treating me that way all along. Don't you think I know exactly what I'm getting myself into? I'm the one out there. I'm the one who has to make the call and decide what I have to do to get what we need. I am doing everything I can to accomplish this mission—"

Jeremy gripped me by the shoulders, and stared intensely into my eyes. "And have you ever *once* stopped to think that this mission might not be worth everything you're risking?"

That stopped me in my tracks. The look of anguish on his face as he held me, his face only inches from mine, was enough to smooth away any trace of defensiveness I felt. "I—I—what are you saying?"

His words came out just barely above a whisper. "Christy—what could possibly be worth losing you?"

His hand moved to my cheek and I pressed into it, even though it felt soft and tentative. I couldn't believe what I was hearing, but I didn't dare doubt it. He pulled me closer and our eyes locked. I bit my bottom lip, and his eyes fell to my mouth.

Way too slowly, his perfect face moved toward me until his lips were a breath away from mine. My lip quivered, and a desperate thrill went through me. I savored his breath mingling with mine before his soft lips touched mine. The rush of emotion that pulsed through me was foreign. This was all new and wonderful. His lips moved gently across mine, his mouth warm in the cold night air, and a pleasant shiver traveled up my spine.

A soft moan escaped his lips, and then he pressed his hungrily to mine. Fire ripped through me, and we crashed into each other, our hands pulling us closer and closer together. My body fitted his as electric desire, hot and sweet, raced through me.

His hands moved gently over my back and drifted over my neck. I pulled him even harder to me and couldn't imagine ever taking my lips off his. My heart was beating so hard I thought I might faint.

Then, something changed suddenly and just as explosively as it had started, it ended. He pulled away, eyes wide, hands trembling on my upper arms.

"No." He stepped back and curled his lips over his teeth. "I'm so sorry. I shouldn't have...that was not..." He swung his head to the side and closed his eyes. His chest rose and fell in a quick rhythm. "Oh, Christy. That shouldn't have happened."

I stepped toward him. "Don't you dare take this moment away from me, Jeremy. Don't you dare. I've waited for this moment for so long, and it was beautiful and right and—" My lungs hitched up, and I couldn't breathe.

He stepped back. "No. It wasn't right. It can't be. I'm your handler. We can't..." He pressed his palms to his forehead and moaned. This was a different moan than the one only seconds earlier. This was a moan of agony, not of pleasure.

"I'm sorry. I shouldn't have, I was wrong to—" "

"You weren't wrong. I want this, and—you want it, too." That discovery had sent my heart soaring just moments before, but now my heart wrenched inside me. It was our first kiss. It didn't have to be so complicated. It had been the most beautiful thing I'd experienced.

"It doesn't matter what we want. This isn't allowed."

He moved his hands back and forth between us. "If anyone found out, we'd lose our jobs." He tilted his head to the side. "I can't take this away from you, Christy. You're too good at this job to throw it all away—everything you could do in this world—just for me."

I knew he was right, but I shook my head. "It's not fair. We shouldn't have to choose." My heart pounded, but all the beauty from earlier had left the beat.

"I know. But we do. And the truth is, we can't think only of ourselves. You are an incredible spy." He put his hand under my chin, his thumb sliding over my bottom lip. "And I refuse to take that from you."

I wanted to say something, anything to keep him there, to convince him that it would be all right, but no words came.

"I'm sorry," he said, finally breaking the silence. "I'm sorry for how I've been acting. I guess I've been kind of a jerk."

I laughed softly. "I thought you were doubting me. I thought you had lost faith in me."

"Never," he whispered, shaking his head. "You have been doing an amazing job—every break we've had in this case has been because of you. I just... I hate watching you put yourself in danger every day. I can't bear the thought of losing you. It's wrong, but I can't help how I feel about you, Christy. It makes me kind of crazy sometimes." He turned to go, but I grabbed his hand and pulled him back.

"If we can't be together, and this is our last moment like this one, then kiss me, one last time." He couldn't refuse me, could he?

The moment stretched on between us until he bent down and brushed his tender lips along my jaw, ending with them on my lips. It was a soft, succulent kiss that buckled my knees and left me paralyzed long after he had left me there and drove away.

I put my fingers to my lips, swearing never to forget what it had felt like to have his lips on mine and wishing things were different. I made my way into the house and went to get ready for some car lifting, my heart aching and yet full at the same time.

Chapter 23

The next day, when I should have been planning and preparing for my dinner with Viktor's uncle, I found I couldn't concentrate on anything but Jeremy. I had pushed away any feelings I had for him for so long—telling myself that I admired him only as a spy and cared for him only as a friend. I'd told myself I only wanted his approval as my mission leader. But when his lips had met mine, it was as though every lie I'd told myself melted away, and what was left was the searing truth that I was falling in love with him. And he cared for me, too—not just as a handler or as a mission leader, but as a man cares for a woman. Knowing that, and knowing it was impossible, set my heart aching.

My thoughts were awhirl, and I knew I had to do something. I needed to prepare for the challenges I'd be facing that evening, but I could barely even focus on putting one foot in front of the other. Jeremy had told the truth—what we had to offer the world was so much more important than anything we might want for ourselves. It wasn't fair, and it didn't feel good, but it was true. I needed to focus my mind on the mission. When I searched my heart, I knew just what to do.

I found a church nearby and attended the service in hopes of finding inspiration and peace. And not surprisingly, I did. I felt centered and ready to tackle the dinner and whatever followed with a renewed vigor and desire to set things right. As I left the building, I thought I saw Jeremy out of the corner of my eye. When I turned to look more intently, there was no one.

I'd packed a lunch in my car, and after the service drove to Central Park for a picnic. The air was cold and crisp, but the sun was out again today and had melted all the snow except what was in the shadiest parts of the city. The ground squished under my feet. I would go over my plan in my mind again with my new focused energy.

As questions arose in my mind about the bratva, stealing cars, or container ships, I looked them up on my phone. It surprised me to learn about the massive ships and how efficient they were when loaded and unloaded. And it surprised me to discover how well-balanced they had to be. The cargo master, the man who mapped out where all the different containers would go on the ship, had to be a great organizer because he had to think about so many different things while mapping. Putting 15,000 containers in just the right spot would be a difficult task. I stayed there until I absolutely had to get back and get ready.

I emerged from my room with a dress and a jacket with boots. I put some extra bobby pins in my hair and wished I could slip a few weapons in my boots and under my clothes, but knew it was too big of a risk. I attached a tracker, cleverly disguised as a mole, to my upper arm then sat in the living room to wait for Viktor to arrive.

Jeremy came into the room while I sat there. "I wanted to touch base with you before you go."

"Okay." My stomach fluttered.

He sat down near me, but not too close. "I know you know this, but I wanted to make sure it was said out loud so that we're on the same page."

Heat spread up my neck. This didn't sound good.

"We can't let on that there are feelings between us. There is nothing that splits up a crew faster than a romantic relationship. In fact, most aren't only separated, but fired. We have to control ourselves and act like there is nothing between us besides a co-worker relationship. Do you know what I'm saying?"

"I do. No secret rendezvous. No flirting."

"It's more than that. No long looks or staring, no lingering touches, or jealousy at any time." He looked a little rueful at the mention of jealousy.

I nodded. "Got it." I felt awkward and silly, so I changed the subject after a pause that lasted longer than I could stand. "What did you mean when you said the mission might not be worth it?"

He squinted his eyes and wrung his hands. "I don't want to burden you with my doubts."

"If you have doubts, I want to hear about them."

"It's just there've been so many suspicious things about this mission. I've been trying to look into why Division wants that particular car, and I haven't been able to find anything. And the secrecy around it is unprecedented. No one knows about it, and any time I ask Director Skriloff for more resources, he shoots me down. That doesn't happen. I've always been able to get whatever resources I need to complete a mission."

"Maybe whoever paid for this mission had limited funds."

"Division wouldn't take on a project that wasn't perfectly funded. I've never heard of such a thing. It would be madness. I have to uncover what's so important about this car. I mean, I'm not willing to risk your life—and Kozlov's, too— to get a car without a really good reason."

"Division rarely tells us everything, Jeremy. We just have to trust that the car is important. I have this feeling we need to stick to this mission. I think in the end, we'll discover that that car is vitally important."

"I don't know if I agree, but I'm not giving up on it, yet."

"Good."

"You ready for this tonight?"

"I am."

"Good, because I hear him coming up the stairs."

Jeremy left the room.

The doorbell rang. I took a deep breath to steady my throbbing heart and went to open the door.

"You look nice," Viktor said, leaning in for a kiss. "Uncle Alexander is going to love you. You'll see."

"He better."

"And yeah, we can't hang out there after dinner. He's got a full schedule. But he did say you could come next week, too."

I raised my shoulders to my ears and let them fall, grinning like a mad cat.

"Have your nerves returned?"

"Nah...I'm excited to really meet him, now that I've been successful at stealing the cars."

He grabbed my hand and squeezed. "You rocked that. He'll be proud of me for picking you. When we first get there, I need you to be perfect. Don't let him have any reason to doubt you. And whatever you do, don't make me look bad. If you can do that, we'll have some fun after the dinner, just the two of us." A deep growl sounded in his chest, and he bit his lip.

"You sure know how to make a girl feel confident." I frowned, feeling my muscles tense in irritation.

He chuckled. "Follow me, and you won't go wrong."

"Okay, Master!" I gave a snarky shake of my head.

I reviewed in my mind exactly what I was going to be doing once I got into the house. An upset stomach would be a perfect excuse to flee for the "bathroom" twenty minutes into dinner.

We pulled into the driveway of an average-looking house, and he stopped the car. He leaned over to me and kissed me lightly. "Remember, follow my lead."

I nodded, and we got out of the car. That's when I noticed the cameras and the two hulking guys near the end of the driveway. Another car pulled in behind us. A strange look of apprehension played across Viktor's face as he looked at them. He led me up the steps to the front door. He rang the bell and then opened the door and entered, pulling me by the hand behind him.

It was like stepping into another time, another place. The flavor of the house was purely old Russia. Intricate rugs hung on walls and covered the wood floors. It seemed every surface was covered thickly with trinkets from the old world. It was impossible to miss the strong smell of foreign spices that hung thickly in the air.

A butler took our coats right after we entered the foyer. Two men entered after us, and Viktor turned to them and said, "I didn't know you two were coming today." He crossed his arms over his chest.

"Uncle called and said you were bringing a friend he wanted us to meet."

Had I just seen Viktor cringe at their words? They passed us into the next room, and he didn't introduce me to them. My heart thudded. Viktor stood firm in the entryway. I grabbed his hand and said, "What was that all about?"

He shook his head in an exasperated movement. "Nothing. They're my cousins, and we don't get along, that's all." His cold fingers told me another story. He swallowed hard. I tried to repress my anxiety by looking at the entryway once again. It was hard to imagine that I was in the average, American-looking house I'd seen from the street. There was a heaviness in the architecture and decoration.

Finally, another man, who was obviously more than a butler, the bulge at his waist front and back confirming it, led us into a large living room. Alexander and five other men, including the two cousins who had passed us in the foyer, sat in various seats around the room. It wasn't hard to notice, however, that Alexander's chair held him higher off the ground than anyone else. I wasn't sure if he'd had the legs on his plush chair raised or if he'd had all the other furniture legs cut off.

Viktor held his ground at the entrance to the room. I looked up at him, but he kept his eyes focused on Alexander, whose eyes were on me.

"Viktor!" he called out in his deep, rough voice, his arms spreading wide to receive him. "Welcome!"

Only then did Viktor move. He nodded, began his procession toward the brigadier and said, "Thank you so much for having us to dinner. As discussed, I've brought Amber Smith tonight."

"Yes. Yes." The bratva leader said, his fingers beckoning us closer just as we reached him.

Viktor leaned into his outstretched arms, and they kissed each other on the cheeks—the typical Russian welcome.

I pretended to be unsure what to do as Viktor backed away and swung his arm out to me, inviting me to receive Alexander's welcome. He nodded at me, and I stepped toward the man I was about to cross. The man who had warned me what the penalty would be if I did. He kissed both my cheeks and gave me a hearty hug.

"Don't be afraid of a good Russian welcome!" He gave a deep chuckle as he released me. "If I decide to let you date my nephew, you will become a pro." His obvious and thick Russian accent was somehow inviting and repulsing at the same time.

Not knowing what to say, but knowing I needed to appear humble, I said, "Thank you, sir."

I thought I saw his eyes narrow slightly, and I wondered if the "sir" was inappropriate. Then again, if I said the right things each time, he'd certainly get suspicious.

"We are only waiting on one more person to arrive, then we will begin. So, tell me. What is it about Viktor that caught your eye?"

All that came to mind was the terrible feeling I had whenever I was with him, but I said, "Actually, I'm sorry to say, I was quite rude to him when I first met him. I can only blame it on nerves of being a new student."

"Is that true, Viktor?"

"It is. But I didn't let that dissuade me."

That's when none other than Jericho stepped into the room. I couldn't help it, I jerked away at the sight of him, and it didn't go unnoticed. Alexander cocked his head to the side and while looking at me, said, "Jericho. Thank you for coming."

The butler entered the room from behind Alexander and said, "Dinner is served."

No one moved until Alexander stood up. Everyone followed him into the dining room. The table was expertly set with dishes of decadent foods I'd never seen lining the center of it. The butler helped Alexander sit and motioned for us all to take our seats. I sat next to Alexander, Jericho was across from me, and Viktor was clear at the other end, sitting next to someone I assumed was Alexander's wife. The others sat in the remaining open seats.

Once again, no one moved to fill their plates with food until Alexander put a skewer of what looked like meat on his plate. He passed it to me, and I took a very small portion.

"Not a fan of lamb?"

I'd never had lamb, but said, "Not at all, there are

just so many new and exciting dishes on the table, I'd like to try them all without having to change into sweats to accomplish it."

He chuckled. "This good Russian meal will change your life forever. American food will have suddenly lost its savor." His eyes laughed as he looked at me.

"S-Dub is quite pleased with your abilities and, quite frankly, I am too. You seem to have made quite a splash." Alexander stabbed a piece of meat.

"It's a bit of a surprise to me, also. I guess I really wanted to impress Viktor—and of course, you." I took a bite of food, convincing myself that it wasn't that bad, and I didn't need to know what it was.

"So, tell me. What is it about stealing an impressive car that turns you on?"

I cleared my throat.

"I mean," he said, stretching the word *mean* out, "What is it that gets you excited about stealing cars?"

I considered my answer. It needed to be one that would make him trust me. "There's a rush when I succeed, that's for sure, but really, I just love becoming the best at something. Give me a task, and I will not only do it, but I will excel."

He bobbed his empty fork in my direction and continued to eat, asking chit-chatty types of questions as he did. The questions, while seemingly unimportant, truly had weight. A large grandfather clock chimed, letting me know we'd been in the dining room for twenty minutes. I needed to make my move soon. I heard a few big booms outside, and colorful lights shone through the sheer curtains to my right. My team had come through with a diversion. I hoped it would at least get the attention of one guard away from the dinner and its guests.

An almost imperceptible nod came from Alexander, and I noticed one guard make his way out of the room. I made sure to drink an excessive amount and made sure everyone noticed that I had. Twenty-two minutes after dinner began, I turned to Alexander, who had kept me talking most of the night, and asked if I could be excused to the ladies room.

He glanced at my empty cup, and I blushed. "Yeah, unfortunately, I tend to drink to calm my nerves." I put a hand to my stomach.

Alexander put his hand over mine. "I'm sorry we've made you feel nervous." His eyebrows rose, and his eyes pierced mine.

I resisted a cringe and said, "Don't tell Viktor. I wouldn't want him to think I did something wrong."

His eyes flicked to Viktor, who was talking to the two men to his right, then landed back on me. "I'll have the butler show you the way." He flicked his finger in the air, and the butler arrived. I hoped he would leave once he showed me the way.

"Would you like me to return to show you the way back?" The butler said once he opened the bathroom door for me.

"Oh, now that would be really embarrassing. I'm sure I can make it back. Down the hall, through the living room, and it's on my left."

"Very well," he said with a bow before heading back down the hall.

I locked and shut the bathroom door without entering it and quickly made it into the locked office, thanks to my fancy bobby pins. I checked for cameras and, not finding any, made the room ready for my search. I made sure the curtains were shut and then turned the light on in the room. I threw a blanket in front of the door to block the light from entering the dark hallway.

In a flash, I had the computer up and running and the contents of its hard drive copying onto a USB stick. I rushed through the filing cabinets, finding nothing. Searching his desk, I found a false-bottomed drawer that contained a gun. Two chairs also had guns shoved between the cushions. I located a large, stunning statue standing in one corner and decided, if anyone walked in, I'd use it to distract the person.

I then searched the walls and under the rugs. I noticed a thick power cord snaking underneath one rug and ending at the floor moldings on the wall. Looking up, I could see a thermostat. That was a huge power source for a simple thermostat. I looked closer. There was a cut in the wall about a foot lower than the thermostat. I put my fingernail into the groove and discovered the cut continued and created a rectangular shape in the paneling. I examined the thermostat and discovered it was anything but. Opening a plastic panel on it, a retinal and fingerprint scanner met me. I was not prepared with any tools to open that safe. I hoped all the documentation I needed wasn't behind that.

I accidentally pushed into the desk as I searched it one last time, and it slid a few inches. It had plastic sliders on each corner that made it easy to move about the rug it sat on. When I pushed it and lifted the rug, I found a trap door that led to a two-foot deep container.

Inside was another gun and masses of papers. I scanned through them, snapped a few pictures on my phone and then continued to scan, setting everything I saw to memory. I was coming up on the ten-minute mark, the time that most people noticed a person's absence was edging on the long side.

I abandoned the papers, even though I was only a good third of the way through them, and closed the laptop despite the fact that I'd only been able to transfer seventy-five percent of its contents, according to the bar flashing across the screen. I didn't remove the drive—it would still download, but it would appear as if the computer was off if anyone looked into the room.

I turned off the light and whipped the blanket back onto the chair in the corner of the room. I used my mirror under the door to assure myself that no one was in the hallway, then I rushed to the bathroom, picked the lock, and went inside, locking it behind me.

Not two minutes later, a knock came on the bathroom door and Jericho said, "Did you fall in, or what?"

"No," I shot back. "I didn't fall in." Why had *he* come looking? I softened my tone. "But I don't feel so good. I won't be much longer, I think." I opened the window a slight bit in hopes it would make anyone checking think I really did have an upset stomach.

I heard him huff and walk away.

I peeked out of the bathroom and when the coast was clear, I hurried back into the office and grabbed the drive. Ninety-eight percent transferred—I couldn't wait for one-hundred percent. The most likely outcome of

Jericho telling Alexander about my bathroom sprint was that Viktor would come looking for me, wanting to chew me out for jeopardizing our relationship by getting sick. I shut the laptop and powered it down before sprinting to the door.

Unfortunately, I wasn't fast enough. I felt him and heard him almost simultaneously. Step. Step. Step. I could even hear his breathing as he got closer. I held my breath. He was just outside the door. I shoved the drive into my boot, leapt to the front of the desk, straightened, and turned to stare at the life-sized sculpture in the corner. I was glad I'd decided on this course of action earlier. That foresight probably saved my life.

Blood coursed through my veins with a ferocity I hadn't felt in a long time. I mentally pressed on my lungs, forcing them to slow their demand for oxygen. I slid into the small, calming box in my mind I'd prepared for moments like this, and with one last deep breath, I evened out my thundering pulse as the door opened.

I pretended not to hear Viktor when he first called my name. I waited for him to place a hand on my arm. I whispered, "That is so beautiful." I didn't take my eyes off the art. I felt his gaze turn to the sculpture, too.

"It is. My great grandfather had it commissioned back when he was in Russia." His hand fell from my arm.

I moved toward the statue, reaching out to it, but then drawing back. "I guess I shouldn't touch it."

"What are you doing in here, Amber?"

I twisted my neck around to see him. He wore a fake

smile, and his lips were pressed flat.

"Oh, I came looking for some meds. Sorry. I shouldn't have been snooping."

A small rush of air escaped his mouth. I could tell he was relieved and also wanted to believe my answer.

"You can be so stupid. If my uncle found you in here, he'd probably kill you. You're supposed to be winning him over, not making me look bad."

"I'm sorry, but there weren't any meds in the bathroom, and I was sick."

"You ask me. Don't go snooping around." He ushered me to the door, and I kept saying I was sorry. I watched him look a bit long at the door handle. He was certainly wondering why it hadn't been locked. Before we reached the bathroom door down the hall, Jericho entered the hall. He looked at us and then further down the hall like he was trying to figure out where we had come from.

"Uh," he narrowed his eyes, "the butler gave me these pills for you." His eyes flicked to Viktor as he held them out to me.

"Oh, wow! Thank you," I said, moving forward and taking the pills from him. "Give me a sec." I went into the bathroom, shutting the door behind me. I turned the water on and then put my hands on the counters and breathed deeply. I threw the pills into the sink and watched them swirl down the drain. I did take several handfuls of water and drank them.

Viktor was waiting for me right outside the door, and relief settled over me that Jericho was nowhere to be seen.

"I'm so embarrassed, Viktor—"

We rounded the corner into the living room, and Jericho stood there, in the middle of the room, as if on watch. "Everything okay now, Amber?" He drew out my name as if he wanted to make me feel bad or even like he didn't quite believe that was my name. All I knew is that it made my insides feel fuzzy. I pulled my muscles in to try to make it stop. Did he know about me?

"I still feel a little sick," I said, which was totally true, "but you came to the rescue with those meds. I hope they'll solve that problem quick." I put my hand on my stomach.

He swished his hand through the opening to the dining room, and we walked through.

"Ah, Amber," Alexander said as I made my way to my seat. "I'm afraid you missed the end of the meal. Of course, there is still dessert."

I leaned back and said, "I'm sure it will be lovely, but I'm not sure it would be a good idea to eat anything for the next little while." I lowered my voice so that only he could hear, "I'm so sorry for disrupting your dinner. I'm terribly embarrassed."

"Don't be. Sometimes trying new things causes upset stomachs." He smiled at me, genuinely, it seemed. Then a flicker of something like suspicion flooded his eyes.

Dessert came and went with me sipping only a glass of water. The creamy cake was definitely something I would normally have devoured. I waited patiently for my chance to escape. I couldn't wait to examine the drive, sure that it would contain the last bit of information we needed to complete the mission. It would be too soon if I never saw Jericho again. And I wouldn't mind saying my last goodbye to Viktor, either.

"Will you be needing us any longer, Uncle?" One of the two cousins said.

Alexander glanced at me and then said, "Actually, I do have a little matter I could use your assistance with."

I got a very bad feeling, and I scraped off my tracker mole, flicking it onto the pants of the guy sitting next to me, just in case they were about to search me or something. I covertly lifted my boot to relieve it of the drive I'd put in there, placing it in a lip of wood beneath the table where I sat. Blood pounded in my ears as the cousin who had spoken leaned down for the brigadier to whisper in his ear. In my peripheral vision, I saw the cousin's eyes flick to me and then to Viktor. This was not good.

The guy moved toward Viktor as Alexander spoke. "Amber, my dear," his voice was syrupy. "I have something downstairs I think you might find interesting."

Viktor's eyes flew wide, and he pressed his hands on the table to stand, but his cousin put his hands on his shoulders, holding him down. "But Uncle," he said, his voice moving from loud to quiet as he spoke. "I thought you had business to attend to."

He knew I'd been in his office. He was going to do something terrible to me.

I forced myself to keep fear from my voice. "I should really get going. I know you're a busy man, and I'd hate to take up any more of your time."

"I've got a couple minutes to spare for my newest star."

Alexander stood and nodded at me.

I stood, too. I looked at Viktor, whose face had turned a pasty white color. "Are you coming?" I asked him.

He stroked his chin. "Nah, it's nothing I haven't already seen." He licked his lips and held tight shoulders. He was totally freaked.

My stomach felt rock hard, and every nerve in my body was on high alert. I had to be ready for anything. We walked through a different wide hallway off to the left of the dining area. After going through the kitchen, Alexander turned and took some stairs down to the basement. Someone was following us. My heart thudded in anticipation.

At the bottom step, he punched in a code on the keypad on the wall, and the door slid open to a dark space. "Please excuse the smell, Amber," he said, as he stepped to the side to let me pass. "It's something we haven't been able to get rid of." The room was small and dank. It smelled of mold and something metallic.

I nodded and walked through the door, every sense I had telling me this was a place touched by evil. A prayer welled up in my heart asking God to keep me safe and help me find a way out of whatever was going to happen without me blowing my cover.

Warm hands urged me forward. I turned around, "You wanted to show me this room made of cement?" It was easy for a trained eye to recognize a wall that moved; slight scrapes rushed along its almost smooth surface. The metal door we'd entered shut with a slight clang. I could see no way out. I could take them both out, but then I'd be compromised, and I had no idea what the code was to open the exit door back up. I couldn't act now. I could only hope he wasn't planning on executing me.

"Okay, Alexander, you're making me scared, now. Are you kidnapping me?"

He smiled a wicked smile. "No, my dear. No. There is something beyond this wall I want you to see...But first, Nikolai needs to search you. I'm sure you won't object."

The cousin, Nikolai, then searched me soundly, even removing my boots and checking for movable heels and all. I said a silent prayer of gratitude for the warning I'd felt earlier.

Nikolai shook his head, and Alexander tilted his to the side and narrowed his eyes at me, like he was thinking. Then he straightened up and pushed a code into the keypad on the opposite wall.

It slid open slowly, revealing another cement room. This room was large, and my eyes immediately fell upon a young boy tied to a chair in the middle of the room. The chair sat over a drain in the floor, and the boy's head lolled forward but then popped up at the sound of us entering the room. I gasped and covered my mouth with my hand. Hank.

Chapter 24

He had obviously been crying, and seeing us caused him to yell out around the gag in his mouth and try to get to us, pleading for us to listen to him.

"Oh, my gosh!" I squealed. "What happened to him?" I moved forward as if they'd let me free him even though I knew they wouldn't. What was he doing here? His smiling, friendly face from lunch flashed before my eyes.

Arms held me back.

"This boy," Alexander said, "is a snitch."

I shook my head. "No!"

"It's true. He was caught tonight trying to send information to the FBI."

"I know him," I said. "He goes to my school. He's a good person. A great person."

"Yes. It is a shame to waste the life of a boy who had so much potential. The police and the FBI don't seem to value the lives of the youth today. It's quite a shame that they would force this boy to die."

"No! Please! He doesn't have to die," I cried. "I

mean, can't you use him to get information on the FBI or something?"

"You watch too much TV. This boy couldn't help me. It's time for him to be punished." He turned to me, faking a sad, forlorn look. "Normally, unless we think we can get information out of someone, we shoot them on sight, but after Jericho informed me of your little snoop fest tonight, I thought it might be good to make sure you and I were on the same page." I guess he thought that since he hadn't been able to find anything of his on me, that I hadn't seen anything I shouldn't have, that I just needed a scare. Nikolai moved toward Hank and pulled out a gun, pressing it to his temple.

I screamed out, my whole body shaking in terror as I threw my hands out in front of me and attempted to run to him. "Please. Please don't kill him!" Tears streamed down my face. "Give him another chance."

Alexander threw up a hand. Nikolai took a step back.

"Maybe there is something we can do for this *good*, I mean *great* young man."

I turned to him. I clung to a desperate scrap of hope.

"I do have a special place I send some of those I find dealing in treachery. It's not a nice place, but he would at least be alive."

I nodded, not sure why.

"You see these others?" He swept his hand out to the room and, for the first time, I noticed four other people in cells around the room. "They're all going to this nice place." There were three boys and one girl. "Those two large boys will be going to the mines to help out and the others will be sold to the highest bidder. I save the best for auction. All have betrayed me in one way or the other."

"Sold?"

"There is always a need for personal or professional slaves to satisfy those pesky physical needs we all have."

I stared at Hank and then the others. Death or a life of slavery? Both terrible. Both unacceptable. But if I could convince Alexander to keep him alive, we could save Hank before he was sold.

"Should I spare him?"

"Please," I whispered.

"Interesting," he said, stroking his chin. "I'm sorry to say that I disagree." He nodded. Nikolai lifted the gun and shot Hank in the head.

I stiffened, and my ears seemed full of cotton.

Alexander clamped his meaty hand on my shoulders, preventing my advance and whispered in my ear, "No," Alexander continued. "He would not have fetched a nice price at auction. I know when you think it over you will understand. We cannot tolerate rats. They spread disease and discontent."

I couldn't take my eyes off Hank's slumped body, blood dripping from the kill shot. My breaths came in rapid, erratic pulls and pushes. The guy who shot Hank took me by the arm and led me out, following Alexander.

Tears coursed down my cheeks. It wasn't that I'd never seen someone killed. I had, many times. It was the sheer brutality, complete disregard for human life. He was only a boy, and on top of it all, he was my friend. The look on his face of panic and pleading was forever imprinted on my mind. Somewhere in my mind I heard echoes that Hank died because of me. I knew that wasn't true. Alexander had told me as much. He would have died had I been there to witness it or not. But I couldn't shake the thought that I caused it. I sucked in for air but seemed unable to get any and clutched my neck as I tried to croak out, "I'm so sorry, Hank. I'm so sorry!" It came out as a broken, raspy whisper, and I couldn't avert my eyes from his still body.

Alexander spoke to Nikolai while looking at me. "Get her cleaned up. I want her back in the living room within five minutes. The transport for those going to auction will be here in ten."

Nikolai punched some buttons on the keypad, and a second door opened and the one leading to Hank's dead body slid shut. He shoved me toward the open door. "Get cleaned up. You have three minutes."

I was in a small washroom with a shower, toilet, and sink, with a shelf full of towels and washrags. Empty of adornment, it was cold and completely still. I grabbed hold of the sink and bent my head forward, renewed tears springing from my eyes.

"Two minutes."

I had to pull it together. I was a spy. I'd seen much worse than this. But I couldn't. Not yet. I screamed out and hit my hand on the mirror, sending shards crashing to the ground. I shook my head. "No! No! No!" I grabbed at my hair. The door slid open, and the guard pulled me out, pushing me into a corner of the room.

"What did you do? You're going to get me into a lot of trouble." He rounded on me as I crouched in the corner and hit me hard on the head, throwing me into the wall beside me. I gasped in pain. When I had the sense to look up again, he was dumping the shards of glass into a waste container. He pulled out a radio and said, "Let Viktor know I need a few more minutes."

He hauled me off the floor and pushed me into the bathroom. "If you don't get cleaned up in the next three minutes, I'm going to go back into that room and shoot the first person I see." He pointed to the room with the prisoners.

"No!" I screamed back at him.

"You have three minutes." He pulled out his radio again, turned around and spoke into it.

I had to pull it together or more people would be killed because of me. My eyes were puffy and red, tear tracks staining my cheeks. My nose was running profusely. I grabbed some tissues and blew my nose, then used a wet rag to scrub my face. There was no way in less than two minutes to hide the fact that I'd been crying. I think that was exactly what Alexander wanted. I felt my head where it had hit the wall, and a goose egg had already formed. Where Nikolai's fist hit my head, it was tender and sore to the touch, and a headache was coming to meet me full bore.

What would the consequences of this be? As I thought about it, I realized my breakdown made it appear that I was who I'd told them I was, and not an agent for Division. After all, what spy would lose it like I had, anyway? Viktor's cousin took me back upstairs and had me in the living room before the second three minutes were up.

Upon my entry, Viktor stood up, eyes wide,

apprehension written all over his face. All eyes were on me as I walked to the chair next to Viktor and took a seat.

The look Viktor had had on his face as Alexander had led me away told me Viktor either knew exactly what was going to happen or just knew it would be bad. But of course, he wouldn't save me from whatever it was either. I wasn't sure what I should say to him when the time came. I said a prayer that I'd come up with the right thing to further the mission. In the meantime, I kept my head down and didn't speak.

"It's been such a wonderful evening, everyone," Alexander said, in a sickly sweet voice.

My insides clenched, and I knew at that moment that I couldn't let this evil man get away with what he'd done. I refused the urge I had to stare him down. We would save those kids. We would. And there would never be another Hank. Never.

"However," he continued, "I have many things to get done and must end this party early tonight." He stood up and walked out of the room.

There was no way I was going to let this awful man get one more cent from his car thieving gang. He would pay for what he did to Hank and those people in his dungeon; they would never get to their destination. We would save them before that happened.

Only then did Viktor reach for my hand. I jerked it away.

"Let's go," he said in a whisper.

I acted like a scared cat as we walked out of the house and to the car. This is how Amber would have reacted after what she had experienced. I sat as close to the door as I could, keeping my head angled so I was looking out the passenger side window.

When he touched my leg, I jumped.

"Amber," he said, speaking in a quiet, stern voice. "Tell me what happened!"

When I didn't respond, he huffed and backed out of the driveway. I watched a black van pull into the drive after we left. That van was transporting those kids somewhere. I wished I knew where. After about ten minutes, he stopped at Prospect Park.

I heard him turn to me. "Amber. What happened? What did you do?" He scowled at me.

I shook my head in tiny little movements against the window.

"Whatever you did, you're going to have to make it right. You hear me?"

In a flash, I turned to him. "Make it right?" I spat. "That would be impossible! He killed Hank. A boy from our school!" I moaned, letting my head fall in a defeated roll. I kept a moan in my throat, and it sounded like a cat crying out.

"What did you do to make him do that?"

"Nothing!"

"It couldn't have been nothing." He brushed his fingers through his hair. "I hope you haven't ruined everything I had planned for us."

"He's the one who ruined it. He's a monster and you...you took me to his house. You lied to me. You told me he was nice. A great uncle."

"He is. I mean, he can be. I just never thought. Why? Did he tell you why he took you down there?"

"Something about me being a snoop and him having

to show me what happens to snitches."

He gasped. "I guess he found out you'd been in his office. I told you—"

"You told me nothing. You told me I'd like him, and I'd feel at home if you took me to that dinner. Well, I didn't, and I hate him. I hate him." My voice evened out, and I set a strong, stony stare at Viktor as I said the last, *I hate him.*

He leaned back and put his hands on the back of his neck. "I get it. But I told you, you needed to be careful..."

I scowled at him, and he shrank back just a bit and, even though it was way out of character for him, his face softened and he said, "I should have gone with you."

I wrapped my arms around him in one swift motion. I'd been waiting for one little show of weakness or maybe kindness in him. "I was so scared. Hank. Oh, my gosh! Hank!" I wept on his shoulder for quite some time.

At one point, he pulled me off him and said, "Do you forgive me?"

"I'm trying. I just—" Was he for real? Did he really have true feelings for me in some small way?

"I get it." His phone chimed. "You feeling up to lifting tonight?" His eyes searched mine.

"I don't know." My mind went to the drive, still trapped under Alexander's table. We had to find some way to get it back.

He looked back at his phone and sighed. "I wasn't really asking. I mean, I was, but you really don't have a choice. You've got to go out." The real Viktor was back.

I huffed. "Figures."

"Looks like your first lift is close to here. I'll drop you off."

I looked down at my clothes. "You want me to go like this?" I really didn't like the idea of being with any of the other lifters without any weapons and in the emotional state I was in.

"I'm sorry, but you've only got twenty minutes to get there, and that's how long it would take to get you home."

"Fine," I growled. "This night couldn't get any worse."

We drove a few blocks when he pulled up to the curb. He climbed out as I did. He didn't make any move to kiss me, but he put his hand on my stomach to stop me when I started to walk away.

"I'll see you tomorrow. Please don't make any mistakes." There was exasperation in his tone, as if all the bad that had happened tonight was my fault, and my strict attention to my duties could clear everything up.

I didn't reply. I simply walked toward the meeting point.

Chapter 25

As I went, I looked for objects lying about that I could use or transform into weapons. There was nothing. I detoured quickly into a hole-in-the-wall eatery and walked casually toward the back as if I was a customer going to use the bathroom. Across from the bathroom was the kitchen, and it was easy to take a few steps in so that I could grab a knife, which I quickly slipped into my boot. It seemed like it gave me back some of the power that Alexander had taken from me. Even if I never had to use it tonight, it would be a comfort. And then I slouched into the bathroom.

I looked at myself in the dirty mirror, my hands clutching the sink, and I couldn't stop the flood of tears that raced down my cheeks. My phone vibrated. Jeremy. I took in a deep breath and tried to pull it together so that Jeremy wouldn't know how completely devastated I felt at the moment. It was good he called. I needed to tell him about the kids in that dungeon.

"Jeremy?"

"I talked to Halluis. He said Alexander took you somewhere in the house that blocked his ability to hear what was going on. He said you left the house completely distraught. What happened? Where did he take you?"

I looked up to the ceiling to help curb my increasing desire to lose it. "He took me to a basement room where...where he's keeping prisoners to ship off with the cars. He's going to sell them as slaves." I took a deep breath. "They're only kids. Not a one older than twenty. And Jeremy," my voice cracked here, and I slapped my hand over my mouth and pressed my lips together.

"Christy?"

I removed my hand. I had to get it out. I had to tell someone who would understand how I was feeling. "They had Hank. Called him a snitch and shot him in the head. They killed that sweet boy." Fresh tears flooded my eyes, and I looked back to the ceiling. I couldn't let the other lifters know I'd been crying.

"I could kill Halluis—he should have been in there the second you were in danger."

Irrational rage was evident in his voice. I forced myself to pull it together, closing my eyes and taking a cleansing breath through my nose. "It's not his fault, Jeremy, and you know it. Besides you can't kill him. We still need him. I put 98% of what was on Alexander's computer on a jump drive on a lip underneath the dining room table. If anyone can get it back, it's Halluis. We'll want the information on that drive, I'm sure of it."

"No, we don't need it. The mission's off. That's what I called to tell you in the first place. You don't have to go out there again."

"What? What are you talking about?"

"I've uncovered the reason the director wants the car. No one hired us."

I furrowed my brow. His breathing sped up. "Apparently, Central Division Director Kettering inherited a car from his father's estate. A 1959 Mercedes Benz 300 SL Gullwing Coupe."

"What?"

"Yep. The Mercedes 300 we've been searching for and putting everyone's lives in danger belongs to Director Kettering."

I let that sink in. "I don't get it. Did he tell Director Skriloff to retrieve it at all costs?"

"No. The car was in probate, and he couldn't take it to Belgium until it cleared. He needed to keep it somewhere secure, and Director Skriloff insisted he store it at his estate because it was so secure and a better place than a storage unit."

"Huh."

"Well, it turns out, Skriloff's son took it for a spin to a nightclub, and it got stolen while parked in the garage. Skriloff was afraid he'd lose his job, so he gave us the mission to retrieve it. It was all to save his butt. It's time to call this mission off. I'm not willing to risk your life and the lives of the whole team for the likes of Skriloff."

For a few sweet seconds, relief washed over me. "I can't tell you how happy that makes me," I blurted. Then reality hit. "But—wait. Those kids. We have to save those kids." Horror gripped me once again.

"What?"

"It's not about the car anymore. Those kids that

were in the dungeon are going to be sold. As slaves. We can't let that happen."

"Kozlov is on the case, remember? He's going to bring the whole bratva down."

"In a year! In a year, those kids will be long gone and at the mercy of who knows who, being forced to do who knows what. I think this is the reason I had that feeling the other day about sticking with this mission. It was for these kids. We have to save them."

Silence.

"Jeremy. I don't care about that car and the Skriloff sent us on, but I do care about those kids." Echoes of Hank's murder rushed through me. "We can save them. We can't quit now."

Jeremy swore quietly. "You're right. I hate it, but you're right—we have to go through with it. I'll get with Halluis and Ace and work out a plan to get the kids from the basement."

"That's the thing. They took those kids to a different location. I have no idea where."

"Nothing can be easy, can it? I guess we go forward with finding the docks where the cars are to be taken and wait for the kids to be loaded. What's your location? I'll tell Halluis, so he can get back on your shadow."

"No!" I insisted. "Halluis has to get that drive. It could tell us where he's holding the kids—we'll need that if we have any hope of getting them out of there before the ship sails."

"All right, then, but if the information is on that drive, then you don't need to go out there at all. We can get everything we need from the files."

"Maybe, but I didn't get a chance to look at them. I only saw the papers in the box under the desk. The information about where they're keeping the kids may be in the files, but maybe not. If I stay in the field, it gives us another chance to find out when the shipment goes out, where they're shipping from, and where they're keeping the kids. We need to do it all."

Jeremy sighed in exasperation. I knew he was looking for a way around it, but there was none.

"Don't worry about me. I'll be careful."

"No, I'm not leaving you on your own with these guys. I'll be your shadow tonight. No arguing."

I paused. I found I didn't want to refuse the offer of his protection.

"Fine, but I don't know where I'll be."

"I'll find you."

I didn't doubt that.

"Be safe. Be careful."

"I'll see you later."

I moved with purpose out of the restaurant, feeling a bit better than I had when I'd entered it, and two minutes later I was in position to meet up with my partner.

Mikado met me again.

"Hey." He rubbed his hands on his pants, probably for warmth.

"You ready?" I hoped all traces of my mourning were gone. I could see my breath freeze in big puffs.

"Yeah. I'm ready for our time off next week." He walked toward the marked car.

"We get time off?" This was interesting news.

"Yeah. Tonight's the last night we can lift for this

shipment. And we always get a week off after a successful shipment."

I nodded. I needed to find an opportunity to give that information to Jeremy and the team. We were not ready for this. We still didn't know which pier for sure the bratva worked out of. I'd text them once I knew which one. We suspected Red Hook because of the information that Carson's family owned a shipping company that worked out of Red Hook, but we hadn't been able to confirm anything. As soon as I could find out, confirmation was on its way.

"Ah, makes sense. I guess they need a few days to load them up. I'm assuming they go on a ship or something." We reached the car and started the process of taking it.

"Nah. It doesn't take that long. Most of the containers got loaded today. An entire ship can get loaded in less than an hour. It's like fifteen thousand containers. It's quite amazing. Of course, this shipment is different. The final containers arrive on the pier in trucks during the night. I mean they just look like semis, you know? Like the ones we drive the cars into. By this time there'll only be a few that haven't arrived yet, and the cars we all steal tonight will be loaded into containers on the pier. The ship will leave as soon as it's loaded—probably before light of day."

I huffed as we finished breaking through the car's security features and started the process of hotwiring it. "Interesting. Do you help load or something?" Information from the box beneath Alexander's desk started playing in my mind, and part of my brain started working on figuring that out.

"Heck, no. But I've seen it done a few times. You'll see it tonight. It makes me sick to see how efficient and effortless it all is for them."

So Kozlov had been wrong—or had he just played up the impossibility of finding the car in order to put us off the mission? It didn't matter. I'd be on the pier where the cars were going out. That meant I'd have a chance of finding those kids—if only I could discover where they were being kept. The car roared to life, and we sped down the city streets, expertly weaving through the traffic.

We pulled up to a closed gate right outside Red Hook, and Mikado typed something into his phone. The gate slid open, and we pulled inside. Only then did I notice the six guards with heavy-duty guns pointed at the car.

"Boy, they take this seriously, don't they?"

He nodded. "This is big business. Like ten million a shipment—just for the cars. There's also all kinds of other stuff on that ship—food, clothes, computer equipment...everything you can think of."

I whistled as he drove the car right into a container. Jeremy had to be seeing what was happening. They had to now know where I was, but just to make sure, I pocket texted the team about which pier we were at and that we were bringing new cars in tonight because the ship sailed before dawn.

We got out, and men rushed in to make the changes to the VIN and the paperwork. Jericho was there in a car near the gate and motioned to us to come to him.

"He's our ride," Mikado said as we walked toward him.

"First one in tonight?" Jericho said.

"Yep." Mikado said as he jumped into the back seat.

I sat in the front, but instead of feeling a chill, I felt heat. We were about to free those kids, maybe this is where that van was headed, and then an anonymous tip could lead the FBI to the shipping yard to retrieve not just one car but all the cars slated for shipment. A pleasant feeling of satisfaction filled me, and a plan started formulating in my mind.

"It's my third. Something slowing you down?" He looked pointedly at me.

"Nah, we were way over in Bensonhurst." Mikado spoke devoid of derision. He'd obviously learned how to handle Jericho.

"Not this time. We're both headed for Prospect Park for this next lift."

He parked the car in a ritzy section near the park, and Mikado and I went one way and he went the other.

We both pulled up to the pier at the same time. I took notice of everything in the pier this time. I knew where every guard was and every camera and every worker. There were no longer any guards at the gate. Only the cameras kept watch.

I watched as Gina and Karina drove out with another guy before we drove in. I guessed everyone was working tonight. We went back out four more times. The third time back in, I saw the director's Mercedes 300 sitting in front of an empty container labeled ABCU 1654347. It would have been an easy thing to get inside and drive away with it, but that was no longer my goal. I had to save those kids, and I had a plan.

I only needed Jeremy to have someone outside the

gates to take us away from this place to safety. I was going to free them tonight. They had to already be at the yard, waiting to be loaded. At least, I hoped they hadn't already been loaded. I texted the team my plan and what I needed from them. Now I simply had to have faith they would be there.

After the last drop, Jericho took us to a subway entrance and dropped us off.

"Looks like the ship will be leaving in a few hours, huh?" My mind was whirring. We had to stop that ship.

"Most likely," Mikado said. "Just think of all the money the bratva will get from this. And we're the ones making it happen." He spat. "Makes me sick."

"Mikado." I touched his arm, his puffy coat sinking under the pressure.

He stopped. Dark shadows hung over us in the meager light from the few streetlights above the area.

"Listen." I kept my voice even, matter of fact. "I'm sorry I didn't listen to you about Viktor. You were right. And your boss, Alexander, he killed a boy right in front of me. It was awful. They shouldn't be able to do this."

"There's no turning back now." He started to walk along the platform, and I stopped him again.

This was it. It was my chance to turn him. "What if there was a way to make a difference?"

He narrowed his eyes at me.

I swallowed hard. "What if there was a way to put an end to it all?"

Chapter 26

He shook his head. "There is no way to end it. I've gone over every scenario I can think of, and there is no way to beat the bratva. You and I, we're stuck. Forever." He started to walk away again, his shoes thudding on the dirty sidewalk.

"Mikado, you know we have to stop this," I blurted.

He stopped, twisted back to me and said, "What are you talking about? There's nothing we can do, and even if we could, it would be suicide. Some rich people lost their cars, sad day for them. You'll have to learn to deal with the guilt in your own way." He turned back and walked on. A car passed by us, but other than that, no one was around.

"Mikado," I yelled out. "It's more than just the cars." He stopped again, and I moved toward him, speaking more quietly. "They're also shipping a container of kids to Africa to be sold as slaves."

"You've lost it." He threw his hands above his head as he walked, clearly exasperated.

I ran after him. I took hold of his arm, and he

stopped and sighed loudly. I walked around him to face him. "I think you know what I'm talking about. You don't want to think about it—you don't want to admit your part in it—but you know it, don't you?"

Mikado just stared at me, but he didn't turn or try to walk away.

"You know I'm telling the truth."

Finally, Mikado looked down, shame marring his features. "So? So I know, what good does that do anyone? There's nothing we can do. And if we tried, we'd end up just like them."

"What if I told you that if you got me inside, I'd be able to get the kids out without getting caught?"

"I'd say you were a liar or delusional. Alexander has an army in there." He raised an eyebrow.

"I have a plan to end this, but I need you."

He didn't move or speak, just stared at me.

"All we need to do is get into the office—I need to get my eyes on the documents and find out where they're keeping the kids. No one would even know. You saw all the chaos. We could make a difference, Mikado."

Something shifted in his eyes and posture, like a weight was just lifted. He looked up to the dark sky.

"If we get caught," I said. "I'll say it was me, that I threatened your family or something."

He snorted. "You think he'd care? Not even." He folded his hands over his stomach.

"You're right. Just get me in and leave me...You get out."

"No way. I'd feel responsible for what happened to you."

My heart thudded with hope for him. He was a really

good guy stuck in an impossible situation. I had to help him. He didn't belong with these awful people. I took a deep breath, leaned into him and whispered, "What if I told you I knew some people who could relocate you and your family and get you out of the bratva?"

He grabbed my arm and whispered back, "Are you telling me you're working for someone? That you're undercover?"

"I can't explain, but I can tell you we're not alone. We can do this, and once it's all over, I can promise you you'll be done with the bratva forever."

"So, this is why you got involved with Viktor?" He rubbed his hand through his hair. "Who is it? The FBI?"

"I can't tell you that. But I do know they can save you and your family, and you would finally be free. All you have to do is get me access to that shipyard." I could tell he was seriously considering it. A nasty wind had picked up. I should have felt cold, but I didn't.

"I don't know." He looked all around.

"Well, I'm going back, with or without you—but it would be easier if I had you to help me." I started back up the stairs when he called out to me.

"Wait." He ran to me. "You swear you can get me and my family out of here?"

"I swear." I looked him directly in the eyes.

"Okay. I'll help you get in. And the FBI or whoever is helping you, they can help you get out, right?"

"Right." Jeremy would never let the bratva get their hands on me.

Mikado stood still in his eerie way for a moment, then nodded.

"Awesome." I pressed a palm to my heart. "You'll see. Everything will work out. Thank you. I'm going to give you a number to call after we're in. What's your number?"

He gave it to me.

"Excellent." My skin tingled and an empty feeling settled in my stomach as nerves about going up against Alexander hit me. I kept to the task at hand to distract me. "I'm texting it to you right now. Call that number and say, 'I can't believe I dialed the wrong number six times in a row.' They will then give you the coordinates of a phone. On that phone you will find contact information that will get you to safety." My mouth went dry and a feeling of giddiness washed over me thinking that Mikado, at least, would be safe.

I knew once I was inside the shipyard, Jeremy would be there with the team watching over me, and as I drove out with the stolen kids, he would be there to back me up and help me get the kids to safety. I sent the team a text telling them Mikado and I were going back in and to stand by.

Mikado and I stole a car from the street, and he pulled out his phone again before climbing in. Looking more closely, though, I could see it wasn't a phone. He explained to me how to use the gadget when I entered and exited the yard. It was essentially a gate opener, but it documented which opener had been used to open it each time and triggered a camera to snap pictures of the car as it entered. The picture of the person driving was then matched to their database. If there was no match, an alarm would be raised and guards would be sent to retrieve the driver.

It seemed to occur to me and him at the same moment what that meant. Mikado had to go inside with me or it would trigger the alarm. I'd hoped to take the opener and have him take off and get into witness protection before I retrieved the car.

"It's no big deal," he shook his head and rolled his eyes. "I'll go in with you, and we'll drive the car out. Then I'll be gone, and you'll be gone, and we can forget about the bratva once and for all."

My chest squeezed, and it felt like a balloon was inflating in my throat. "I don't expect it to, Mikado, but it could go very wrong."

"My life is already really wrong. At least this will give me and my family the chance to get out of this. Let's go." He slid into the driver's seat, and I ran around the car and hopped into the passenger seat and then slid down so that no camera would pick me up. He drove the couple blocks to the yard and pushed the button on the opener.

"It's opening. That's a good sign. They didn't only restrict me to a particular number of opens today. Sometimes they do that." After a thirty-second pause, the car moved forward through the gate. Since I was out of sight, I checked my phone and quickly scanned through the messages I'd received from Halluis and Jeremy. Halluis had retrieved the drive, and Ace had started decrypting files, looking for information about the kids. Jeremy said they would be ready for us when we got out. The car stopped, and Mikado said, "All right. You can sit up."

I pocketed the phone and sat up. He'd parked next to the office building. "I'll go in and search for the container with the kids. You wait here." People were rushing about, loading cars into containers and working on the VINs and documentation of others, some workers just ran from place to place, and I had no idea what they were doing.

"Wait here, act like you belong, and we'll be out of here in no time," I said, climbing out of the car.

No one seemed to be paying me any attention, and I opened the door to the office. I knew from my study of cargo ships only a few days ago that one guy organized exactly where each and every container would go on the ship before they were loaded according to weight and contents. Each container was tracked using a specific code. That information was fed to the crane operators and truck drivers to get the right containers located in the right spot at the right time. It was a very complex process. All I had to do was get my eyes on the list of containers and look for the one with the kids in it.

Since loading was in process, I'd have to disable the man behind the computer, and if the container with the would-be slaves had already been loaded, I'd have to disable a crane operator, too. I could do this. I peeked quickly through the window in the door—the reception room of the office was empty. I opened the door and walked into the office, acting like I knew exactly what I was doing.

Just as I entered, I got a text from Halluis. *Slaves not listed as cargo. They are using code. Try these three words for the description of contents: livestock, auction, new merchandise. Cars are listed in code also, but the code varies with the different cars.* I checked out the empty room. Nothing of consequence caught my eye, but there was a door behind the counter. I headed toward it.

It was obvious that I'd found the right room. A thin man with wire-rimmed glasses and super pale skin looked up at me. He must be the man who pulled the strings and told the crane operators where each container was to be put. I pulled out my knife and in two steps, I had it on his neck and his hands behind his back before he could react to my presence.

"I need you to pull up the cargo manifest."

"Never." He spoke through clenched teeth. I didn't wait; I didn't have time to negotiate. I slid the knife into my boot and with one pressured movement at his neck, I knocked him out. I slid him off the seat and called Ace.

"I'm sitting in front of the computer." I then explained to him what I was seeing on the screen.

"Okay, you'll need to access the ship's cargo manifest," he said. I felt a twinge in my heart as he patiently walked me through the process, utter calm emanating from his voice. I hadn't stopped to think about the consequences of going off mission—for all of us. If we didn't retrieve the car tonight, Director Skriloff would probably find a way to have us all fired.

"Ace—Jeremy told you and Halluis what's going on?"

There was a pause on the line. "You got that last step, right?"

"Yeah, I got it. But listen, I just want—I mean, I need to make sure you guys understand—"

"Christy." Ace cut me off. "What did we tell you? You're our girl, and we're with you one hundred percent."

"Ace—"

"Don't worry about us. If we lose our jobs, big deal. Those kids are more important than any job, and we all agree on that."

Suddenly, Halluis's voice was coming over the line, muffled as if he were trying to pull the phone away from Ace.

"Of course, if you could pull off a miracle and rescue the director's car at the same time, we would not be ungrateful."

There was a brief scuffle, then Ace was back on the line. "Don't listen to him. You do what you have to do to save those kids and get yourself out of there safe."

"You've got it, Ace," I said, barely containing a grin.

"All right, last step," he said, and mere seconds later I was looking at the ship's cargo manifest.

"I'm in. I've gotta go."

"Okay. Just remember—don't be out past curfew, young lady."

He hung up, and I scrolled through the manifest, my photographic memory seeing and cataloging the information in an instant. No livestock. Twenty new merchandise and one labeled auction. A zing touched my heart, and I just knew the container had to be the one labeled auction. I captured the container code and location. It had already been loaded. Crap! I went to the Internet and pulled up a guide on operating an onboard crane on a ship. I scrolled through it, the much-needed information now trapped in my brain, but not yet understood. I clicked back to the cargo manifest and stood up. If I were quick, I'd have the container back on the pier before the man woke up. I hoped no one would go into the office before then.

A fierce chill hit me. Carson stood by the door staring at me, betrayal and question all over his face.

Chapter 27

My first instinct was to reach for the knife, but I overrode my training and said, "Carson. Give me one minute to explain, and then if you still want to you can alert someone to my presence after that." Of course, I wouldn't allow that if it came to it, but I hoped it wouldn't. He could help. "Alexander put a container of kids onto this ship to be sold as slaves. I'm here to save them. I found the container and with your help I can unload it and save their lives."

"What?" His eyes narrowed. "Who are you?"

I knew repeating my name wouldn't be enough. "I work with some people who are trying to bring down the bratva."

He tilted his head to the ceiling and huffed. "No wonder you went for one of the worst guys in school. It didn't make any sense."

"I'm sorry I lied to you, Carson, but the clock is ticking." I looked down at the guy on the floor.

Carson took a step forward and pulled on a drawer. My hand grabbed his, and I stopped him, afraid I'd lost the battle with him. He didn't struggle, just said, "Whoa! I'm getting some tape."

"Oh." I released my hold. He was going to help.

In the drawer were all kinds of various tapes. I grabbed the duct tape and taped the fallen man's mouth and his arms, attaching him to a locked cabinet. Carson grabbed something from the drawer and pocketed it. As we walked out of the inner office, Carson locked the door and looked up at me grimly. He knew what he was sacrificing to do this. He knew the risks, and he was doing it anyway. A new layer of respect for him fell over me.

"Thank you, Carson. I will do everything I can to keep you safe."

"I believe you want to, but I know you may not be able to. I've been a coward my whole life. It's time I break free and do something my conscience has been telling me to do for a long time." His look was sad and resigned, and yet totally determined. "I hate these guys. Let's do something that will really hurt them."

I smiled. "But let's do it carefully and not get caught." I moved around the counter toward the door that led out of the main office.

"No problem." He followed me.

Mikado still sat in the car. I wanted him to stay there, he was in the getaway car, so I didn't approach him. I continued past the car toward the large crane, keeping my pace even so I wouldn't draw any extra attention.

I walked with purpose, like I belonged, and I hoped Carson was just as confident.

I was about to climb the safety escape ladder of the

crane, when Carson put his hand on my arm. "Hold on."

I turned to him.

"Do you even know how to operate one of those?"

"I read the manual."

"Oh, man. It takes practice. Lots of practice, and if you expect to do it unnoticed, you need someone experienced."

"I'm all there is, Carson." I turned and started to climb.

"Get down. I can do it."

"Are you sure?"

"Yes. I've filled in for crane operators a bunch of times."

I started down, then realized the crane operator would need to be taken care of. "You can operate it, but I need to take the crane operator out."

He pulled out a radio. "John. I'm seeing sparks from the underbelly. Come on down."

Almost immediately, the box began to lower. I stepped off the ladder.

I nodded at him and thought, *Please be ready, Jeremy.*

I crouched behind some large boxes to get out of sight.

"I can't reach Grayden," Carson said to the crane operator. "I think he's helping someone out in the dead zone on the ship. Could you get him? I need to check in some cars real quick so we don't fall even further behind."

"He was supposed to have fixed this last week."

"Yeah. I think someone may be searching for a new

job soon." Carson turned to go and so did the crane operator. After he walked a few more steps, Carson turned back to the crane and hopped inside. "Amber?"

I came out of hiding. "Yeah?"

"Tell me you know the container number."

I gave it to him, and he wrote it down on a sheet of paper. "I'll hurry as fast as I can. I know just the place to set it down."

"I'll be here." I watched as he grabbed the container with the hooks. It had been right by the bridge, I guessed for easy access to feed the prisoners. I would have thought they would have hidden the container so that the chances of it being searched would be less. He worked with precision and made it look easy, even though I knew it couldn't be. The precaution and trouble-shooting sections of the manual had been quite daunting.

Immediately after the container touched ground, Carson popped out and moved quickly toward the container. I caught up with him and stopped him. "You're done, Carson."

"What?"

"I want you safe. You've done your part. I know where the container is. I'll get the kids out. You go back to your office, and as soon as you see Mikado and me drive out the gate, go free your cargo master."

"Do you have one of these?" He pulled out a tool from his pocket. It was the item he'd grabbed from the drawer after handing me the tape. "You need it to get into the containers." He started walking again.

"Just give it to me. I don't want you involved any more than you already are." I grabbed his arm.

"Sorry. I'm already involved, and I need to show you how to use it. I thought we were in a hurry."

As soon as we rounded the corner on the container with the slaves in it, he used the tool to open the container. I reached to pull it open, but I heard a voice that froze my hand.

"I'm hurt. Really, Amber." Alexander spoke.

I swallowed hard, closed my eyes, and turned slowly but surely, opening my eyes before I faced him. I would not cower. Instead, I glared.

"What, did those kids tug at your heart? And you thought you, little old you, could save them?"

A new guard showed up and put a padlock on the container Carson had just unlocked and then the arms of the crane came down and lifted it up. Men with rifles descended on us, and Carson put his hands in the air. It seemed like the proper thing to do, so I did too.

I looked quickly around, hoping beyond hope that Jeremy was seeing what was happening. His name even slipped from my lips. Carson's face was blank as he stared forward.

I needed to run. I needed to fight. Instead, tears rushed out of my eyes as a guard threw me to the ground. My cheek burned as it slid over the rough asphalt ground. I couldn't even scream out. Hollowness filled me.

The guards tied my hands behind my back with a thick plastic zip tie—one of the hardest bonds to get out of. I could do it with my hands in front, but with them tied behind me and plenty of guards watching, there would be no escaping this.

Two guards lifted me and shoved me roughly to the

ground in another spot. I stared up at Carson next to me, he looked forward, his body stiff. Seconds later, Mikado's body slammed into mine, shifting me up against Carson and forcing him to sway to the side. He recovered quickly, returning to his stony look and position. I wriggled myself into a sitting position, and Mikado followed my lead.

"Don't worry about me," he whispered. "It's better that I die now and end the shame I've brought to my family. I will take the blame."

"No," I hissed. "You will not." In my mind, I thought of Jeremy and Division, and a hope lit inside me that we would all be saved. "I'm taking the blame."

I glanced up when someone cleared his throat. Alexander, flanked by four guards with guns stood before me, a slight smile on his lips. He tsked. "You know, Amber, I would have thought that my demonstration earlier tonight would have been enough to curb that hot will I sensed in you. Instead, you choose to try to steal from me?" He chuckled. "And you seem to have roped these two soldiers into your little scheme. What exactly did you do to turn them? What promises did you make them? What promises have already been fulfilled?"

A rumble of people shifting and muttering came from behind the brigadier, and Agent Kozlov appeared out of the crowd to the side of Alexander's guards.

"What in the devil? We're already behind—" His voice was deep and yet somehow sharp. His eyes lit on mine, recognition flitting through. His lips pressed together, and air rushed from his nose. I was saved. Jeremy had sent Kozlov to save us. Relief washed over me.

"Alexander? What is happening here?" He spoke in Russian.

"Nothing you need to concern yourself with. Just a tiny rebellion that I am about to put down." He nodded to his guards, three of whom raised their guns, pointing them directly at our heads.

Kozlov pressed down on the arm of the guard directly next to him. "I asked," his voice was insistent, "what was going on here."

I'd never been so glad to see anyone before, but a tightness gripped my heart. In order to save me and the others, he would end up exposing himself.

"Sorry, sir," Alexander said. "I didn't want to bother you with the details. Vlad never wanted to know."

Kozlov raised an eyebrow. "I am not Vlad. And you know he's indisposed. We've already had this discussion. If you have a problem with that, then you need to bring it up with the *Pakhan*."

It occurred to me that even though Kozlov was technically above Alexander in the bratva's pecking order, he wasn't even on the same branch as Alexander. How had he gotten here?

Alexander spoke, "I don't. It's just, this girl was attempting to steal from us and convinced these two boys to help her."

"Really?" Kozlov stared down at me like I was a piece of meat as he circled the three of us. I suddenly felt unsure of his role as our savior. "I wonder how she did that? Is she the lead *vory*?"

"No. That's Jericho."

"And where is Jericho, and why hasn't he been able

to control his crew?" Kozlov snarled.

"He's on a run. Should be arriving soon with his last car." Alexander seemed to be groveling a bit.

"Looks like he should have had his attentions elsewhere." Kozlov kicked Mikado. He switched to English. "And you, Carson. How did you get caught up in this little revolt? We've worked so well with your family for so long. You know we don't deal well with betrayal. What will your parents say?"

"Don't blame him," I shot. "He didn't know I was planning this. He was in the wrong place at the wrong time."

Someone kicked me from behind, and I barely had a chance to turn my head before it smashed into the ground.

"Don't speak unless spoken to, girl!" Alexander huffed.

"I wasn't thinking, sir," Carson said. His voice flat, but void of fear. "She tricked me. I'm sorry to have betrayed you and my family."

Kozlov snorted. I rolled to my side just in time to see a car pull into the yard. Jericho. I closed my eyes and breathed in hard.

He marched up to us after parking the final car. "What's going on?"

"Jericho?" Kozlov said. "Are these pieces of dirt part of your crew?"

His eyes widened in terror. "Yes, sir. At least Mikado and Amber."

"And did you not teach them about loyalty and honor?"

"I did, sir." Jericho's face actually blanched.

"Then why were they caught in the act of trying to steal from the *Pakhan*?"

Jericho looked confused, but didn't seem to want to ask any questions. "I don't know, sir. I'm sorry, sir."

"Perhaps you should be on the ground with them."

Alexander stepped forward. "I have a better plan for him, sir, if you will allow it."

Kozlov turned his attention to Alexander. "And what would that be?" The menacing look he gave Alexander made me shudder.

"He should be the one to administer the punishment." One of Alexander's guards stepped forward and handed his gun to Jericho.

Jericho immediately pointed it at me.

Kozlov stepped forward. "I don't think so. I have a better idea for these sorry little beggars." He picked me up, forcing me to stand. His eyes were hard as he stared into mine. This was Jeremy's friend? Had he gotten himself assigned to this ship just to stop us from succeeding? Had our meeting backfired on us? Once again I thought of Jeremy and hoped he was watching. "I bet she used her womanly wiles to get you to act tonight. Is that how she tricked you?" His gaze landed on Carson.

He nodded.

"I couldn't hear you." He kicked Carson.

"Yes, sir. Sorry, sir." Carson's face angled down.

"Yes." His hand held my chin up as he examined my face. "She has a good face. A little scraped up at the moment. But that will heal." He spoke as if to himself. "You a virgin, girl?"

My eyes involuntarily turned the size of apricots.

277

This was not good.

He squeezed my chin, hard. "Well?"

I spit in his face.

"I think that gives me my answer. Excellent. I'll get a high price for her."

"What?" I spluttered.

He let go of my chin and turned to Alexander. "Instead of you shooting her, we will send her somewhere her skills will be appreciated." An ugly smirk fell on his face, and Alexander chuckled. An awful sound that sent a hailstorm through my gut. "Don't you think that is fitting punishment, Alexander?"

He nodded. "Yes, sir."

He turned on Mikado. "And you. I won't have any trouble finding a place for a pretty boy like you."

Mikado growled, showing his teeth. "I won't. You'll have to kill me. You may as well get it over with right now."

Kozlov's vengeance was swift and hard. His hand sent Mikado flying back with an extremely hard blow to the head. Mikado didn't move from his awkward position on the ground. Only Carson remained to discover his fate.

But Kozlov turned to Jericho instead. "And you. You will accompany me on this journey to ensure my two new prized possessions arrive at their new home. Maybe I'll be able to teach you how to inspire loyalty on the way there. We don't have any containers available for their shipment. They will need to be kept in the belly of the ship. You don't have any plans for the next two weeks do you?"

Jericho's eyes narrowed at me. "No, sir." I guess he figured he didn't have the option to say he did.

"It's settled then." Kozlov smiled. "And as for this boy," he swung his head toward Carson. "It's unfortunate that his parents didn't teach him well enough to keep him alive. I think his parents need a little lesson too." Kozlov nodded to Alexander, who nodded to Jericho and with the click of Jericho's trigger, and deafening bang of a gun, Carson slumped to the ground.

I screamed, lunging toward his lifeless body. A fist hit me in the side of the head. Stars and blackness met me.

Chapter 28

I woke to discover my body tied spread eagle on a bed in a small room with no window. Panic trilled through me. I was on the ship. My head pounded. I looked at the zip ties that bound me to the bed. I tested them, they were tightened perfectly. Not too tight and not too loose. Because I was spread eagle, none of the methods I knew for breaking the ties would work. I did spend some time trying to slip my hand out, but the ties only dug into me more. I couldn't shim them, and I couldn't use brute force against them. I was a sitting duck.

Memories of Carson's body slumping to the ground hit me. There was no mistaking it. I was the reason he was dead. Me and me alone. He'd tried to warn me about what happened to people who got involved with Viktor, and now my actions had ended his life.

Mikado. Where was he? I looked around the room. He was not with me. I had to find him and save him. I could not let more blood be spilt on my account. I played with my bonds for a little while longer and had to accept the reality that there was no way to undo them without help. I would have to take my chances with the guards.

"Help me!" I yelled. "Help! I need to pee. Please. Please. Somebody! Anybody! I need to pee." I had to have someone untie me. Once I was free, I would take them out. I hoped my body would respond to my call and function as I needed it to. I continued to yell until my voice started to strain and go hoarse.

Two bulky men finally came.

"I'm so glad you're here. I totally have to go. Untie me, please."

"Not happening," one of the guys said. "I couldn't care less if you wet yourself." He turned to go.

The other guy said, "But that guy said he had plans with her later." He made a rude gesture when his partner looked back. "What harm would it do? It's not like she could do us any damage."

The other guy laughed. "You got that right." They cut me loose. They pushed me toward the bathroom where I actually did use the bathroom. There were towels and even soap waiting for me to use. I did and then collected the ceramic covers for the bolts that held the toilet to the floor, a body towel, the bar of soap, and the two-foot mirror that hung on the wall above the sink. These guards had totally underestimated me. I then stood in front of the door and waited.

At long last, a guard knocked on the door once. I didn't respond, I simply readied myself. When he knocked again, I threw the door open, capitalizing on surprise. The door slammed into the guard who'd knocked and sent him flying back into the metal bed frame where he smacked his head hard and slid to the floor. I didn't waste a single second.

With speed and accuracy, I flung one of the hard ceramic bolt covers directly at the Adam's apple of the other guard. He clutched at his throat and bent over at the waist, trying for air that would not come. I whipped around and chucked the second bolt cover at the guard who had stumbled and hit his head. He flinched to the side, and it barely missed him. I set the mirror down, resting it on the doorjamb.

His eyes gleamed with hatred, and he stormed toward me. In one step he'd be upon me. I wound up the towel and took a step back, whipping him in the face, momentarily blinding him. The other guard was now writhing on his back, hands still clutched around his throat. The guard I whipped struck out with his foot, sending the door sailing into me as it tried to close. I stumbled back, still clutching the towel. The door swung back toward the whipped guard, who kicked it again. It slammed into the mirror that I'd propped on the doorjamb as I'd flung the door open.

He lunged for me, and I jumped onto the bed, snagging the pillow as I went and sliding the cover off it. He lunged again, and I'd intended to jump off the bed, but the pressure made me sink into the soft bed, slowing me down. His hand got a hold of my ankle, and I fell backwards off the bed, landing with a thud into the wall opposite us.

My head cracked back, and a moan escaped my lips. Stars scrambled my eyes, and I shook my head to catch my bearings. He was upon me, his thick hands crushing my neck. I let go of the towel and in one swift motion, grabbed the other end of the pillowcase and pushed it up at his neck, then brought my knee up for a nice groin hit. His hands released their hold, and he rolled over in pain, clutching his crotch, fire in his eyes. I grabbed the lamp beside the bed and whacked him over the head with it. It didn't stop him; it only seemed to make him more mad.

His legs shot out, clipping mine and throwing me to the floor. All the air whooshed out of me, and my hands flew above my head, one landing in the pile of mirror fragments. He was now sitting on the edge of the bed, a gun pointed at my face.

"I give," I called out, palming a shard of glass as I brought my hands to my waist. "I give."

He kicked my leg. "If I didn't have strict orders not to kill you, you'd have a bullet in your head right now."

I sat up, noticing that the guard I'd hit with the bolt cover no longer struggled. I swallowed hard, tasting bile.

"Get up here," he said in a flat voice, the gun trained on my chest now.

I stood and he did too, giving me access to the bed. In effect, we switched positions. I lay back, ready to be tied up only to cut myself loose after he left the room. But then he sneered at me. "I know what you'll be doing in Africa, and I think after what you've done, that it's only fair that I get a piece of you before you go."

A shiver that turned into a flame flowed through me as he moved toward me, a horrid look of nasty anticipation on his face. I let him get close enough that it would only take one double strike to disable him. One of my arms jutted out to whack his gun hand and the other pushed the shard of glass into his eye. I had been aiming for his jugular, but missed as he adjusted to my initial strike. He called out in pain, dropping the gun. I grabbed the gun and hit him hard in the temple. He fell on the bed.

I tied his arms using the restraints they'd used on me and pulled the glass from his eye. I used the pillowcase to tie around his head to stop the bleeding. There was no sense in letting him die, too, even though he was a total scumbag. I hoped he would be around when the bratva fell. I'd be the first one in line to testify against him.

I tucked the gun into my waistband and used a piece of the mirror to look under the door and see if the way was clear. We'd been so noisy, no one could have been anywhere near or they would have heard us. Then I remembered how long I'd had to scream in order to get anyone to come. We must be far away from anyone.

I walked out into a narrow, completely white hall. I was in the last room in the hallway. I hurried to the opposite end of the hall and found a door. A locked door. I felt in my hair for bobby pins, but found none. I looked back to the room. One of those two guards had to have keys. I rolled my eyes and headed back. In my rush, I'd left a lot of valuable things that, had I been in my right mind, I never would have left behind. I stuffed the other guard's gun in one boot, then took both sets of keys.

I hurried back down the hall to the door and unlocked it, prepared to find more guards just outside, but no one was there. I must have been in the bottom-most accommodations in the belly of the ship near the front third of it. The rear was filled almost exclusively with containers or cells. Above me were more accommodations, the galley, and then the bridge. Once I found Mikado and the kids I'd have to deploy a lifeboat. I had no clue how I'd accomplish it without running into others. And I had no idea how loud such a process might be or how long it would take to lower the boat. Unfortunately, besides the engine room, the majority of people were to be found in the area I'd have to traverse. I prayed that the others were sleeping soundly.

I sifted through all the information I'd ever read or learned about container ships. While they weren't all the same, they had the same elements. I had a long way to go to get out, and I most likely would not find a clear path. I wondered how long I'd been on the ship, just how far I was out to sea. There were no windows to judge by, so I had no idea what time it was—we could have been moving for hours or days, I wouldn't know. I had to push that thought away for fear that the idea would overtake me as I began my precarious ascent. I had to focus on the fact that I would soon be outside in the fresh air.

Typically, a ship like this, even as huge as it was, would only need ten to twelve crew members, but something told me there would be many more on this ship. Usually only one third was awake at any given time, which worked to my advantage—at least I hoped it did. If they doubled the amount of crew members to help ensure the arrival of the containers, then I had somewhere around fourteen people I had to avoid in this area alone. With any luck, there wouldn't be a shift change as I made my way up.

I very carefully and methodically made my way up, stopping only long enough to look at a clock in an unoccupied room. The clock read five a.m. We had at least an hour and a half of darkness before dawn hit. There was such relief in not being time deficient any longer.

Someone walked out of a room about twenty feet in front of me. I froze. To my sides were only ship walls, no doors. I was completely exposed. But he didn't see me—he was facing the other way and made his way quickly up the hall and through a door at the end of it. The door shut with a clang behind him.

I shoved a hard breath out and stared forward again until I heard footsteps. At this point, I was only a few feet from a door. I flung myself inside and readied to fight if need be.

I realized someone was behind me only seconds before a hand went over my mouth. I twisted, ready to strike and stopped just in time. It was Jeremy. My legs wobbled slightly, and I covered my mouth with a trembling hand. I fell into his arms, and he dragged me to the open closet and said, "Shh!" as he pulled the door silently shut. We heard the click of a door opening, and light filtered under the door. A person walked across the floor, opened a drawer, shut it, and then walked back out, the door clicking shut behind him.

When the coast was clear, I couldn't help releasing a little sigh of a laugh and wrapping my arms tightly around Jeremy.

"You're here! I can't believe you're really here."

"Of course I am," he said gently, holding me even

closer. "I told you I would find you."

I nodded, not trusting myself to speak. My insides sparked with happiness at being with Jeremy, and so close at that. Everything suddenly looked bright and possible. He smelled of sweat and salty air and water. I never wanted to leave the closet, but when Jeremy asked if I was ready, I nodded. Jeremy opened the door and stepped out. I followed.

"We'll deploy a lifeboat to get us all out of here once we've found everyone. The trick is getting there. It's likely that we'll have to jump a great distance. We'll take the ladders down as far as we can, but there is no guarantee, and the water...it's cold. It won't be easy." His eyes looked pinched with worry.

"Do you know where Mikado is? He wasn't in any of the rooms near mine."

"I didn't see him on my way down here, so he must be somewhere else. We'll find him, and then go get the intended slaves. I sent in an anonymous tip to the FBI about the cars, but I doubt anything will get done, considering they have a man in the field. However, they don't always make the right calls. We can hope, but that's about it. Let's get moving." His muscles were tight, and his jerky movements told me he was completely immersed in the mission. "There should be a shift change in about twenty minutes, so we need to hurry." He consulted his watch.

"I hope Mikado is okay." My stomach filled with squawking birds.

"If they didn't kill him, he will be okay."

I was suddenly aware of a sharp chlorine smell. Bleach of some sort. The captain must require total cleanliness in the rooms. "Agent Kozlov is onboard, and..."

"I know. I arranged for that." He headed for the door without further explanation.

Shock filtered through me. "But he had Carson killed."

He stopped his advance on the door. "I don't have time for you to tell me the details, but I'm sure if he had someone killed, it had to be done to save you or himself."

"Didn't you see it happen?"

"No. I got to the pier as quickly as I could, but when I got there, they had the place completely locked down. It took me too long to find a secure way in, and by that time you were nowhere to be found. Ace said he hadn't heard from you since he walked you through finding the shipping manifest. I knew something must have gone wrong, so I snuck onto the ship before it sailed. I've been looking for you ever since."

I nodded my head slowly. It was all starting to make sense. Mikado and I had been completely alone as we entered that shipyard.

"I'm sorry about Carson, but we've got to go. Now."

"How are we getting out?"

"We need to find a lifeboat, and get as far away from the ship as possible. Halluis and Ace are supposed to be working on our extraction, but with no official sanction for resources from Division, they may not be able to do anything at all. We have to operate as if we're on our own."

"All right. We'll make this work. I think I know where the kids are. At least they were there earlier. In the rows next to the captain's deck. Maybe Mikado got put in there with them."

"Let's hope so."

I nodded, and he led me up to the next level. As we walked down the short hallway on the next level, two men exited a room to our left. Without a thought, I pulled out one of my guns and said, "Hands up!" Jeremy rushed forward and pushed them back into the room they'd come from. The dining room.

I kept my gun pointed at them, and Jeremy grabbed some dishtowels and gagged and tied them up. After taking away their radios, we locked them in the refrigerator. Only twenty minutes to shift change, and their replacements would find them and free them.

We slinked up one more set of stairs that let us out onto a small deck. I could see the horizon, the thin sliver of the distant sun's rays poking through the darkness. I couldn't make out a single landmass. A burst of wind whipped through my hair as we climbed up a metal ladder on the outside of the ship. Jeremy looked down at me and mouthed, *This is it.*

I knew it would mean he was going to slow down, and I'd have to be even more careful. He stopped for a minute or so and then moved quickly to the top and disappeared over the edge. There must be people moving about. I hurried to the top and peeked over the edge.

Someone on the crew was smoking, just outside the entrance to ship's controls. I hung on, peeking over the edge occasionally to see if he had gone back inside. It took a good three minutes before he did. We were wasting too much time. Shift change was only ten minutes from now. I hurried over the edge and found shelter under an overhang. I heard some movement to my left and saw Jeremy's foot protruding around the corner of a container—*the* container. We'd found the one where they were keeping the kids.

The foot moved. I followed. Jeremy stood, his hand on the handle that opened the door to the container. I was relieved to see he had one of the same tools Carson had used to open the container. He winked at me before opening it and going inside. I rushed to the side of the container where Jeremy had been and waited. I couldn't hear what happened next, but the fact that he was in there for a few minutes was a good sign. He'd definitely found the kids. I knew he must be instructing them on our escape plan. I took a deep, steadying breath. It was going to be super tricky to get seven people off the boat without being seen by someone.

Once the door opened, Jeremy came out first, then a bruised Mikado. I grabbed him into a silent hug as the four kidnapped kids made their way out. They looked pale and terrified, but they didn't say a word as we led them around the corner. We all huddled behind the container as Jeremy filled me in on the plan.

"We're going to climb down two containers lower. From there, we should have a clear shot to the middle of the ship, where we should find a ladder that leads to the main deck. We'll see. If it's not there, there will be one at the back of the ship."

"I was hoping you weren't going to suggest we jump from here. We must be 200 feet up."

"No way. No one would survive that jump. We need to get a lot lower. You lead the way. Mikado and I will bring up the rear to make sure no trouble comes after us. I already told them they would be crouching to the middle of the ship. Let's get moving."

I was glad we wouldn't be far from the water, and we could easily pull an inflatable lifeboat in with us. The four former prisoners were eerily docile. They shuffled along behind us, wordlessly, and I was disturbed that their faces didn't register any emotion—no hope, no fear. Just acceptance. They must have been captive for quite some time.

We scurried along like squirrels until I found the ladder. It felt secure, and I couldn't see anyone on the deck. Jeremy took up a position of watch about ten feet down from us. I pointed to the area of decking right next to the ladder.

"Lie flat," I whispered. "When it's your turn to climb down, keep as low as possible. I'll go down first and make sure the coast is clear. Mikado, you take up the rear. Make sure everyone gets down safely."

Mikado nodded, and the four prisoners lay down on their bellies beside the ladder. I quickly looked over the edge and, seeing no one, started down the ladder.

Once my feet hit the deck, I immediately located a little alcove for everyone to get into while we waited for everyone to get down. It should keep them out of sight of anyone walking along the deck. I hid behind a container and kept watch as they climbed. Once the first two boys had made it down, I put my hand up for Mikado to hold the others, and I ducked into the alcove with the first two. I had heard footfalls. Two shipmen passed us.

"Just keep an eye on that one. We may have to

transfer all of its contents if it continues blowing fuses like it has."

"Got it."

Shift change was in full motion now. It was probably a good thing because the crew was focused on informing each other about what had happened on the previous shift and what needed to be done instead of looking for rogue passengers. I figured they wouldn't be paying attention to much else. I checked to make sure the guards were gone before having Mikado send down the others.

One by one, the last boy, the girl, Mikado, and Jeremy made it down the ladder. I watched nervously for guards as each one descended, pulling them all into the shadowed alcove.

"Shift change is in full swing," I said, quietly. "I'm sure the men in the fridge and the one I killed are about to be found. We don't have much time before the whole ship starts searching for us." We really had to speed it up. We heard footfalls and pushed closer together.

The shipmate who had been explaining what was going on with the refrigeration section walked past us in a hurry.

"We need to find a lifeboat." Jeremy's eyes darted around the ship, and he scratched at his hand. "Amber, you look that way, I'll look this way." We went opposite directions along the ship's main deck, leaving the others to hide in the alcove. Everyone else stayed put with Mikado.

Voices echoed from a nearby stairwell. "I have no clue," one of the crew said as the door opened.

I scampered into a cubby just to the right of the

stairs and hoped Jeremy had heard the men coming.

"They're going to be in so much trouble when they're found," the other crew member said. They passed me. I peeked out as the men turned into the maze of refrigerated cargo. The temperature gauges had to be checked several times a day, and I was guessing it took several crewmen to do that. To my relief, I couldn't see Jeremy, which meant he had heard the men coming.

We both emerged and began our search for a lifeboat icon again. I had to walk in the direction the men had come, but stayed near the railing instead of entering the cargo area. About a quarter of the way down the almost 220 foot walkway, I found the icon painted on the wall of the ship. I pulled on the lever and started to yank the boat out.

A screaming alarm sounded. The removal of the boat must have triggered it. Jeremy came barreling toward me, dropping all effort at silence. He stopped at the alcove and reached in, bodily pulling the kids out of the hiding place.

"Come on! Run!" He pointed to the boat, and then ran to help me carry the heavy boat to the side. He jumped up on the railing. "Jump, or we all die!"

We jumped, hearing the sounds of shouting and yelling as we propelled ourselves as far out as possible. Mikado and the rest jumped seconds after we did.

As I fell, I kept telling myself that when I hit the water, I had to swim hard, away from the ship. All my thoughts left me, however, when I hit the water. Cold shock slammed into me. It forced me to take a breath of the salty ocean water. I gagged as I kicked my way up to the surface and what I hoped was out and away from the ship. I sputtered and coughed as I hit the surface, trying to stay above the waves, but failing as I gasped for air.

In a pop of bright yellow, the boat inflated about ten feet from me. Jeremy appeared at my side and pushed me toward it. He grabbed hold of the boat and shoved me hard up into it. I felt helpless, unable to control my coughing. I couldn't get the air into my lungs that I needed to relax and calm down.

When my face hit the bottom of the boat, I threw up, an extremely watery mess that pooled at the side of the boat. I sucked air after that. Other bodies fell into the boat all around me. Jeremy and Mikado were helping all the rescued kids into the boat. I couldn't seem to lift myself up to help. Finally, Jeremy's hands grabbed me, helping me get as much exposure to fresh air as possible.

The ship was so close to us, I feared it might hit us or suck us under. Jeremy and Mikado started rowing. We were slowly but surely moving away from the ship. I coughed and sputtered, unable to be excited about our escape yet. The four escaped prisoners looked worse than I felt, clutching the sides of the lifeboat and struggling for air.

Suddenly, buzzing filled the air and two boats appeared, surrounding us. As my eyes rounded in fear, Jeremy saw what I already had. He took a deep breath and said, "You still have that gun?"

I felt around my waistband, neither gun had survived the plunge. I shook my head. I was just getting my air back, when one of the boats pulled up right next to ours and two big, buff men leapt aboard our boat.

One man tried to grab Mikado, but Mikado kicked out, sending the man overboard. The other headed for Jeremy. "Watch out!" I croaked, but my voice wasn't loud enough to warn Jeremy. The man punched Jeremy in the head, and he swayed, but managed to stay on his feet. Jeremy ducked, the momentum of the strike throwing the attacker over the puffed up edge of the boat and into the water. Without a moment's pause, another solid and large man flew into the boat, taking Jeremy at his waist. I wanted to help more than anything, but I barely had the strength to move, much less fight. I did the only thing I could. I crawled over to where the four kids were sitting, watching the fight with dumbfounded expressions. I reached out and wrenched them down one by one.

"Duck," I squawked. "Get low!"

Mikado fought another man who had come aboard our ship. Suddenly, he fell and the man overtook him. I sucked for breath again, trying to get myself ready to be useful to Jeremy. As Jeremy and the man struggled, I felt the unmistakable click of someone cocking a gun and the cold, hard feel of one touching my temple. "Call him off, Amber. Now." That cold, cruel voice could only belong to one person: Jericho. He yanked my hands behind me and fastened them with plastic ties that cut into my skin.

"Jeremy," I called in a weak voice. I hacked a few more times before I could try again. And by that time, Jeremy had taken the knife of the man who had attacked him and slit his throat, throwing him overboard. I'm sure the man had been a well-trained guard, but going against Jeremy was never a good idea.

"Jeremy!" I called, finally finding a voice that could be heard over the rushing water and the struggle.

He turned, a swift, even movement. When his eyes took in the scene, they changed from being on fire to a smoky ash pit. He could see that he was beat. He dropped the knife.

Jericho laughed out. "We'll save our introductions until after we get back on the ship."

A boat with another three hulking men with square jaws, motored up to us, and the men boarded our lifeboat and rounded up the other kids. Two other guards crossed over to our boat and threw Jeremy down, securing both his hands and feet with plastic ties. They moved us to the metal boat and secured it to large carabineers attached to winches to haul the boat up. The seven of us were attached to rings on the boats with more zip ties. Four of the guards, along with Jericho, joined us. We weren't going anywhere.

After the guards attached four ropes to the boat, winches pulled us up to the deck. Jericho emerged from the boat first. Two guards cut our hands free and then re-tied them behind our backs with new zip ties. I stood shivering on the deck, continually clearing my throat. I still had water in places it didn't belong.

"First things, first," Jericho said. He raised a thick stick into the air, and before I could even think to duck, he brought it straight for my head.

Chapter 29

I closed my eyes, but the hit never came. When I opened them, I saw Agent Kozlov holding Jericho's arm, the stick high in the air.

"I thought you understood that the *merchandise* was not supposed to be damaged any more than it already is." He sneered at Jericho and then at me. He took a step toward me and grabbed my chin, digging his fingers into my jaw. I cried out in pain, sure I already had bruises. "You do something foolish like that again, and I will personally hold you down for my crew to break you in."

Fury tinged with raw fear rushed through me. Had Jeremy been right? Was he really only doing things that protected us both? Why was he being so cruel to me now?

He jerked my head to the side before removing his fingers. My jaw ached.

"And who do we have here?" He turned his attention to Jeremy.

"I'm her uncle. Can't you see the resemblance?" His tone was sarcastic and smart.

Kozlov backhanded Jeremy, making his whole body sway. I thought I heard something crack, and I cringed. "You think you can disrespect me? If you're a Fed, you can kiss your life away. If not, I have a nice little coal mine picked out for you in West Africa." He punched Jeremy in the gut, and he doubled over. The crew laughed. Kozlov turned to one of the guards and said, "Get a picture of him to Alexander, let's see if we can find out who he is so we can apply the correct punishment. Put the merchandise back where it belongs, and bring the others back to their new little home, container RT 264. And no one gets near it until we pull up to port." His eyes traveled over the crew and stopped on Jericho. "You understand?"

He nodded, his Adam's apple working hard in his throat.

Kozlov lowered his voice. "I won't tell Alexander about this little slip up, but if anything else happens, I'll have to report it. I don't understand how you allowed this to happen. Unbelievable."

It took me a second to realize it, but Kozlov was speaking in Russian. I flipped my head to Jericho. He clenched his jaw, and a vein pulsed on his temple. He had definitely understood Kozlov's words. Did that mean that Jericho knew Russian? Did he have a Russian heritage? Were his parents Russian? Or had he been working for Alexander for a while and had taken Russian classes in order to fit in better? That made more sense to me. Besides, it seemed obvious, now that I knew him better, that he was involved with the bratva for the status, the power of it.

The fire in his eyes told me he would find a way to

make me pay. Of that, I was sure

I thought Kozlov would leave now that he had laid down the law, but he didn't. He stood there, waiting to watch Jericho succeed or fail.

I watched, despondent, as the kids we'd come to save were led away with the same hopeless acceptance they'd shown when we'd taken them out of the container in the first place. It broke my heart.

With military-like precision, Jericho ordered the rest of the guards to take up positions along the path to some container that would be our home for two weeks. I glanced at Jeremy. What was going to happen to us? Would Halluis and Ace be able to send someone? And even if they did, how would we be able to get to our would-be rescuers?

Jericho assigned two guards to each of us, who held onto us as they led us up stairs until we reached the deck just below the captain's deck.

Two rows of twenty-foot containers sat even with this deck, but directly behind the second row, they were stacked one higher. Two guards stood outside a red container labeled RT 264. I figured that was our destination. I took a deep breath as a guard shoved me forward, almost forcing me against Jeremy's back. Jericho pushed his way to the door of the container and, using a key he pulled from his pocket, unlocked it. With a little shove, the door swung open. If it hadn't been for the rope light wound around the bottom of the container, it would have been pitch black inside.

I gulped, thinking about the absence of windows. If for some reason we had to remain in the container for the whole two-week voyage, I'd lose my mind.

"I'd say ladies first, but I see no ladies here," Jericho mocked, pushing Jeremy inside. His foot hit the lip of the container, and he stumbled into the container.

Jericho stepped toward me and, wanting to mitigate whatever action he was going to take, I attempted to enter the box of my own accord, but he stopped me, his arms wrapping around me and his temple resting on mine. A sticky wetness ran over my ear as he licked it. "I'll be back for you, to teach you a little lesson in being humble."

Ignoring the shiver that overtook me, I smashed the side of my head into his. He called me a bad name as he stepped back. I spat on him. He raised his hand to strike me, but stopped, I'm sure thinking of Kozlov only feet behind him.

Despite my attack on him, he still moved in close and said, "I'll see you soon." He ran his tongue around his lips as he moved back. I hurried forward, stepping over the threshold and into the dank darkness of the container.

Inside, I found Mikado huddled in the far right corner of the twenty-foot container with Jeremy sitting only a foot or so away. I took a seat on the cold, hard metal and slid my arms under my butt to the front of me. Jeremy already had his bound hands in front of him, and he had his hands raised above him ready to break the ties.

I immediately brought the bonds to the front of me and tightened them until they hurt. Raising my hands above my head, I puffed out my stomach and slammed them into me, breaking the clasp. The plastic fell to the floor. Mikado followed suit. Mikado sat back down with his knees to his chest, and his arms wrapped around them.

That's when I noticed all the bruising on his hands, arms and face. I reached out, but he shrank back as I got near. "What did they do to you?"

"Jericho gave me a nice welcome party."

I hissed. "I think we need to plan our own welcome party for when he returns."

"Definitely," Jeremy said, moving next to me.

"Because we could totally overpower him with all our weapons, right?" Mikado huffed.

"We are weapons, Mikado," Jeremy said. "I watched you fight at your martial arts studio. You were amazing—powerful beyond belief."

He laughed bitterly. "Haven't you ever heard, don't bring a knife to a gunfight? We don't even have a knife. I'm decent on the mat, but what could I do against semi-auto weapons?" He shook his head, then looked at Jeremy accusingly. "And why the heck were you watching me fight?"

Jeremy chose not to answer the last question.

I started to talk. "Don't sell yourself short. You're a machine, and you can easily take Jericho."

"Not when he has a gun and is surrounded by four or five other guards with guns." Mikado tsked.

"We can teach you how to disarm not only one attacker, but all of them all by yourself...of course, it will be easier with all three of us," I said.

"You're always the optimist, aren't you?" Mikado mused.

Jeremy nodded. "Yes, she is. Definitely."

"I try. I try," I said. "Let's get busy."

"Now?"

"Of course. We don't have a spare minute. We need to be ready when the next person comes through that door."

We practiced for a good while until I could see that Mikado needed to rest. His injuries had taken a big toll on him. I was feeling tired, too, and I pushed up against Jeremy.

"I'll take first watch," I said.

"No, I'll do that," Jeremy argued, but I cut him off.

"We all need some rest, don't deny it. I'm so tired, I don't know if I could get up to take my shift if I fell asleep now. Better if I take the first watch."

Jeremy nodded, a bit hesitant.

It didn't take long for their breaths to even out.

Chapter 30

I jerked awake to someone pulling me up by my arms and twisting a rope around my waist and chest, binding me tight. I'd fallen asleep on my watch. He held me to him in a chokehold. It took me about two seconds too long to realize who had me. In that time, guards stepped behind me, restraining both Jeremy and Mikado who had obviously been sleeping just as hard as I had been. Gut-wrenching fear sliced through me. I was exposed, about to become Jericho's plaything, and I had no way of stopping it. It only took Jericho three more seconds to have me at the door.

Jeremy called out, "Leave her alone. You heard what your boss said." Both he and Mikado were on their feet moving toward me, pulling against the men who had them restrained. Two more guards stepped over to help keep them in check.

At that, Jericho stopped and gave a menacing chuckle, throwing his head back. "Oh, don't worry. I won't do anything that he'll be able to see." Then he licked my cheek.

Resisting the urge to gag, I hit my head into his with a sickening thud. He didn't gasp. He hit his head back into mine, making me see stars as he said, "Ooh, I do like it rough." Then he bit my ear. I screamed out. I tried to yank my hand up and feel if he'd removed a chunk, but the ropes held me firm. My breathing turned rapid and short as panic took hold of my heart.

"Yes, this is going to be fun," he said in a breathy whisper. "A lot of fun."

The sharp pain in my ear seemed to crescendo at his words. Both Jeremy and Mikado were having an epic battle with the men holding them, grunting as they fought for their freedom to help me. Jericho took two more steps, and we were outside on the deck of the ship. I took a deep breath of fresh air and tried to calm my mind enough to figure out a way out of the mess I was in. A prayer leapt out of my heart. A prayer that both calmed and reassured me. I closed my eyes and pulled hard on the brisk air as the guards pushed the door to the container shut and locked it.

Just as I was going to place the heel of my foot in Jericho's groin, he moved me a couple feet away from him, and two guards took hold of my arms. A grotesque smile played on his face. He turned and headed for the stairs. The guards pushed me forward.

I would not have a chance to escape until I was untied. And that most likely wouldn't happen until I was alone with Jericho. The thought of being alone with him shot furious dread through me. I fought hard to quell the terror and work on finding a way out of this. As I walked, I could feel the rope around me slacken little by little. As we tromped down the stairs, I purposefully shook with each step to help loosen it. With any luck, it would be loose enough for me to get the drop on Jericho.

I figured he was leading me to the living quarters, and I visualized how I would stop him from following through with his plans and hopefully detain him so that I could help Jeremy and Mikado escape.

We took the door leading to the bedrooms, and I focused. So much was riding on my ability to stay calm and execute my plan flawlessly. He opened the first door on his right, which increased my optimism. I would not have to run down the whole hallway and avoid anyone in it in order to escape. It would be simple to get to the stairwell door once I'd incapacitated him. This was going to work. I had to crook my arms slightly to prevent the rope from falling off me as I stood outside the door. I assessed the room, taking stock of every last thing that could help me escape.

My head throbbed at the spot where Jericho had hit me. I'd have a hefty goose egg for sure. Jericho walked into a room with a bed, a side table with a lamp, and a dresser. The guards pushed me inside, closing the door behind me as they left. Their job was done. Or would they act as guards outside the door? Jericho stood by the dresser, too far away from me to go through with my plan. I'd have to be patient. I just hoped he wouldn't notice that the rope was no longer tight around me.

He turned on some music. Classical music rang out around us, and my throat tightened. He was setting the stage. "I love Bach." He breathed in deeply through his nose and closed his eyes.

I stood still, waiting for him to come closer. My insides churned.

With steps that swayed with the music, he moved toward me. I rehearsed my plan in my mind. Two more steps, and I could see it through. One more step. The music hit a crescendo, and he took that last step.

It was time.

I let my tied arms fall to my sides, and the rope fell to the floor. I struck him first with my bound hands, under his chin, causing his head to fly back. I immediately twisted on one foot inside the puddle of rope and kicked with the other, the hit slamming into his groin with a vengeance. He leaned forward, gasping. I slammed my hands into his back, and he fell to the ground, his head hitting the leg of the bed. He didn't move.

I quickly tied his hands to the bedframe and used a pillowcase to gag him. I only needed to delay him long enough for me to get back to the container and free my friends and then the other kids. From there, we could try to escape with another lifeboat. We'd have to find a way to disable the alarm. If we had known about that, we might be long gone by now. I cursed myself for that mistake. I searched Jericho's pockets and retrieved the keys. I ran to the door and swung it open only to find the two guards right outside it.

I lunged at them before they knew I was there. I smacked one with my bound hands on the back, sending him into the opposite wall. As the other guard turned to investigate, I grabbed his shoulder and kneed him, and he bent over, calling out in pain. I slipped between the injured guards into the hallway and grabbed hold of the doorknob to the stairwell.

Someone grabbed my hair and pulled me toward him. I twisted and kneed him hard in his outer thigh, irritating all the nerves there. He let go of my hair and collapsed, screaming out in pain. As the other guard charged forward, I ground my heel into the arch of his foot, stopping his progress all together. He bent down and grabbed his foot, hopping around on the other one. That's when my focus fell on Jericho, who stood just outside his door with a gun pointed right at my head. I froze. The two guards between us moaned in pain.

"That's quite enough, wouldn't you say?" Jericho's voice was almost a growl. An angry red mark, darker in the center, stood out against the white skin of his temple.

I didn't speak. I only stared. I had failed. He had me. This time I would not escape.

"Come along now. We have some unfinished business to attend to." He beckoned me with his hand.

Cold and hot assaulted me all at once as pure fear sank into me. I was breathing hard from the fight. I refused to enter the room, and was rewarded by the guards shoving me in. Before Jericho could enter the room, however, a call came over the radio.

"What is Jericho's location? Please advise." It was Kozlov's voice.

I suppressed the hysterical snigger of relief that bubbled up inside me.

One of the guards spoke into the radio through clenched teeth. "He's in his room, sir."

"Well, wake him up. I need him on the bridge. Right

now."

"Yes, sir."

Jericho huffed before turning to me and saying, "Don't worry, darling. We've got almost two weeks to see this through. We don't need to rush it." He turned to the guards. "Well, you heard him. Get her back to the container. I'm needed."

They pushed me into the container, and I stumbled inside, landing in Jeremy's arms.

"What did he do to you? I'll kill him." He glanced in my eyes before shifting to look at my bloody, sore ear. "Good grief, he almost bit it off."

My relief was so great at being back with him, I couldn't speak. He'd gotten out of his zip ties again, deep gouges of blood and bruises ringed his wrists. He'd fought hard to get them off. He took off his shirt, exposing his firm, muscled chest. Even in the dim light, it made my heart race. He bit into the shirt, tearing a strip from the bottom edge. He wrapped it around my head, securing my ear tightly to it.

"Did he touch you? If he did—"

"No. He didn't." My words felt hollow. I'd simply been lucky. "He got called to the bridge. It was a close call."

I felt hot, stinging tears rise up in my eyes so I turned away and looked up, hoping to stop them.

"I'm sorry I let him take you."

"Don't be sorry. You did everything you could have. You couldn't have stopped it. And it all turned out okay...but he promised to come for me later."

"I won't let that happen." The earnest way he looked at me left no doubt he was speaking the truth. "The next time someone comes to that door, we will be ready."

We came up with a plan and moved toward the door so we could be ready. Mikado slept, but Jeremy and I kept watch, holding hands against the darkness.

Chapter 31

An hour or so later, the lock on the door rattled softly. Jericho was back. Cold permeated my heart, and it thudded a hard, slow rhythm. Using the wall, I stood. Jeremy did too, rousing Mikado, who got into position.

A sliver of light shone through a small crack in the door. Every muscle in my body was set to spring. The beam widened as the door opened. Before we could act, someone spoke.

"Don't attack me. I've come to get you out." Kozlov's thickly accented voice echoed through the container as he stepped inside, pulling the door shut behind him.

Warm relief filled me.

"You must get off this ship, now. I've got Jericho and the others busy with other things. You're going to have to get to the back of the ship and jump from there. I hope your people know where you are, Jeremy. I can't send you with a boat, but there are suits in a compartment thirty feet from the point of the stern. Don't activate the light until we are out of view, or you hear your people arriving. If you've messed this up for me, Jeremy..." he let that hang out there. Jeremy and I moved toward the exit, but Mikado stayed.

"Aren't you coming?"

"No. This is the end for me."

"You don't want to reach the destination they had planned for you, Mikado." Kozlov's voice was harsh. "If you want to hurt yourself, there are better ways. Just throw yourself into the propeller or something. But don't stay here." He held his arm out for Mikado to exit the prison.

"Don't you dare," I said, glaring at Kozlov. How dare he make it seem that Mikado had nothing to live for. "You are going to live, Mikado. Free from the bratva. Free. You and your family. Now get it together."

Kozlov shrugged.

"She's right," Jeremy said. "Fight it. Don't let Alexander take another life. Reclaim yours."

Jeremy looked out the crack in the container and motioned for us to come. Something felt wrong. It was so quiet. I couldn't put my finger on it, but something was wrong. He only opened the door just wide enough for us to slip through.

My spidey senses flared, sending my heart racing. "Are you sure?"

He looked again. He nodded, taking a step out.

I followed. With hesitant steps, I checked the area, holding my hand out behind me, urging Mikado and Kozlov to wait. My chest felt heavy, and my body screamed for me to step back into the container. Jeremy was already five feet onto the deck and nothing had happened. I was being paranoid. I pushed past the fear and took a couple steps out, looking all around.

"What's this?" A familiar voice grated over me, sending a spasm up my back as I looked up toward the voice. I shook my hand behind me, warning them not to come.

"Amber." He tsked. Jeremy froze. "I'm not sure I understand what is happening here, but it doesn't look good." Alexander, the brigadier, peered over the edge of the triple-stacked containers. Four guards' rifles pointed right at us.

I opened my mouth to speak, but nothing came out.

"Don't worry, *myshka*," he said. "I will come down and give you the chance to tell me everything." He started down with two guards while the other two remained, guns still pointed at us. "When Kozlov sent me the pictures of the man who had been sent to save you, we searched all our databases for his face. Interestingly enough, he didn't show up anywhere. That made me wonder. What kind of a man would be skilled enough to get onto my ship and get his hands on my prisoner and not show up in the databases? I knew it could only mean one thing. He was a spy of some sort. I had to come to meet this spy and be a part of his interrogation. And the interrogation of my little *myshka*, because if he was a spy, it followed that my *myshka* must also be one. We have an exciting day in front of us."

Jericho burst out of the stairwell where we had been headed, only he came from the bridge above us. Shock played all over his face as he spotted Jeremy and me, but it turned to utter fear as his eyes lit on Alexander emerging from the containers with his two guards.

"Jericho, my boy. I'm glad you're here. I needed you

to tell me why *myshka* here was roaming freely about my ship when Kozlov told me he had her secured to meet a fate worse than death. This hardly seems to fit. And where is Kozlov? I have interesting news to tell him."

Jericho looked at the container. "It was locked," he cried, moving past Jeremy, causing him to move back toward me, closer to the container. He turned to Jeremy. "How did you get out? How?" His face turned dark red, and he clenched his teeth as he pulled a gun from his waistband and pointed it at Jeremy.

"You're a little late to the party, Jericho. Don't you think?" Alexander waved his hand at the guards beside him, who had their rifles pointed at us. The other two guards came up behind those two and spread out, two on each side of the brigadier.

"I didn't know you were coming, sir," Jericho said, his eyes shifting to Alexander. "It's an honor to have you here."

"Lip service will do you no good at this point. You are a failure. I asked you where Kozlov was. I think it might be a good idea to have him here right now."

Jericho pulled a radio out of his pocket and called for Kozlov. I closed my eyes. This would give Kozlov up if he had a radio on him. I doubted he would have thought to turn it off before coming for us. I took a deep breath, but I didn't hear a sound from the container. Had Kozlov really left his radio somewhere or thought to turn it off? What luck.

Crew members spoke back through the radio, saying Kozlov had headed to his room. "His radio must be off. Could you send someone to his room and tell him

Alexander is waiting for him by the container."

"Which container?"

"He'll know. Just tell him." He was fighting to keep control. He licked his lips and looked at me like a man who had lost his last cent in a poker game.

"Mikado. Is he still secure or is he also running around the ship?" Alexander's piercing stare even made me cringe.

"He was in there," Jericho said, waving the gun toward the container.

"We should check and see if that's still the case, don't you think, Jericho?"

"I'm sure he's still there." He stalked forward. Alexander and his men took a few steps forward also, until they'd created a semi-circle, with us on the end of one side and two guards on either side of Alexander. Two guards' guns were trained on Jeremy and me; the other two guards shifted their guns and pointed them toward the slightly ajar container door. My stomach ached in anticipation, and my hands began to sweat. Jericho pulled on the door, swinging it out.

Out of the darkness, Mikado leapt, kicking the gun from the guard closest to Alexander, forcing him to sway and hit into Alexander. He fell back. While still in the air, Mikado twisted, punching the second guard next to Alexander in the face, sending him flailing in the opposite direction. At the same moment, Kozlov emerged, chucking his radio at the face of one of the other guards, who dropped his rifle and threw his hands up to deflect the blow. Kozlov then slice kicked the final guard, taking his feet right out from under him and sending his face into the deck.

I was closest to Jericho now that he'd moved the door, so I kidney punched him, then locked my arm around his neck and yanked. He didn't give in, however. Instead he rolled, whipping his hands around my neck and squeezing the air out of me. I leaned over, trying to get my hands back on him.

Jeremy was on top of one of the downed guards, trying to extricate the rifle from his grasp. Mikado fought one of the other guards, and Kozlov fired a rifle at a third guard who plagued him. The man fell back and remained. Kozlov then aimed the gun at the final guard, who was pointing his gun at Kozlov.

Alexander had righted himself against a wall and pulled a knife out of his boot. I leaned my head back and head butted Jericho. He staggered back, but bared his teeth and came at me again, but not before I had the chance to shout out a warning, "Knife! Alexander!"

Everyone turned their attention to Alexander, including Kozlov, who turned the gun on him, waving it back and forth between the guard and the brigadier. It took my attention away from Jericho just long enough to give him the opportunity to grab hold of me again. I hit his arm with mine, and his gun shot across the deck.

We both flew to the ground for the gun, our arms outstretched. I pushed with my feet and snagged it before Jericho could, and I rolled, the gun pointing directly at his face as he twisted toward me. It didn't stop him. He kicked my leg and then clamped my legs in his, effectively stopping me from moving.

I still had the gun pointed at his head. Kozlov, Alexander, and the guard were in a showdown, and Mikado had finally knocked the guard he'd been tangling with. He sprung to his feet and froze, taking in the situation. Jeremy snatched a rifle from one of the three downed guards and without a moment's hesitation, shot the guard challenging Kozlov, freeing Kozlov to send a slug into Alexander just as he released the knife. It stuck into Kozlov's leg, and he cried out.

Jericho glanced away to see what made the awful sound. I took the opportunity to hit Jericho over the head with his own gun as hard as I could from the awkward position I was in. That was it. He must've blacked out because he didn't move. I could have shot him, but I wanted him to suffer and go to prison.

We could hear the stomping feet of others coming down and up the stairwell.

"Kozlov! Get out of here." Jeremy shouted.

He didn't wait, but shouted to Jeremy, "Shoot me, Jeremy, now."

Without hesitating, Jeremy obliged. He shot him once in the shoulder and once in the leg, and Kozlov fell to the ground. I screamed out before I could reason out why Jeremy had shot him.

"Mikado, Amber, get your hands on a gun," Jeremy barked.

I rolled out from under Jericho and wrapped my hands around a rifle. Mikado grabbed one, too. I looked toward Kozlov, lying inert on the deck. He had to pretend to have been overtaken on the ship so that it wouldn't look like he was involved. It was the only way he'd keep his position. And we wanted him to keep his position to bring down the entire bratva. He'd need medical attention fast or he'd bleed out. We needed to hurry.

We all aimed our guns at the crowd of guards that spilled out of the stairwell.

"If," Jeremy said to the five guards packed up against the stairwell door, "you turn around and go back the way you came, we'll forget we saw you, and we'll be gone in three minutes flat. Or you can choose to take us on and you will lose, just like your comrades here."

Eyes perused the deck and one by one, the guards disappeared back down the stairwell.

"Check everyone," Jeremy said. "And make sure there aren't any more guards around before we take off. There can be no witnesses to Kozlov's treachery."

I could hear the blades of a helicopter coming, but I could tell it was still very far away. Was another of Alexander's helicopters coming? I pointed up and then to my ear, and Jeremy furrowed his brow. "Maybe Halluis was able to pull through after all." I didn't dare hope. I braced myself for another wave of attackers when the helicopter arrived.

Jeremy checked the other five. All were dead. I didn't dare check Jericho, even though I could have reached my hand out and done it easily. I stared at him, hoping he wasn't dead one second and hoping he was the next. Both Jeremy and Mikado made their way to me. Jeremy reached out and felt for a pulse on Jericho's neck.

"He's still with us," Jeremy said.

Without any ceremony, Mikado shot him in the chest, anger blazing in his eyes.

I screamed, covering my mouth.

"He can never hurt another person now. He was

pure evil." He spat. "They all were."

"What now?" I asked Jeremy. There were no more guards, and no one to order them after us, anyway, but there was still the small matter of getting off the ship. Mikado stood guard at the stairs and kept watch for any sneak attacks from above or below.

"It's not one of Alexander's," Jeremy said, and he motioned toward the sky. "That's a chinook helicopter—government issue. We're saved." He smiled wryly and pointed in the direction of the shore. "And we won't even have to get wet."

I looked up and saw, far off in the distance, the huge helicopter moving steadily in our direction, a large black shadow against the inky sky.

"Why are they sending such a huge chopper?" I asked, incredulous.

"I told Halluis we'd need something big enough to transport a car and a bunch of prisoners."

"A car?"

"I figured, since we're here..." he shrugged and smiled.

"You don't mean—?"

"Yep, our mission's not over, yet. Come on, didn't Ace get you a look at that shipping manifest?"

"Well, yes, but I only saw it once," I floundered. It was true that with one look at the shipping manifest I'd memorized the container number of the director's car— and every other car on the ship, but Jeremy wasn't supposed to know I had that talent. "I was looking for the information on the kids," I finished lamely.

Jeremy just looked at me expectantly. He knew what I could do.

"It's in container AFG 145."

"Attagirl," Jeremy grinned, and we set off for the car, Mikado following along in silence.

We found the container. Luckily it was one on the end, or we'd have had no hope of getting the car out. Jeremy shot open the lock with one of the guards' guns, and we were inside.

I looked at Mikado. "Still have your tools on you?"

He reached for his pocket and pulled them out, a look of absolute shock on his usually stoic face. "I can't believe it, but I do."

We heard gunfire as the helicopter landed. Someone must've looked dangerous to those in the chopper.

We hotwired the car. and I backed it out then drove it into the chinook.

"Let's go get those kids." We raced to the container with the would-be slaves.

I wrenched open the door, and the four of them blinked back at me in surprise. I'm sure they weren't expecting anyone to open the door again so soon.

They were a little hesitant to leave the container, and I couldn't blame them.

"Don't worry," I said, entering the container to grab the girl by the hand. "This time, we have a helicopter."

Hope registered on their faces for the first time; one of the boys even cracked a smile.

Watching the prisoners climb into the helicopter made my heart pound with excitement and relief. Jeremy climbed in last.

As the helicopter pulled away from the ship, I looked back at the carnage behind me and wished I could feel pity. Triumph swelled inside me, and a smile of relief graced my lips. Jericho would never get his chance to hurt me or anyone else ever again. As we flew away, bright lights shone up into the air around us. I saw the brigadier's pilots lying dead on the opposite end of the ship.

Jeremy put headphones over my ears and then took one of my hands in his. I leaned my head on his shoulder, right in the soft little nook that cradled it so well. His thumb caressed the back of my hand, and I took a deep breath and closed my eyes.

Chapter 32

To my surprise, the helicopter didn't take us to Division HQ. Instead the pilot landed almost immediately after reaching the shore. When Jeremy questioned him, he told us he'd been given instructions to take the car, the rescued kids, and Mikado back to HQ, but we were to return to the brownstone until further notice. Though surprised, I was grateful not to have to debrief just then. The adrenaline from the battle on the ship had worn off, and I was exhausted.

Jeremy climbed out of the helicopter, pulling out his phone to call a cab, but I stayed behind a bit longer.

"Mikado," I said gently. He looked up at me, his face completely blank, as usual. "What we did tonight," my eyes flicked over to the group of kids, now lying huddled on the floor of the helicopter, apparently asleep. "It would have been impossible without you. Whatever else you've done, whatever else haunts you, you have to know that you saved lives with your courage."

He blinked once, and I thought I caught a gleam of moisture in his eye, though I could have been imagining it.

"Thank you, Amber," he said, then his mouth twitched in a slight smile. "Or whoever you are. For what you've done for my family. I won't forget it."

He reached out a hand, and I shook it and nodded. There was nothing left to say. I climbed out of the helicopter, and as soon as I was clear of it, it lifted into the sky.

Moments later, a cab had arrived, and Jeremy and I crawled in. The ride was a blur, and before I knew it we were back at the brownstone. Jeremy and I trudged up the steps and went inside. Halluis and Ace were waiting just inside the door for us.

"Young lady, you are way, way past your curfew," Ace said, crossing his arms and looking stern.

After the intensity of the last 24 hours, his comment was too absurd—I started laughing, but it came out closer to a choked sob. Ace dropped the stern look immediately, his face melting into panic as I leaned against the entryway wall and cried and laughed hysterically.

"I didn't mean—I'm sorry—are you—" he faltered.

"*Crétin*," Halluis muttered, pushing past him to pull me into a tight hug. "Can't you see our girl has had a hard time? And here you are making jokes!" He pulled me down the hall, and I managed to get my hysterics slightly under control.

"I'm f-fine, really—it was funny, Ace, I p-promise," I laugh-cried.

"Come, we will make some *chocolat*, and you will

soon feel much better," Halluis insisted. His kindness threatened to undo me again, and I buried my face in my hands, trying to keep a shred of composure.

Ace, Jeremy, and I sat around the table, and Halluis busied himself making hot chocolate. I focused on steadying my breathing. Once I had calmed down, I noticed that Jeremy had his arm protectively around my shoulder. He didn't seem to realize what he was doing, and I made no move to call attention to it. Right then, I needed his arm around me more than anything in the world.

Halluis set mugs in front of each of us and sat down.

Jeremy said, "You guys really came through for us tonight. I don't know how you got that chinook, but you saved the day."

"That was all Ace," Halluis said generously.

Ace ducked modestly, then said, "There may have been a little bit of illegal maneuvering going on to override the resource restrictions we were given. I might have impersonated an officer of the U.S. military—digitally, at least. I did it, but it was Halluis's idea, to be completely honest."

"So you were the ones who gave the 'order' for us not to go to HQ?" I asked.

"*Mais oui*," Halluis nodded. "We thought you could use a break before facing that."

I raised my eyebrows at him. "Impressive. Both of you."

"But the helicopter would have been useless if the two of you hadn't been able to subdue the guards on the boat. Pretty great work, yourselves," Ace said.

"If you think about it, it was quite the miracle it all

worked out." Halluis laughed.

We all grinned at each other for a second, reveling in the successful end of the night. Then Halluis cleared his throat, breaking the silence.

"There is something I have to say," he said. "And I think I should probably say it now, because we probably won't get another chance."

I frowned in confusion. What was he talking about?

"This has been the finest team I have ever worked with in all my career—and though I regret what will happen to us all after this night, I have never been more proud of my work than I am right now."

"What do you mean?" I asked, my brain still felt fuzzy, and I couldn't make sense of his words. It sounded like he thought we were about to be punished. "We completed the mission—we even retrieved the director's car!"

Halluis looked at me in surprise. "Well, you must know—oh, well, I suppose not, you being so very, very young." His tone was mocking, but gentle, and his eyes flashed. He smiled a bit sadly. "Skriloff won't want anyone to know the car was ever missing. This mission has been a dead-end for us all along. Fail, and we would lose everything. But even in our success, we will still lose everything." He shrugged.

I looked at Jeremy. He sighed. "Halluis is right, of course. Skriloff will probably assign us to separate remote locations where we can never tell what happened, and where we can never use it against him. It's just the way things work."

I stared at the three of them, all taking this so stoically, and my mouth hung open in shock.

"Hey, but we were a pretty fantastic team while it lasted, don't you think?" Ace said.

I held back tears as Halluis raised his mug. "To us?" he suggested.

"To us," Jeremy and Ace agreed.

"To us," I echoed, and we all clinked mugs.

The noise of a phone vibrating broke the mood. Jeremy pulled out his phone. "That's our cue." He looked around the table at all of us. "Thank you all for what you've done here. We did good work."

Everyone nodded.

"What the heck? Let's get this over with," Ace grinned.

***

We sat in silence in the conference room, waiting for Director Skriloff to arrive. He walked in, chest pushed out and obviously feeling pleased with himself. Once he made it to the head of the table, he remained standing.

"I wanted to commend you on all your fine work. For a minute there, I thought you weren't going to come home with the prize. Agent McGinnis here made it sound like you were all jumping ship a day or so ago. Let this be a lesson to you that with a little persistence, all things are possible." He smiled down on us condescendingly.

The four of us sat calmly, knowing what was coming, but not wanting to give him the satisfaction of a reaction.

"Of course, you'll be reporting for your next assignments immediately. I think it will be best if we split you all up—I think you'll all do better with a totally new challenge."

"And you wouldn't want us talking to each other—or anyone else—about your unethical misuse of Division resources for personal gain," Halluis said calmly.

Skriloff sighed. "Yes, it's exactly that sort of attitude I need to quell in my ranks. Thank you for confirming my decision. Despite your success on this mission, you have all proven insubordinate. I think a little time...away...will do you some good."

"Why don't you just come out and say it?" I demanded, sick of his condescension and simpering. "You don't want the director to find out what you did."

"Too late for that," we all heard a voice say, and then the head director, Malcolm Kettering, strolled in. I'd seen him many times while I was in training, and he looked the same as always. Despite his serious and risky job, his kind, dark blue eyes sparkled with happiness and expectancy. The laugh lines around those eyes were pure evidence of his choice to seek joy and laughter. His handsomely trimmed, thick beard, mustache, and eyebrows had turned a dark gray, the only evidence of his gaining years.

"It is inconceivable that you would lose my priceless car and keep it from me, but it is unconscionable that you would take four of my most valuable operators and put them up against the mafia without proper backup to retrieve it. You are a coward, and as a fit punishment, you'll have a remote assignment of your own. Maybe we'll forget you're even there, who knows? Despicable." He nodded, short clipped nods.

He turned from Skriloff to us. "You all, on the other hand, deserve commendations for what you accomplished. Well done. Thank you for finding and retrieving my car, but most of all, thank you for saving those kids from a terrible life of slavery."

He led a sputtering Skriloff to the door, where he was met by two suited men. The door closed behind them. The relief I felt at seeing him go was mirrored in the faces of my team members.

Director Kettering returned and shook each of our hands.

"Really, you've done fine work. You've proven yourselves to be among the very best of our agents here at Division 57."

"So, will we get to stay together?" I blurted before I even thought about what I was saying.

He laughed. "Well, that's up to you. We don't usually do this, but I think it's deserved in this case. I'm offering you your pick of assignments."

We grinned at him and at each other. It was too good to be true.

"So, what'll it be? Which of the Division headquarters would you like to be assigned to?"

No one said anything for a moment, then Halluis spoke up.

"Well, if no one else has a preference—what about Paris? After all, Christy could really use some work on her French."

I laughed and found myself nodding. Ace shrugged, and Jeremy said, "I could do France, I guess."

The director smiled. "Excellent choice."

***

A few days later, I looked at Hank's grave. Mounds of wilting flowers lay on top of the freshly filled grave. I added a huge fresh bunch on top of his headstone. New tears tracked my cheeks. Inside, I ached. Feelings that it was my fault ate at me.

Jeremy came up beside me. "I need you to remember that this was not your fault." How had he known my innermost thoughts? "You were just unfortunate enough to witness it. And if you think about it, he was blessed in a way. He had a friend there when he died and someone who knew the truth about what happened to him."

And what about Carson? His death had truly been my fault. If I hadn't asked him to help me, he'd still be walking the earth. Then I remembered the look in his eye, and his words as he told me he knew exactly what he was doing and what danger he was putting himself in. He'd done what he thought was right. Flashes of his selfless nature and kind heart flashed through my mind until I saw the moment Jericho pulled the trigger and killed him. My tears became rivers. I took Jeremy's hand and squeezed hard, trying to make myself stop crying.

He grabbed me into a hug. He smelled so wonderful, and I felt safe and loved. I snuggled deeper into the hug. "I can't stand the fact that the mafia is going to live to see another day, and according to Kozlov, probably another year."

"A year is only moments in time. The bratva will end, and Kozlov will bring it down."

In those few words he'd answered lingering questions I had about Kozlov. I had wondered if he was dead for not being able to stop the coup on the ship. He must have been awarded for surviving or something.

He spoke into my hair. "You know, we'll be working

on our next mission together."

"I'm so glad." My words were muffled in his shirt.

"The hard part will be keeping it professional between us. But we have to."

I nodded.

"Do you understand, Christy?" He pulled back slightly and looked down at me.

I nodded again and said, "I do. Unfortunately." At least I would be near him, even though it wouldn't be romantically.

***

The next day, I was packing in my room when I heard a knock at the door.

"Come in," I called, but the door didn't open and no one answered. I heard stifled laughter—Ace's—and a muffled groan from Halluis.

"What's going on, you guys? Would you just come in? I don't have time for this," I sighed in exasperation. They still wouldn't open the door, and I could still hear Ace tittering behind it.

I threw the shirt I'd been folding onto the bed, marched over to the door, and wrenched it open. "What do you want?" I demanded. Then my jaw dropped in utter shock.

Ace and Halluis stood in my doorway—both wearing tight-fitting, sequined gowns, fishnet stockings, and full makeup. Ace was sniggering uncontrollably, and Halluis had a look of pure misery on his face. I noticed Ace was holding him by the elbow—perhaps it was the only thing keeping Halluis from bolting.

"Um," I said, as calmly as I could. "What are you—? Um. Wow. Just...Wow."

"I told you she'd forgotten all about it!" Halluis hissed.

"A bet's a bet," Ace laughed. "And when you give your word, you have to follow through." Ace held up a bag of crickets, and Halluis held up one containing snails. I pressed my hand to my mouth, fighting back bursts of laughter as he filled his own hand and Halluis's with the disgusting-looking critters. He raised his eyebrows at me.

"Oh, you want me to give you the cue?" I laughed. "Okay, then. On three. One, two, three!"

They both downed the crickets in one gulp. They repeated the process with a snail each, using a tiny fork to pull out the fried glob from the shell, then Ace took a bow, pulling Halluis into a bow beside him. "Ta-da!"

"You guys—you're nuts. But you're the best." I laughed. I gave them both hugs, and they turned to go.

"You know, those crickets really weren't all that bad," Ace said as they moved down the hallway. "Kinda crunchy, kinda salty. I think I might pick up some more before we leave."

"You just wait until we get to France. There you will find real cuisine."

I leaned up against the doorjamb and listened to them argue, laughing as I watched their sequined figures disappear into their respective rooms.

I went back to packing, and a few minutes later Jeremy appeared in the door. He informed me that once I was through packing, we'd have a chance to visit one place that I'd always wanted to visit in New York City. Tourist attractions filled my mind.

"Only one, eh?" It felt strange to think of visiting

tourist spots, but I had to move on. If I were to sit here and dwell on what happened to Carson and Jericho and how the bratva turned Mikado and so many others into murderers and thieves, I would have to curl up on myself, and I'd never recover from the pain. No. I locked those terrors into their own little box in my mind and threw away the key. I hoped to never have to think of them again.

"If it's only one, then I want it to be a walk along the Brooklyn Bridge. I've always wanted to do that."

"Your wish is my command." He swung out his hand, inviting me to go out the front door and begin our New York tourist excursion.

Jeremy and I sat on the train with our thighs touching. I had to force myself not to unclasp my hands and put one on his knee. It seemed like the natural thing to do. Instead, I took a moment to draw in his smell. Musky. Soapy. Delicious. I had learned quickly to breathe only from my mouth when entering the subway tunnels to avoid the nasty, pervading smells of B.O., urine, and old trash, but Jeremy's smell overpowered it all.

"I thought you'd choose the Empire State Building or even the Statue of Liberty. I don't think I would have guessed the Brooklyn Bridge. You've driven over it and everything." His eyebrows raised in question.

"But I haven't walked along it. And besides, it's sure to look different on foot, walking above the cars. Thank you for taking me."

He leaned into me, a smile tugging at his lips. "I don't want to burst your bubble, but a lot of sightseeing in New York involves being above the cars."

"Ah, but none where the exhaust and car noise fills the space around you. I simply can't wait."

He shook his head. "Yeah, I can't think of a place that says New York better than that."

Despite my teasing, I knew there was no better place to view Manhattan, the rivers, and Brooklyn than that bridge, and it was such an iconic spot for travelers to visit. We got off at City Hall and entered the walkway. All kinds of people were on the wide, wooden bridge. Cyclists, runners, tourists, and lovers. The cars and trucks that rumbled below us seemed to disappear the farther we walked.

My stomach filled with tingles as we looked back where the East River met Manhattan. Leaning on the rail, we looked out at the Empire State Building. The air smelled crisp, fresh, and I breathed it all in.

"Can you think of a more romantic place than this?" I sighed.

A mischievous grin spread across his handsome face. "In the interest of making this the best moment ever, I'm going to agree. But I reserve the right to show you a place I think you may find just as romantic if not more so."

I bit my bottom lip and glanced at him. "I will definitely need to see this fictitious place one day."

Sure, I'd seen masses of pictures of the city, maps, and even live satellite aerial shots of New York, but that was nothing compared to having the cold, windy air hitting my face as I looked out over the city. And I was with Jeremy.

"This is seriously amazing."

He stepped back and took a picture of me on his

phone. I crossed my eyes.

"Hey! Give me at least one decent one," he chided.

It made me nervous. He'd have this picture of me forever. I wanted it to be a good one. I tried to smile, but I'm sure my nervous energy made it look more like a smirk.

He laughed. "Did you just catch a whiff of something gross or what?"

I tipped my head back and laughed. He snapped a picture.

"Hey!" I yelled, putting my hand on my hip.

He snapped another.

"I reserve the right to delete any picture you take today."

He shook his head and mouthed the words, "I don't think so."

I reached out for the phone, and he held it away from me. A girl with a ponytail came up to us. "Do y'all want me to snap one of both of y'all?" she asked sweetly. Her Southern drawl was thick, and she wore an "I Heart NY" hoodie. Obviously a tourist.

"That would be awesome," Jeremy said.

We made funny faces for the first picture. Then we made stone faces. After that, he smiled at me, and I heard the camera click. We both looked at the camera and smiled for the final one.

"I hope you like them." She handed the phone back.

"Thank you. I'm sure we will."

"You two make a cute couple."

To that, neither of us replied, but heat crept up my neck.

I pulled out my phone and snapped a picture of us

that was sure to only get a small section of our faces. "Now that's a fine picture," I said, looking at it on my phone and then showing it to him.

"Here." He took the phone from me with one hand, and his other rounded my hip as he pulled me close. I sucked in a deep breath and a heavenly heat spread through me. "Smile!"

And I did. I couldn't help it. It was totally involuntary. My cold nose was no longer cold, and as he snapped away, a rush of warm liquid settled in my gut. I leaned my head on his shoulder and laughed. The moment ended much too quickly.

We continued across the bridge, and he pointed out Wall Street, the Manhattan Bridge, and the many different skyscrapers. We didn't talk much after the picture session, but instead enjoyed every sensation that came to us.

"Do you feel it?" he asked, stopping, at a point where Governors and Staten Islands were visible.

"What?"

"The energy? The wonder?" His eyes scanned the area.

"Yes! And the beauty." I threw my hands in the air, unable to contain my excitement.

He looked at me, his eyes sparkling. "Yes. And the beauty." He touched my face, his fingers tracing my jaw, and I took a sharp intake of air.

I wished with all my heart he would tell me there was no reason we couldn't be together, that we could have anything we wanted. But I knew it couldn't be.

His brown eyes hit mine, and I knew he was lamenting the same thing. His hand dropped from my face, and he looked away.

I took my water bottle out of my jacket and held it up. "To us never having to work on a case without each other." He pulled out his own bottle and raised it to mine. I smiled and tapped my bottle to his.

"Here. Here." The way he said it made me think he didn't believe it would happen.

I continued to grin and took a drink. It was okay if he was losing faith. I had enough for both of us.

We were at the end of the bridge, and made our way to the Brooklyn Bridge Park that was bustling with people getting pizza and even ice cream. We walked along a trail, joggers and bikers whizzing past us. Children, all bundled up, played on the playground and the sky above the East River caught my eye as a helicopter entered the space. Jeremy pulled out his phone and looked at it.

"What would you say if I told you we were about to go on another adventure together?"

"I'd scream out with joy."

"Really? Well, get ready then."

The beating blades of the helicopter got louder and louder as it neared. While all the people around us scattered to avoid the pounding wind, Jeremy and I moved out onto a wide grassy area.

Two cables fell from the sky, and both Ace and Halluis waved to us from the belly of the chopper.

"No way, Jeremy! This is too cool."

Jeremy handed me one of the cables. He took the other. We stepped into the foot loops, and the cables rose. I leaned my head back and gave the loudest scream of excitement I'd ever given.

Let the adventure begin.

Acknowledgements

My husband was ecstatic about this book because it took us to one of his favorite places in the world, New York. I knew I wanted to write a book set in New York, but I was uncertain of what I wanted to write about. As we walked along the Coney Island boardwalk, we couldn't help but notice how the closer we got to Brighton Beach, the more Russians we saw. Bill told me a story a friend of his told him about car thieves who were shipping cars to West Africa, the friend's homeland. They were making a fortune—and the idea for *Hotwire* was born.

Amazingly enough, the newspapers in New York echoed my husband's friend's stories, and I started my research. It was easy to be inspired by such an interesting and eclectic city, and it seemed natural to bring Division there.

As always, my readers, my critique groups, and my editor, Charity West played a huge role in the shaping of this story. I've won the editor lottery and feel blessed and amazed at her ability to help me find the right words. Without her, *Hotwire* would not be what it is today. And in a twist of fate, my agent, Michelle Wolfson, played a huge role in putting the team that appears in this book together. Her advice was for *Fatal Exchange*, but played perfectly into this book.

Thank you all.

Thank you for going to Amazon.com and BarnesandNoble.com and leaving a review of this book. That helps me more than you know!

Know first when Cindy's new books come out and get awesome extras when you sign up for her newsletter. Sign up on her website: cindymhogan.com

Watch for *Fatal Exchange*, the next book in this series. And be sure to read *Adrenaline Rush*, the first book in the series.

If you loved this book,
Jump into the exciting adventures of the *Watched* trilogy: *Watched, Protected,* and *Created* to learn how Christy became a spy.

Immerse yourself in a great mystery with *Gravediggers*.
And laugh and cry with Brooklyn in *Sweet and Sour Kisses*.

Visit Cindy on her blog: cindymhogan.com

For series trivia, sneak peeks, events in your area, contests, and fun fan interaction, like the Watched Facebook Page: Watched-the book

Follow Cindy M. Hogan on twitter: @watched1

About the Author

Cindy M Hogan is the bestselling and award winning author of the Watched trilogy. She graduated with a BA in education and is inspired by the unpredictable teenagers she teaches. More than anything she loves the time she has with her own teenage daughters and wishes she could freeze them at this fun age. If she's not reading or writing, you'll find her snuggled up with the love of her life watching a great movie or planning their next party. Most of all, she loves to laugh.

To learn more about the author and the books she has written, visit her at cindymhogan.com or on Facebook at watched-the book